Mr. Wu

Based on the Play "Mr. Wu"
by H. M. Vernon and Harold Owen

Louise Jordan Miln, Harold Owen,

Harry M. Vernon

Alpha Editions

This edition published in 2023

ISBN : 9789357957861

Design and Setting By
Alpha Editions
www.alphaedis.com
Email - info@alphaedis.com

Contents

CHAPTER I
Wu Ching Yu and Wu Li Chang

A LOOK of terror glinted across the eyes slit in the child's moon-shaped yellow face, but he stood stock still and silent—respectful and obedient.

The very old man in the chair of carved and inlaid teak wood saw the glint of fear, and he liked it fiercely, although he came of a clan renowned for fearlessness, even in a race that for personal courage has never been matched—unless by the British, the race which of all others it most resembles. Old Wu adored little Wu, and was proud of him with a jealous pride, but he knew that there was nothing craven in the fear that had looked for one uncontrolled instant from his grandson's narrow eye—nothing craven, but love for himself, love of home, and a reluctance to leave both; a reluctance that he was the last man in China to resent or to misestimate.

Wu the grandfather was eighty. Wu the grandson was ten.

Rich almost beyond the dreams of even Chinese avarice, the mandarin was warmly wrapped in clothes almost coolie-plain; but the youngster, who was but his senior's chattel, would have pawned for a fortune as he stood, a ridiculous, gorgeous figure of warmth and of affluence, almost half as broad as long, by virtue of padding. His stiffly embroidered robe of yellow silk was worn over three quilted coats, silk too, and well wadded with down of the Manchurian eider duck, and above the yellow silk surcoat he wore a slightly shorter one of rich fur, fur-lined and also wadded. The fur top-coat was buttoned with jewels. The yellow coat was sewn with pearls and with emeralds. Jewels winked on the thick little padded shoes and blazed on his little skull cap.

For himself the mandarin took his ease in unencumbered old clothes, but it pleased his arrogant pride and his love of the gorgeous that his small grandson should be garbed, even in the semi-seclusion of their isolated country estate, as if paying a visit of state to the boy Emperor at Pekin. As little Wu was of royal blood himself, he might indeed by some right of caste so have visited in no servile rôle, for on his mother's side the lad was of more than royal blood, descended from the two supreme Chinese, descent from whom confers the only hereditary nobility of China. Perhaps the yellows that he often wore hinted at this discreetly. The sartorial boast (if boast it was) was well controlled, for true yellow was the imperial color, sacred to the Emperor, and young Wu's yellows were always on the amber side, or on the lemon; and even so he might have worn them less in Pekin than he did here in the Sze-chuan stronghold of his house.

The room was very warm, and seemed no cooler for the scented prayer-sticks that were burning profusely in the carved recess where the ancestral tablet hung, and as he talked with and studied the boy, whom he had studied for every hour of the young life, the upright old man with the gaunt, withered, pockmarked face fanned himself incessantly. Little Wu had run in from his play in the bitterly cold garden, all fur-clad as he was. The mandarin had sent for him, and he had not stayed to throw off even one of his thick garments. Old Wu was not accustomed to be kept waiting or the grandchild to delay.

"Well?" the old man demanded, "you have heard. What do you say?"

The quaint little figure kotowed almost to the ground. It was wonderful that a form so swathed and padded could bend so low, wonderful that the jewel-heavy cap kept its place. His little cue swept the polished floor, and his stiff embroideries of gem-sewn kingfisher feathers creaked as he bent. He bent thrice before he answered, his hands meekly crossed, his eyes humbly on the ground: "Most Honorable, thou art a thousand years old, and, O thrice Honorable Sir, ten thousand times wise. Thy despicable worm entreats thy jadelike pardon that he pollutes with his putrid presence thy plum-blossomed eyes. Thou hast spoken. I thank thee for thy gracious words."

"Art thou glad to go?"

"Thy child is glad, Sir most renowned and venerable, to obey thy wish."

"Art glad to go?"

The boy swept again to the ground, and, bending up, spread out his pink palms in a gesture of pleased acceptance. "Most glad, O ancient long-beard."

The grandfather laughed. "Nay, thou liest. Thou art loth to go. And I am loth to have thee go. But it is best, and so I send thee." He held out his yellow, claw-like hand, and little Wu came and caught it to his forehead, then stood leaning against the other's knee, and began playing with the long string of scented beads that hung about the man's neck.

"Well," the mandarin said again, "say all that is in thy heart. Leave off the words of ceremony. Speak simply. Say what thou wilt."

"When do I go?" It was characteristically Chinese that such was the question, and not "Must I go?" or even "Why must I go?" The grandfather had said that he was to go: that point was settled. From that will there was no appeal. The boy scarcely knew that there were children who did not obey their parents implicitly and always. That there were countries—in the far off foreign-devils' land—where filial disobedience was almost the rule, he had never heard and could not have believed. Of course, in the classics, which even now he read easily, there were runaway marriages and undutiful offspring now and then. But the end of all such offenders was beyond horror horrible, and even so little Wu had always regarded them as literary makeweight, artistic shades to throw up the high lights whiter, shadows grotesque and devilish as some of his grandsire's most precious carvings were, and scarcely as flesh and blood possibilities.

In all their ten years together there had been between these two nothing but love and kindness. No child in China (where children are adored) had ever been more indulged; no child in China (where children are guarded) more strictly disciplined. The older Wu had loved and ruled; the younger Wu had loved and obeyed always. They live life so in China.

"When do I go?" was all the boy said.

"Soon after your marriage moon: the third next moon, as I plan it."

The child's face glowed and creamed with relief. He was only ten, and—at least in that part of the Empire—older bridegrooms were the rule. If the dreaded exile were not to begin until after his marriage, years hence, all its intricate ceremonial, all its long-drawn-out preliminaries, and happily to be delayed again and again by the astrologers, why, then here was respite indeed.

"Nay," the mandarin said, shaking his old head a little sadly, "think not so. Thy marriage will be when the cherry trees in Honan next bloom."

"Oh!" the boy just breathed his surprise.

"I think it best," the old man added. "Your wife was born last month. The runners reached me yesterday with the letter of her honorable father."

Little Wu was interested. He had read of such marriages and he knew that they really took place sometimes. He rather liked the scheme—if only he need not go to England for hideous years of wifeless honeymoon! He had heard none of the details of his exile—only the hateful fact. But his Chinese instinct divined that in all probability young Mrs. Wu would not accompany him. Yes, he rather liked the idea of a wife. He was desperately fond of babies, and often had two or three brought from the retainers' quarters that he might play with them and feed them perfumed sugar-flowers. He hoped his grandfather would tell him more of his baby-betrothed.

But the grandfather did not, now at all events, nor did he add anything to the less pleasant piece of news, but rose stiffly from his chair, saying, "Strike the gong."

The boy went quickly to a great disk of beaten and filigreed gold that hung over a big porcelain tub of glowing azaleas, caught up an ivory snake-entwined rod of tortoise-shell, and beat upon the gong. He struck it but once, but at the sound servants came running—half a dozen or more, clad in blue linen, the "Wu" crest worked between the shoulders.

"Rice," the master said, and held out his hand to the child.

"Lean on me, lean on me hard," pleaded the boy; "thy venerable bones are tired."

"They ache to-day," the octogenarian admitted grimly. "But untie thyself first, my frogling. Thou canst not eat so—we are going to rice, and not into thy beloved snow and ice."

The child slipped out of his fur, and cast it from him. His quick fingers made light work of buttons, clasps and cords. Garment followed garment to the floor, and as they fell servants ran and knelt and picked them up almost reverently, until the boy drew a long free breath, clad only in a flowing robe of thin crimson tussore: a little upright figure, graceful, and for a Chinese boy very thin. Then the old man laid his hand, not lightly, on the young shoulder; and so they went together to their rice.

CHAPTER II
AT RICE

JAMES MUIR was waiting for them in the room where their meal was served. There were but two meals in that household—breakfast and dinner—or rather but two for the mandarin and those who shared his rice; the servants ate three times a day, such few of them as ate in the house at all. But there was a fine mastery of the art of dining, as well as a good deal of clockwork, in the old Chinese's constitution; and Muir, at liberty to command food when and where he would, found it convenient and entertaining to eat with his pupil and his host.

For three years the young Scot had held, and filled admirably, a chair in the University of Pekin. The post had been well paid, and he had enjoyed it hugely, and the Pekin background of life no less; but old Wu had lured him from it with a salary four times as generous, and with an opportunity to study China and Chinese life from the inside such as probably no Briton had had before, and far more complete and intimate than the no mean opportunity afforded by his professorship in the capital.

Chinese to the core and Chinese to the remotest tip of his longest spiral-twisted and silver-shielded fingernail, Wu Ching Yu, astute and contemplative even beyond his peers, searching the future anxiously saw strange things ahead of this native land of his burning love, and he had boldly mapped out an unique education for his grandson.

Europe was coming into China. It was too late to prevent that now; Wu Ching Yu doubted if it had not always been too late. Well, what would be would be; Confucius had said so. Europe was coming into China, and Wu Li Chang, his grandson, should meet it at an advantage which other Chinese were not wise enough to prepare for themselves. Wu Li Chang should know Europe before Europe came to reap the wealth of Shantung and Peichihli and to fatten on the golden harvest of four thousand years of Chinese thrift, frugality, and sagacity. The boy should have an English education and a facile understanding of English thought and of English ways.

Quietly, remorselessly, the grandfather had studied the individuals of the Aryan races already permeating in official and mercantile trickles into Pekin, Hong Kong, Shanghai and Hankow. The Germans commended themselves to him in much. His Chinese thoroughness liked their thoroughness. His concentration liked theirs. But they had other qualities he liked less. The French and the Americans he understood least, and he somewhat under-estimated both. He liked the Russians; but he gauged them to be threatened by the future rather than being themselves seriously threateners of China.

It was the British, he decided deliberately, who most threatened China and promised her most; they, above all others, were to be dreaded as foes, desired as friends. He thought that they had staying powers beyond all other races save his own, honorableness and breeding. He disliked their manners often, but he liked the quality of their given word. He suspected that the English would win in the long run in any contest of peoples to which they set their shoulders and their will: and it was to England that he determined to send his boy, that there the child might learn to hold his Chinese own in China in the years to come, let come to China from the West what would. Cost them both what it might—and would—of heartache, the boy should go, but he should go with such equipment, such armor of *savoir faire* as was possible or could be made possible. He should learn to speak English, to ride a horse English fashion, and to use a fork before he went. And so James Muir was selected and secured as tutor, mentor and general leader to the little yellow Chinese bear.

Mandarin Wu had met Muir in Pekin, had studied and liked him. And Wu's great crony, Li Hung Chang, knew the Scot and respected him. The rest was easy; for Wu was masterful, diplomatic, and the length of his purse was almost endless. Muir had lived with the Wus for three years now, and had known from the first what little Wu had only learned an hour ago: that the boy was going to England and Oxford.

Not for a moment had the mandarin neglected the Chinese furnituring and decorating of the boy's mind. Such a course would have been unthinkable. Already almost the lad might have been presented at the great national examination, and very possibly ennobled as one of the literati, but the mandarin had not thought it necessary. The boy could recite the Li Ki (the old, old Book of Rites that has had more influence than any other secular book ever written, and has done more to make and shape Chinese character and Chinese customs than have all other books put together) and recite it without mistake or hesitation; he could write decorous verse, paint swiftly and accurately the intricate Chinese characters, and he knew his people's history. He could wrestle and tilt, and once he had beaten his grandfather at chess.

He had worked well with Muir, and Muir with him. They liked each other. And after three years of constant drilling, always followed industriously and often enthusiastically, the young Chinese had a glib smattering of European lore, dates, grammar, facts. Europe itself—real Europe—was a closed book to him, of course. The mandarin understood that. But a few years in the West would mend all that: and then the beloved boy should come home, to serve China and to rule his own destiny.

Between the old Chinese mandarin and the young Scotchman a sincere friendship had grown—and almost inevitably, for they had so much in common, and so much mutual respect. Each was honest, manly, and a gentleman. Each had self-control, generosity, deliberation, taste and a glowing soul. Three years of daily intercourse, and something of intimacy, had destroyed completely such slight remaining prejudice as either had had against the other's race when they met at Pekin.

Wu the grandfather was never long or far from the side of Wu the grandson. James Muir had taught one Wu almost as much (though not as systematically) as he had taught the other. And they had taught him more than he had taught them: the child unconsciously, the mandarin with conscious glee. All three had been eager to learn, the men more eager than the boy; and the teacher who is at home always has a wide and deep advantage over the teacher who is abroad. Background, environment, each smallest detail and petty reiteration of daily life, aid the teacher who instructs in his own country, but impede and thwart the teacher who instructs aliens in theirs.

Chinese families who live in some state usually eat in the great hall—the k'o-tang, or guest-hall—of their house, as far as they have any usual eating place. But more often than not when in residence here the Wus "dined" (of course, they used for it no such term: it was, as were all their meals, just "rice") in the chamber in which the two men and the child now sat. This house had more than one great hall, and several rooms larger than this, though it was far from small.

It was a passionate room. It throbbed with color, with perfume, with flowers, with quaint picked music and with a dozen glows and warmths of wealth.

High towards the red and sea-green lacquered roof, carved and scrolled with silver and blue, a balcony of pungent sandal-wood jutted from the wall. The floor of the balcony was solid, and from it hung three splendid but delicate lamps, filled with burning attar. The railing of the balcony was carved with dragons, gods, bamboos and lotus flowers, and within the railing sat three sing-song girls. They were silent and motionless until, at a gesture of the master's hand, the eunuch, who was their choirmaster and their guardian, spoke a syllable, and then they began a soft chant to the tinkling accompaniment of their instruments. One played an ivory lute, one a lacquered flute, the third cymbals and bells; and the eunuch drew a deeper, more throbbing note from his chin or student's lute—five feet long, with seven strings of silk, its office to soothe man's soul and drive all evil from his heart. In the corner farthest from the table squatted, on the mosaic floor, a life-size figure of the belly-god. He wore many very valuable rings, an unctuous smirk, a wreath—about his shoulders—of fresh flowers, and very little else. He was fleshed of priceless majolica, but his figure would have been the despair of the most ingenious corset shop in Paris; his abdomen protruded several feet in front of his knees; his was a masterly embonpoint of glut.

There must have been a hundred big joss-sticks burning in the room—not the poor, slight things sold in Europe, but Chinese incense at its best and most pungent.

The mandarin used chop-sticks. The boy and his tutor ate with silver forks.

The food was delicious, and Muir ate heartily. But the child and the old man ate little. Both were sick at heart. Five of the mandarin's concubines brought in fruit and sweetmeats. The boy took a glacé persimmon, and smiled at the woman. He knew them all by name (there were a score or more in the "fragrant apartments"), and he liked most of them and often played with them. The mandarin paid no heed to them whatever. Such of their names as he had once known he had quite forgotten. The old celibate lived for China and for his grandson. But he kept his Chinese state in China, and always would. And his women were well clad, well fed, well treated and reasonably happy. And if one of them died she was replaced, and so was one that took the smallpox and was disfigured. But one was rarely scolded, and never was one beaten. Wu Ching Yu rarely remembered their existence. When he did it bored him. But they were part of his retinue, and it no more occurs to an important Chinese to discard his retinue than it does to a portly and decent Scot to discard his kilt in broad daylight on Princes Street. The one discard would be as indecent as the other. Manners make men everywhere, and they have no small share in making manhood, in China as in Edinburgh. They differ in different districts, but, after all, their difference is but of thinskin depth. It is their observance that matters: it is vital.

A great snake waddled in and came across the floor—a fat, over-fed, hideous thing. Muir knew the creature well, and that it was perfectly tame and harmless, but, for all that, he tucked his feet between the rungs of his chair. Little Wu flung sweetmeats and bits of sugared fat pork to the monster, and presently it waddled off again, crawling fatly, and curled up at the feet of the belly-god, and went to sleep with its sleek, slimy, wrinkled head under the lea of the god's wide paunch.

CHAPTER III
THE MARRIAGE JOURNEY

WU LI CHANG enjoyed his wedding very much. He enjoyed all of it (except the enforced parting with his young wife)—the wonderful journey to Peichihli, brightened by anticipation; the more wonderful return journey, not a little dulled by homesickness for his bride and by the near-drawing of his voyage to England; the six weeks' stay in the palace of the Lis; and most of all—decidedly most of all—his wife.

He would have been ingratitude itself if he had not enjoyed his visit at his father-in-law's. Never went marriage bells more happily. Never was bridegroom more warmly welcomed or more kindly entertained. The wedding ceremonies interested him intensely; they went without a hitch, and never in China was bridal more gorgeous. The honeymoon was best of all—if only it might have been longer!—and had but one jar. (Most honeymoons—at least in Europe—have more.) The one in Wu Li Chang's and Wu Lu's honeymoon was acute and plaintive: it was the day that his wife had the colic and wailed bitterly. Wu Li Chang had colic too—in sympathy, the women said, but James Muir suspected an over-feed of stolen bride-cake, gray and soggy, stuffed with sugared pork fat and roasted almonds. Probably the women were right, for Wu Li Chang was not a gluttonous boy, and he had eaten sugared pork fat with impunity all his life; but, caused no matter by what, the colic was real enough, and Wu Li Chang could have wailed too, had such relief been permissible to a Chinese gentleman.

The cavalcade started at dawn on an auspicious day in early spring, when the nut trees were just blushing into bloom and the heavy buds of the wistaria forests were showing faint hints of violet on their lips. The return journey was made when the short summer of Northern and North Central China was turning towards autumn, and the great wistarias creaked in the wind and flung their purple splendor across the bamboos and the varnish trees, and the green baubles of the lychees were turning pink and russet.

The marriage ceremonial took quite a month, for the mandarins would skimp it of nothing; and a Chinese wedding of any elegance is never brief. The engagement had been unprecedentedly brief—made so by the exigencies of Wu Ching Yu's plans—and to have laid on the lady the further slight of shabby or hurried nuptials would have been unthinkable, and most possibly would have been punished by three generations of hunchbacked Wus.

Mandarin Wu kept his own soothsayer, of course, and equally of course that psychic had pronounced for the brevity of the engagement, and himself had selected the day of the bridegroom's departure and the marriage days. His commandments had synchronised exactly with his patron's desire. The mandarin's wishes and the necromancer's pronouncements almost invariably dovetailed to a nicety; and when they did not the mandarin took upon himself the rôle of leading seer, and then changed his fortune-teller. It had only happened once, and was not likely to happen again. Wu Ching Yu was a very fine clairvoyant himself.

The prospective parents-in-law were old and warm friends, Wu Li's senior by thirty years. The older mandarin had dreamed a dream one night, just a year ago, and in the morning had sent a runner to Pekin with a letter to his friend:

"Thy honorable wife, who has laid at thy feet so many jeweled sons, will bear to thy matchless house a daughter when next the snow lies thick upon the lower hills of Han-yang. Thy contemptible friend sues to thee for that matchless maiden's incomparable golden hand to be bestowed upon his worm of a grandson and heir"—and several yards more to the same effect, beautifully written on fine red paper.

The offer had been cordially (but with Mongol circumlocution) accepted. The match was desirable in every conceivable way. And when Li Lu was born she was already as good as "wooed and married and a'" to the young Wu, at that moment teaching James Muir a new form of leap-frog.

The cavalcade formed at daybreak, and Wu—both Wus—and the tutor came out of the great house's only door, mounted their horses, and the journey began. It was a musical start, for each saddle horse wore a collar of bells that the pedestrians might be warned to stand aside.

The palanquins of state and their ornate sedan chairs were carried by liveried coolies that the three gentlemen might travel so when they chose; and those provided for Muir were as splendid as those for the mandarin and little Wu. Teachers are treated so in China always, though not always are they paid as the mandarin paid Muir.

The presents for the bride were packed in bales and baskets—pei tsz—of scented grass, slung by plaited bamboo straps from the shoulders of the carrying coolies. There were three hundred bales in all, their precious contents of silk and crêpe and jade and gems, of spices and porcelains and lacquers, wrapped in invulnerable oiled silk of finest texture and impervious to the sharpest rain. There were silks enough to clothe Li Lu and Li Lu's daughters forever, and the materials for her bridal robes were as fine as the Emperor's bride had worn.

There were five hundred bride's cakes, sodden gray things, quite small in size but heavy with fat pork. There were sixty tiny pipes—all for the bride—of every conceivable pipe material and design. There were a hundred pairs of shoes, to be worn a few years hence when her feet had been bound. There were birds to sing to her—living birds in jeweled cages, and birds made of gold, of coral and of amber. There were ivories and rare pottery and mirrors of burnished steel. There were jades—such as Europe has not yet seen—bronzes beyond price, tea, tortoiseshell and musk, paint for her face, and a bale of hair ornaments. There were a score of slave-girls—ten for her, ten for her mother. In a great bottle-shaped cage of rush a tame tortoise rode at ease. It had been procured from Ceylon at great expense for a maharajah's children in Southern India, and trained to carry them on its back. It were jeweled anklets now, and was for Li Lu when she should be old enough to straddle it. Wu Li Chang had tried it, and he said that its gait was good. And Muir had named it "Nizam." But it had its own servants; for the tortoise is one of the four sacred animals in China. A hundred and thirty musicians followed the mandarin's cooks and bakers—a musician for each instrument of Chinese melody, and for many two; ten more for the flutes, four for the harps, nine for the bells, and a dozen for trumpets, drums and gongs—the women carried in chairs, the men on foot. There was much, much more, and at long last the mandarin's bannerman brought up the slow rear.

Beside the old noble's palfrey a servant carried his master's favorite linnet in its cage.

There was a long wait at the temple, some yards from the house. Wu and his grandchild went in to make obeisance and to worship before the temple tablets of their dead, while Muir sat outside and smoked an honest meerschaum pipe and drank scalding tea.

The road climbed hillward, and soon after they left the temple they passed a magnificent paifang. The mandarin bowed to it reverently, dismounted, and passed it on foot; and so did the child, knowing that it marked the spot where his grandfather's mother had hanged herself—in her best robes—at her husband's funeral.

On the summit of the first hill they halted again. The old man and the boy took soup and sweetmeats and tea, and Muir munched fishcakes and savory rice; and the child looked long at the house in which he had been born.

The carved screen, standing a few feet before the door to keep the evil spirits out, was dyed deep with sunlight, and its peaked roof's green and blue and yellow tiles were darkly iridescent, as were the green and yellow and blue tiles of the old dwelling's many tent-shaped roofs.

When they moved on, the boy trotted on foot beside his grandfather and twittered to the linnet, and the linnet twittered back; the mandarin smiled down at them, and Muir lit another pipeful.

All this was most irregular—so irregular that only a Wu could have compassed it. The bride should have been coming to her husband, not the bridegroom going to his wife. But Wu and the necromancer had managed it. Wu was an iconoclast—China is full of iconoclasts. Moreover, it was scarcely feasible to bring so young a bride across China in the early spring—treacherous often and uncertain always. And Mrs. Li, who was not well and who hated travel, had insisted upon conducting the details of the wedding herself. That clinched it. Mrs. Li ruled her husband. It is so in China oftener than it is in Europe.

It would be delightful to chronicle every hour of that marriage journey and of the splendid festivity that closed it. But this is the history of an incident in Wu Li Chang's maturity, and the boyhood that was father to that manhood must be hinted in few, swift syllables.

They traveled as in some highly colored royal progress. Now and again they passed an inn. But they stopped at none. They squatted by the roadside for "rice" whenever they would, and they fared sumptuously every day. There was whisky and mutton for the Scot, and any number of other things that he liked almost as well. When it rained—and in the month it took them to reach Pekin it rained in angry torrents four or five times—they stretched out in their padded palanquins and slept. Each night they rested in comfortable bamboo huts that relays of the mandarin's servants had erected in advance; and when they had eaten and had wearied of chess, the musicians sat outside and tinkled them to sleep, and often the crickets joined in the throbbing music—and sometimes the pet linnet too.

Because they traveled in such state, the peasants, with which many of the districts through which they passed teemed, never pressed near them. But in the wildest parts there were a hundred evidences of human life and industries. Tiny homesteads jutted from the rocks, perched on the crags, hung beside the waterfalls. Wood-cutters, grass-cutters, charcoal-burners passed them hourly and made obeisant way for the shên-shih or sash-wearers, as the Chinese term their gentry. On every sandstone precipice some great god was carved—Buddha usually—or a devout inscription cut in gigantic letters—gilded, as a rule. Each day they passed some old temple, ruined or spruce and splendid; some days they passed a score; and nearing or leaving each temple was its inevitable stream of pilgrims with yellow incense bags slung across their shoulders—for Buddha shares the imperial yellow in Northern China. Each pilgrim cried out "Teh fu"—acquire bliss—or "Teh lieo fuh"—we have acquired bliss—and to them all the mandarin sent cash and rice or doles of cowry shells, and sometimes bowls of liangkao, the delicious rice-flour blancmange, colder than ice and more sustaining than beef-tea, or plates of bean-curd, the staff of Chinese coolie life.

They passed through groves of tallow trees, winged willow, hoangko, walnut, acacia, poplar, camellia and bamboo; through miles of brilliant fire-weed, arbutus, peanut and golden millet; through jungles of loquat, yellow lily and strawberry.

Everywhere there was running water, jade-green or musk-yellow or frothing white: water clear and unpolluted always, for in Asia it is a crime to befoul or misuse water.

When the short twilight died into the dark, from every temple or hut, by path or on hill, glints of lamp radiance sprang into the night, and lamps glowed along the river banks; from every traveler's hand a jocund silk or paper lantern danced, and everywhere the kwang yin têng—"lamps of mercy" the Chinese name these will-o'-the-wisps—darted and burned.

The days were golden, and the nights smelt sweet.

And from then Muir had but one quarrel with China: it had made Japan seem to him forever commonplace.

James Muir had never enjoyed himself so intensely before: every moment was a picture and a feast. And often now, sitting alone in London, he closes his book-tired eyes and dreams that he is back once more in China, crossing the Sze-chuan hills with a mandarin he admired and a boy he loved, or sipping hot perfumed wine at the indescribable kaleidoscope that was the marriage of Wu Li Chang and Li Lu, and thinking sometimes, not without a sigh, of all he relinquished when the great boat on which Wu Li Chang went to England took him—the tutor—as he well knew, forever from China.

CHAPTER IV
WEE MRS. WU

IT was love at first sight. The bride crowed at the bridegroom, and he forgot his grave new dignity and his ceremonial mandarin robes, and clapped his little yellow hands and danced with delight.

The bride's part might have been performed by proxy, and there had been some talk of this, Mrs. Li volunteering for the vicarious rôle. But Wu Li Chang's lip had quivered mutinously, and so the suggestion had gone no farther.

All was performed punctiliously—or nearly all. One "essential" had been discarded perforce. The baby bride had torn off her red veil and screamed her refusal to wear it. So Wu Li Chang had seen his betrothed's face some hours before he should. It was a brazen bride, but very bonnie. She wore less paint than an older bride would have worn, for Mrs. Li feared for the new, tender skin. Li Lu was a gleeful bride. The feigned reluctance and the daughterly wailing had to be omitted with the veil. She played with the strings of bright beads that hung over her from the bridal crown, and peeped through them giggling at her bridegroom. She laughed when their wrists were tied together with the crimson cord. Wu Li Chang thought the hot marriage wine less nice than that he usually drank at home; but when a few drops from his cup were poured upon her mouth she sucked her lips eagerly and pursed them up for more.

Even Muir, who had small flair for babies, thought this one very pretty. She was as fat as butter, but not nearly as yellow as Devon butter is when creamed from kine that feed on buttercups and clover there. Her tints were more the color of a pale tea-rose. She had bewitching dimples and the exquisitely lovely eyes which are a Chinese birthright. And her grandfather-in-law thought that she would be surpassingly lovely as a woman; for Mrs. Li, whom he saw now for the first time, was as beautiful as any woman he had ever seen, and his proud old heart was much content, for he knew well how a wife's beauty comforts her husband's years.

She was married on a daïs, of course, but instead of sitting—as she should have done—on a chair of state, she was tied upright in her cradle, the perpendicular bamboo cradle of Chinese babyhood, very much the size and exactly the shape of the huge tins in which farmers send milk to London—to be seen in their hundreds any morning at Victoria or Paddington.

When the last of the hundred rites was over, Li lifted up the mite to carry her to her own room; but she stretched out her arms to little Wu in unmistakable desire, and he sprang to her and gathered her into his arms and carried her himself up to her nursery and her women: the happiest and the proudest bridegroom that ever was—and the mandarins almost chuckled with delight and the Scot felt oddly queer.

After that the boy was free of the women's quarters (the fragrant apartments) in the inner court. He had many a good game of battledore and of kites in the spacious grounds and in the courtyards with his wife's brothers—she had six, and they were all very kind to him; but most of his time he spent squatted on the polished cherry-wood floor of her room, nursing the babe. He liked that best of all. She was a placid mite, but she seemed to like his arms, that never tired of her, almost as much as they loved nesting her so—and she slept longest or, waking, smiled sunniest when they encradled her. Even the day the foul fiend colic came and cankered them both, she seemed less tortured in his holding, and it was he who soothed her first.

And so they spent their spotless honeymoon. And much of it they spent alone. Her amah watched them from the balcony where she sat sewing, and Li's prettiest concubine tottered in now and then on her tiny feet, sent by Mrs. Li to see that all was well. But amah and concubine counted scarcely as more than useful, necessary yamên furniture to the boy, and were no intrusion.

No man of his rank in all China had more or comelier concubines than Li, and none concubines that were finer dressed. Mrs. Li saw to that. She was a strict and punctilious stickler in such things. Her lord had grumbled sometimes at the expensiveness of "so many dolls"—for he was thrifty—and once he had flatly refused another semi-matrimonial plunge. But Mrs. Li had lost her temper then, called him bad things, and smacked him with her fan, and after that he had let her be, and she had enlarged his string of handmaidens as she chose, and he had paid for them; for he loved his wife, and feared her too, and she had borne him six strong sons. But he saw to it that all the concubines served her well. In English (and in the other tongues of Europe) more exquisitely ignorant nonsense has been written about China than about any other subject, and far the silliest and crassest of it all about the facts of Chinese womanhood.

Mrs. Li did not neglect her baby, and she was too good a mother and too proud not to nurse the little girl herself, and she toddled into the nursery as often as the hour-glass was turned thrice, coming in slowly, leaning on an attendant's arm because her own feet were so very small and useless. As a matter of fact, she could move about quickly enough, and run too (as many of the small-footed women can), so skillfully had her "golden lilies" been bound. But she did it privately only or when she forgot. It was not a fashionable thing to do.

She nursed little Mrs. Wu, but she did not linger in the baby's room overmuch. The mother of six sons was not inordinately proud of a daughter's arrival, although the great marriage had gilded it considerably. And she was greatly occupied in playing hostess to her husband's older guest. It is not etiquette for a Chinese lady to chat with men friends or to flutter about her husband's home beyond the female apartments, but a great many Chinese ladies do—ladies in most things as canonical sticklers as Mrs. Li. Of course she never went beyond her home gates except in the seclusion of her closed chair. The Emperor himself would as soon have thought of showing his face freely on the Pekin streets.

So the boy and the baby were practically alone much of the time. He sat and crooned to her and rocked her in his arms, and she crooned to him and grew fast into his warm young heart. And each week passed in added delight.

But they passed! Wu the mandarin had much business in Pekin, aside from the paramount marriage business that had brought him so far; he had not been in Pekin for years till now, although his official yamên was still here, and much of his revenue. The yamên was a bleak, empty place that he had never used as "home," and now given up to compradores and other underlings. He visited it daily after the wedding had been completed, and well scrutinized his deputies' accounts and doings. It took time. Nothing is hurried in China except the waterfalls. But Lord Wu's Pekin business was done at last, and he took his elaborate farewells of the Lis, and turned towards home, taking Wu Li Chang reluctant with him.

The boy had asked to take the baby too, even venturing to urge that she belonged to them now. (And to Muir he confided in an unreticent moment that he'd dearly like to include her in the ill-anticipated trip to England.)

The grandfather agreed that she was indeed theirs now. Of course she was. A Chinese wife is the property of her husband's patriarch. That is alphabetic Chinese fact. But they would lend her to the Lis until her husband returned from Europe. The boy grieved secretly and at heart rebelled, but outwardly he was smiling and calm, made the thrice obeisance of respect and fealty, saying, "Thy honorable will is good, and shall by me, thy worthless slave, be gladly done," took a stolid (but inwardly convulsive) leave of Mrs. Wu, fast asleep on her crimson cushion, and turned his slow feet heavily toward his homing palanquin.

CHAPTER V
HOMING

BUT the homeward journey was even more delightful than the journey coming had been. The mandarin was very good to the boy, even a little kinder than his wont, watching him narrowly with a gentle smile glinting in the narrow old eyes.

The air was pungent with the smells of coming autumn. In the wayside orchards the trees bent with ripening fruit and were heavy with thick harvest of glistening and prickly-sheathed nuts.

There were still strawberries for the gathering, and the raspberries and blackberries were ripe. The wayside was flushed with great waxen pink begonia flowers and fringed by a thousand ferns. The air was sweet and succulent for miles from the blossoms of the orange trees, and on the same trees the great gold globes hung ripe. And the feathery bamboo was everywhere—the fairest thing that grows in Asia.

They passed groups of girls gathering the precious deposit of insect wax off the camellia trees—blue-clad, sunburnt girls, singing as they worked.

Once—for a great lark, and just to see what such common places were really like—Wu Li Chang and Muir had tea at an inn, a three-roofed peaked thing built astride the road. The mandarin did not join them, but stayed to pray at a wayside shrine dedicated to Lingwun—the soul.

One day the three friends (for they were deeply that) saw the great Sie'tu, the Buddhist thanksgiving-to-the-earth service, in a great straggling monastery that twisted about a mountain's snowcovered crest, and blinked and twinkled like some monster thing of life and electricity, for its dozen tent-shaped, curling roofs were of beaten brass.

The Scot got a deal of human sight-seeing out of that return journeying. But it was its silent pictures and its wide solitudes that the boy, child though he was, liked best. They moved on homewards through a pulsing sea of flowers and fruit and ripening grain, of song and light and warmth and vivid color, but above them towered the everlasting hills, imperial as China herself, white, cold, snow-wrapped.

The soul of China pulsed and flushed at their feet; the soul of China watched them from her far height: China, Titan, mighty, insolent, older than history; China, lovely, laughing, coquetting with her babbling brooks, playing—like the child she is—with her little wild flowers.

There was a tang of autumn in the air, and the cherries were growing very ripe.

Often at night they lit a fire of brush beside their wayside camp, and sitting in its glow the old man talked long and earnestly to the child. To much of their talk Muir listened, smoking his sweet cob in silence. Some of it was intimate even from his trusted hearing. Nothing was said of the voyage to England or of the years to be lived out there. It had been said for the most already, and almost the subject was taboo. But of the home-coming to follow and the long years to be lived at home the old man said much. And most of all he talked to the boy of—women. Again and again he told him, as he often had even from his cradle-days, of the women of their clan. There are several great families in China noted above all else for their women, and the Wu family was the most notable of all.

Most of the ladies Wu had been beautiful. Many of them had been great, wise, gifted, scholarly. Their paifangs speckled the home provinces. One had been espoused by an Emperor and had borne his more illustrious Emperor-son. All had been virtuous. All had been loved and obeyed. To treat their women well was an instinct with the Wus; to be proud of them an inheritance and a tradition.

Wu Li Chang just remembered his own mother, and his father's grief at her death. The father had died before he had laid aside the coarse white hempen garments of grief that he had worn for her. The epidemic of smallpox that had pitted the mandarin's face for a second time had killed the only son— the father of this one child.

A great-great-aunt of the mandarin had been a noted mathematician. Another ancestress had invented an astronomical instrument still used in the great observatory at Pekin. On the distaff side the old man and the boy could prove descent from both the two great sages—descent in the male line from whom alone gives hereditary and titled nobility in China, except in such rare, Emperor-bestowed instances as that of Prince Kung. Wu Ching Yu and Wu Li Chang were descended through their mothers from Confucius and from Mencius. One foremother of theirs had written a book that still ranked high in Chinese classics, and one had worn the smallest shoes in all the eighteen provinces.

They had cause to be proud of their women, and to boast it intimately from generation to generation.

Li—perhaps in compliment for the tortoise—had given his son-in-law a tame trained bear and a skilled juggler, and Mrs. Li had presented Wu Ching Yu with two of her husband's choicest concubines. The older mandarin had graciously appointed them attendants upon his granddaughter and to stay with her in Pekin. But the bear and the juggler were traveling with the home-returning Wus; and when the inevitable chess-board and its jeweled chessmen and the flagons of hot spiced wine were laid between Muir and the mandarin, Bruin—Kung Fo Lo was his name—danced and pranced in the firelight for the boy, who clapped his hands and shook with laughter; the heart of a man-child cannot be for ever sad for a baby-girl, known but two months and not able to crawl yet. But Wu Li Chang did not forget Wu Lu. He often wished that she might have come with them. He'd willingly have traded the dancing bear for her, with the juggler thrown in (he had two better jugglers at home); and for permission to forego the journey to Europe he would have given everything he had: his favorite Kweichow pony (a dwarfed survival from the fleet white Arabs that the Turkish horde of Genghis Khan brought into China), his best robes, the little gold pagoda that was his very own, everything except his cue, his ancestral tablets, and his grandfather's love and approval—yes, everything, even his wife.

CHAPTER VI
HEART ACHE

BUT it was summer again before he went. The mandarin was taken ill soon on their home-coming, and all through the cold northern winter only just lived. Death means little to the Chinese, but somehow, for all his relentlessness of purpose, for all his iron of will, the old man could not bring himself to part with the child while his megrim was sharp. With spring he grew better, and when the great tassels of the wistaria were plump and deeply purpled he sent the boy with his tutor to Hong Kong.

They took their parting in a room in which they had passed much of their close and pleasant companionship. James Muir understood that the old man avoided, both for himself and the lad, the strain of the parting, long drawn out, that the cross-country journey must have been. And Muir suspected also that the mandarin did not dare the bodily fatigue of such a journey, no matter how easily and luxuriously taken.

Muir was right. But chiefly, Wu chose to say good-by in their home—the home that had been theirs for generations and for centuries.

Except a few pagodas there is not an old building in China. The picturesque houses, with their pavilions and their triple roofs, flower-pot hung, curling and multicolored, spring up like mushrooms, and decay as soon. Houses last a few generations—perhaps. Great cities crumble, disappear, and every trace of them is obliterated in a brief century or two. The Chinese rebuild, or move on and build elsewhere, but they do not repair. Their style and scheme of architecture never alter. The tent-like roofs (or ship-prow survivals—have it as you will, for no one knows), painted as gayly as the roofs of Moscow, make all China tuliptinted, and looking from a hillside at a Chinese city is often oddly like looking down upon the Kremlin. It is very beautiful, and it looks old. But unlike the Muscovite city, it is all new.

But this house of Wu, where both the old man and his grandson had been born, was far older than a house in China often is. The Wus were a tenacious race, even in much that their countrymen usually let slide; and here, in these same buildings, or in others built on the same site, the Wus had made their stronghold and kept their state since before the great Venetian came to China to learn and to report her and her cause aright.

And it was because of this, far more than because his old bones ached and his breath cut and rasped in his side, that Wu Ching Yu chose to take here what must be a long and might well be a last farewell.

The actual "good-by" was said standing beside the costly coffin which had been the man's gift from his wife the year their son was born. Wu the grandson had played beside it when still almost a baby. He knew its significance, its great value, and that there was no finer coffin in China. The precious Shi-mu wood, from one solid piece of which it had been carved, was hidden beneath layer after layer of priceless lacquer and Kweichow varnish, both inside and out. And little Wu, who knew each of its elaborate, fantastic details as well as if it had been a favorite picture-book, had never been able to determine which was the more gorgeous—the vermilion of its surface or the gold leaf of the arabesque that decorated it.

The old man laid one thin claw-hand on the casket, the bleached and taloned other on the young shoulder. "I hope that you will be here to stretch and straighten me in it at my ease when my repose comes, and I take my jade-like sleep in this matchless Longevity Wood. If so, *or if not*, remember always that you are Wu, my grandson, a master of men, the son and the father of good women, and a Chinese. You have always pleased me well. Now go."

The boy prostrated himself and laid his forehead on the old man's foot. The old man bent and blessed him. The child rose.

"Go!"

Without a word, without a look, Wu Li Chang went. And James Muir, waiting at the outer door, noticed that not once did the child look back—not when they came round the devil-protection screen, not when they passed the ancestral graves, not when they went beneath his great-grandmother's memorial arch, not when they crested the hill—nowhere, not at all, not once. He folded his hands together in his long sleeves and went calmly, with his head held high and with a sick smile on his pale face. They were to sail from Hong Kong in a few days, but that was a small thing: this was his passing from China and from childhood.

And as they passed south, bearing east, the boy said little. He neither sulked nor grieved—or, if he grieved, he hid it well. But he wrapped himself in reticence as in a thick cloak.

His eyes went everywhere, but his face was expressionless and his lips motionless.

Villages, cities, gorges, lakes, hills, highways and by-ways, he regarded them all gravely, and made no comment. Even when they crossed the Yangtze-Kiang, he looked but showed no interest. And when at last Muir pointed into the distance, the boy just smiled a cold perfunctory smile, and bent his head slightly in courtesy; nor did he display a warmer interest when the exquisite island lay close before them.

The old rock that used to be the Chinese pirates' stronghold and tall look-out, but on which England has now built Greater Britain's loveliest holding—there is no lovelier spot on earth—sparkled in the hot sunlight. The bamboos quivered on the peak, the blue bay danced and laughed. The sampans pushed and crowded in the harbor, the rickshaws rolled and ran along the bund, Europe and Asia jostled each other on the streets and on the boats.

Muir stood on the ship's white deck holding Wu Li Chang's hand, and taking a long last look at the city of Victoria and at the old island it threatened to overspread, and in parts did, bulging out into and over the sea. His thoughts were long thoughts too. He had come to Hong Kong little more than a boy, academic honors thick upon him, but life all untasted. Few Europeans had seen China as he had, and almost he sickened to leave her. He was going home. In a month or two he would see his mother, who was very much to him. But China quickened and pulled at his heart. He knew that he would not forget China.

The boat slipped slowly off, backing like a courtier from the queenly place. And the man and the boy stood without a word and watched the unmatched panorama dim to nothingness. The small yellow hand lay cold and passive in the big, warm, white one. Presently Wu drew his palm gently from his friend's, and turned quietly away and walked to the saloon stairs. Muir turned too, and watched the quaint, gorgeous figure as it went—so pitifully magnificent, so pathetically lonely—but did not follow. He understood that the boy wished to be alone. And he himself was glad to be alone just then.

Two hours later, when the dressing warning went, he found his charge in their cabin. Wu had no wish for dinner. He had been crying—almost for the first time in his life; the Chinese rarely weep—and besides, he was very sick. Muir dressed without speaking much, and when dinner was served mercifully left the boy to himself and his pillows.

Across China an old man in shabby robes left his rice untouched, and bowed long before the ancestral tablets of his race.

And that night in her sleep Wu Li Lu gave a little cry; she had cut a tooth.

CHAPTER VII
A TORTURED BOYHOOD

ON the whole, young Wu enjoyed the voyage. He liked the way the foreign women eyed his clothes; not one of them had garments half so fine. He liked the motion of the boat when once he had mastered it. There were snatches of absorbing sightseeing at Colombo and at Malta. And in those days one had to change boats between Hong Kong and Southampton. He had much to think of when he chose to sit alone. He had Muir to talk with when he liked to talk. And the captain, on whose left hand he sat at table from Hong Kong to Colombo, was friendly without patronage and played a good game of chess.

And by some strength of will and childhood's splendid resilience he had thrown off (or laid away) his heart-broken apathy with his sea-sickness. He enjoyed the voyage, on the whole.

When they landed at Southampton Wu thought that he had found Bedlam, and wondered, as he had not done before, why his grandfather had condemned him to such hideous exile. Everything he saw revolted him. He thought that nothing could be uglier. He was not even interested. The very novelty had no charm. His little gorge rose. Europe—seen so and so sounding—was a stench in his nostrils and rank offense to his eyes. He held up his heavy embroidered satin skirts and tucked them about him close, as a girl in Sunday-best might pick her way across the malodorous street slime in a low and squalid neighborhood.

It was late afternoon, and as they were not expected at their London destination until the next morning, Muir put up at the hotel of which Southampton was proudest. Wu was measurably accustomed to English food. The mandarin had seen to it. And on the liner the young Chinese, eating tit-bits and prime cuts from the joints at the captain's table, had found them good. But this was English food with a difference. James Muir was not a selfish man—far from it—but he exulted, for the time at least, at being at home; and he ordered a truly British dinner in a burst of patriotism (not the less deep because its expression took such homely form), forgetting to consult the boy's tastes, which he knew perfectly. They began with oxtail soup and finished with three kinds of inferior cheese and a brew of "small" coffee which *was* very small indeed. Wu thought it would have been an unkindness to the palate of a coolie. And in the big, strange bed he lay awake half the night, grieving for his old grandfather, and trying to make up his homesick little mind which was nastiest, apple tart or salt beef and carrots, and wondering why the gods let a people be who made and ate such salad. His tutor had taken two helpings, and had praised the abominable beef.

The train frightened him. The little (first class, reserved) box into which they were locked, appalled and then offended. Waterloo was purgatory. The hansom he liked. They drove to Portland Place, and Wu went up the steps with dignified eagerness. This he knew, was the Chinese Legation—the London yamên of a distant kinsman. This would be better—almost something of home. They expected him here. But it was not better; it was worse—a purgatory and a drab, dull one. Even James Muir was struck that the hall and the drawing-room had been subjected to unhappy furnishing. And instead of the friendly countryman that Wu had expected to greet him at the threshold, a sleek young English attaché, with oiled yellow hair and a lisp, came forward leisurely, saying, "Oh, it's you. Hello then! Come on in." A Chinese servant opened the door to them, but he scarcely seemed real to the disappointed lad, and there was nothing else in the least Chinese to be seen.

Why the Chinese Legation in London should have been furnished from the Tottenham Court Road passes respectful understanding; but it had. It was magnificently furnished. It had been done completely and with no stint by a famous firm. Probably that firm would have done the work less crudely if it had been left to its own well-experienced professional devices. But it by no means had. The youngest attaché—he of the fair, sleek locks—suffered from conscience. He suspected that he might never shine at international diplomacy, but he intended to do what he could to earn his "ripping" emolument. And among other self-imposed activities he had elected to direct the great house furnishers and decorators. The red and yellow, about equally proportioned, of the hall and the reception-rooms were not his own first favorites. A nice Cambridge blue with rose trimmings he'd have liked better for himself. But the Chinese Government was paying him, and he meant to play the game by that Imperial Body of an imperial people; and he played it by some hundreds of yards of red silk plush and bright marigold-yellow satin that he considered utterly Chinese. Wu thought it barbaric, demoniac. The Chinese Minister saw both the intended kindness and the joke, and enjoyed the joke very much indeed, laughing slyly and good-naturedly up his long, dove-colored crêpe sleeve.

The Minister was out, the attaché explained: had had to go—"to the F. O., don't you know?"—Wu had no idea what "F. O." meant—"sorry not to be here. Back soon," and he ushered them up into the long, draped and padded barrack of a drawing-room, and said again, "Hello!" but added in a verbose burst, "I say, sit down."

It was better when the Minister returned at last from the Foreign Office. And after lunch he took Wu into an inner room more like China, less like Hades. But until he died Wu hated the Chinese Legation at Portland Place. And he stayed there for five years. Then he went to Oxford.

London he never learned to like. There was no reason why he should. But he did learn to like the country places all over the kingdom's two islands. For he and Muir traveled together at Christmas and at Easter and in the summer.

Muir had a British Museum appointment—it was waiting for him when they landed. But his hours and his duties were easy, and he still drew his larger income from the coffers of the mandarin in Sze-chuan, and he gave much of his time and labor to his old pupil. But for the Scot and a few of the Chinese at No. 49 the exiled boy might have gone mad, so shaken and cramped was he by homesickness. But they were an enormous help and refuge. He worked hard and learned prodigiously, as only a Chinese can learn. And, being Chinese, what he once learned he never in the least forgot.

Oxford he liked from the first. Always his soul ached for China, for her people (*his* people), her ways and her scenes: the smell of her, the sound of her, the heart and soul of her matching to his: the haze of her peaceful atmosphere, pricked by the music of her lutes, and throbbing with the mystic beat, beat of the tom-tom. He thought there were no flowers in Europe, no repose, no balance, no art, no friendship.

But, for all that, Oxford thrilled him, and though he counted every hour that brought him nearer to China, he counted them not a little good in themselves because they passed by the Isis and in the classic droning of Oxford days and ways.

All the sunshine seemed to find him in Oxfordshire, all the shadow at Portland Place.

Small things rasped him at the Legation, and two heavy trials—one a humiliation, the other a grief—found him out there. A few months after his arrival they cut his cue and dressed him in an Eton suit. His rage and shame were terrible. For months he did not forgive it—if he ever quite did. Child as he was, they might not have encompassed it had they not assured him that it was his grandfather's will. That silenced but did not console him. And he treated his new garments to more than one paroxysm of ugly rage. Chinese calm is as great a national asset as any of the many assets of that wonderful race. Heart disease is almost unknown among the Chinese, and probably they owe their happy immunity from that painful scourge to their own placidity and equable behavior. But when they do "boil over," as they do at times, the eruption is indescribable—they foam and froth, and until the fit (for it is that) has spent itself and them they are uncontrollable and beyond all self-control or semblance of it.

Wu did not mind being laughed at in the London streets for his "pig-tail" and his gold-embroidered satins. He was sincerely indifferent to it. When English urchins called after him, "Chin-chin Chinaman, chop, chop, chop," he did not care a whit. Partly this was good-nature—for he was good-natured as yet—and partly it was vanity: the centuries-old vanity of a descendant of an interminable mandarinate. He understood how immeasurably superior he was to those who presumed to laugh at him—how much better clad, how much better bred—and tolerated them and their peasant mirth very much in the spirit of the old fellow in Æsop's fable who scorned to resent the kicks his donkey gave him because he "considered the source," and with, too, the quiet pride of the MacGregor who, when his acquaintance expressed surprise that the great "Mac" had been seated below the salt at some feast, asserted with bland arrogance, "Where MacGregor sits is the head of the table." But to be shorn of the cue and stripped of the finery at which the canaille jeered maddened him and made him very bitter.

In ten years the Chinese in exile made many acquaintances, but only one friend. Probably he filched some profit, some equipment for his years to come, from each of the acquaintances; but, for all that, he found most of them no small nuisance. A Mrs. Cholmondeley-Piggot was his infliction in chief. She was a distant connection of the blond attaché's mother, and had gone to school with a second or third cousin of Sir Halliday Macartney. And she had no doubt that those two facts, by the strength and the charm of their union, made her *persona grata* at the Chinese Legation. She called there at the oddest times, and dropped in to lunch uninvited; and the Chinese Minister, trained from his birth to make great and chivalrous allowance for the vagaries of women and of lunatics, would not permit his exasperated staff to cold-shoulder, much less to snub, Mrs. Cholmondeley-Piggot. And so she came to Portland Place frequently and unrebuked. She called the Minister "my dear Mandarin." She doted on China, and did so hope to go there some glad day. She loved the Chinese, poor dears. And once, when she gave a dinner party, she borrowed the Legation cook; but she only did this once. The Minister would have condoned a second time, but the cook would not. Mrs. Cholmondeley-Piggot had called him "John," and asked him if Chinese children loved their mothers, and the kitchen-maid had taken liberties with his cue.

But there were others of his race—more highly born than he—whom this lady also called "John," among them the Minister's private secretary, a very proud and solemn man who was a nobleman by inheritance—there are a few in China—and who often longed to boil the friendly Englishwoman alive in oil.

She took Wu to her heart at once; and, what was far worse, she took him for "a nice long day" in Kew Gardens.

That awful day! And she meant so well! At first she merely bored him. Then she infuriated him. It was scarcely fair to ask a Chinese boy to think overmuch of Kew's prized Wistaria sinensis—there were miles of better on the estate at home. He thought the picture of the House of Confucius hanging in the Museum an impertinence—no red scroll of honor above it, no joss-stick burning in homage beneath it. The Chambers imitation of a pagoda was to him even more unpardonable. What right had this English tea-garden sort of place with a shabby mockery of a sacred thing of China? And the bamboos and the golden-leaf flowers of the hamamelis and the fragrant cream blossoms of the syringa made him newly homesick. What right had the dear home-flowers to grow in Europe, transplanted, dwarfed, caged, exhibited—as he was? And his hostess's remarks upon opium, as they stood beside the poppy beds, did not tend to soothe him. Wu Li Chang did not know much about opium in those days, but he knew considerably more than Mrs. Cholmondeley-Piggot did, and he knew that these were not opium poppies, for all the lady or the guide-books said—she had presented him with a guide-book, of course. There was not much poppy culture in his part of Sze-chuan, but he knew that much. Decent brands of opium were made from the white poppy. Some inferior sorts, such as coolies chew, are made from the red-flowered plants, but not such as these.

To his angry young eyes the expatriated lotus plants seemed little better than weeds; and when she expatiated upon the wonders of Kew's banyan tree (a picture rather of banyan fragments) he scorned to tell her of banyans he knew well at home, trees under any one of which a thousand men could shelter from the rain, and of one his grandfather had seen under which twenty thousand men could hide from storm or sun.

The day at Kew was a ghastly failure. But happily Mrs. Cholmondeley-Piggot never suspected it, and was sincerely and generously sorry that the boy could never seem to find time to go anywhere with her again.

The second trouble that came to him was on a grander scale than the cutting of hair or the enforced wearing of strange, uncomfortable garments. It was tragedy indeed, and almost broke his affectionate, homesick heart. When he had been in England about a year word came that his grandfather was dead.

Wu was desperate. And now he was quite alone. He belonged to no one in all the world. And in all the world no one belonged to him except a baby-girl just learning to walk across a floor of polished cherry-wood, nearly eight thousand miles away in old Pekin.

CHAPTER VIII
SOME BALM

THERE was a great deal in the Oxford life that reminded Wu of China: the beauty and the dignity, the repose, the dedication (and of some the devotion too) to the finer things, and not less the riot of the "wines," the crash and clash of the "rows," the luxury and the elaborations. It was reminder that he found, and not resemblance. Oxford was intensely English. He liked it none the less for that. Nothing at Portland Place had annoyed him more than the mongrel mix-up of West and East, the fatuous attempt to blend the unblendable. It was neither English goose nor Chinese mongoose, and he loathed it. Oxford was good, downright English dog, and well pedigreed; he liked the bark and the bite of it and the honest look in its eyes.

The crass mistakes so often made by his rich countrymen at such places he avoided, partly by his own good sense and partly by Muir's counsel and the dead mandarin's command. He spent of his great income lavishly, but not too lavishly. He kept good horses, but not too good; and he kept no valet. His entertainment was generous, but nothing much out of the common, and never beyond the convenient return of the richer men. He made much pleasant and useful acquaintance, but no friends. He indulged himself a little in the furnishing of his rooms, but they scarcely smacked of China. His jade lamp had cost a great deal, but a young duke had one that had cost more. He had a little bronze and some lacquer, but he had no kakemonos and burned no incense. Quite a number of the other students had kakemonos by the half-dozen, and burned joss-sticks elaborately.

Wu worked prodigiously at Oxford and played industriously. He enjoyed the work. There were some brilliant men at Oxford then, but no mind better than his, and no industriousness to equal his. He took nothing much in honors—that was not in his grandfather's scheme; but he assimilated an immense amount of alien fact and thought. He learned Englishmen. He read many books and mastered them. But he had been sent to Europe to study men and peoples, and he never forgot it or swerved from it for an hour. None of his fellow undergraduates particularly liked him, but few disliked him, and he interested many. Several of the dons and fellows did like him; with one he might have had intimacy if he had cared to, and from studying Wu two of the wisest reversed a lifelong estimate of China and the Chinese.

He excelled at all he did there. But almost always he was at pains to be surpassed at the last lap; and when now and then he won, he made it his inexorable rule to win by but a hair's breadth.

Not all his fellow undergraduates treated him with entire courtesy. Some laughed at him openly at times and called him "Chops." And because these presumably were gentlemen he was not so altogether indifferent to it as he had been to the gibes of the gamins on the London streets. He was young enough to wince at the criticisms of companions he was Chinese enough to despise.

He studied women too when he had the chance, but with all them his relations were impeccably ceremonial and on the surface. His being was in China still, and no English girl stirred his pulse or fogged his subtle shrewdness. James Muir, who watched over him faithful as a mother, had somewhat feared for him when the passing of adolescence into first raw manhood should come pounding at the door of sex. Muir knew that in that experience Englishmen in exile usually found some impulse toward vagary irresistible. But Wu lived on unruffled—alone in Europe, and content with loneliness.

He did not forget Li Lu, but he rarely thought of her now. No doubt she would do well enough when the time came to assert his ownership and desire sons. In the meantime, he was absorbed in carrying out to the minutest particle his grandfather's behest.

There was a girl at a parsonage where he sometimes visited that he thought less uninteresting than the others he met, less like a horse or a tornado or a pudding, more like a girl. And Florence Grey made him shyly welcome at her tea-table and taught him to play croquet. She played a beautiful game, and in their second match he could have beaten her. He gave her father's church a new organ, and made her first bazaar an unprecedented success: he half stocked the tables, and then saw that they were swiftly stripped. She knew of many of his "kind contributions," though not of all his re-purchases—they were indirectly made, and Mrs. Muir in Scotland was not a little aghast at the frills and flummeries her son sent her in three big packing-cases. And the Vicar looked a little askance at the presence of a smirking heathen god, conspicuous, but not for being overdressed, on his daughter's stall.

After the Oxford years came several years of travel, sometimes with Muir, sometimes not. One summer Wu was the Muirs' guest in their simple Scottish home.

After her first sternly concealed qualm or two, the friend's mother took an immense liking to the young Chinese, and her he liked at once, perhaps better than he had ever liked any one but his grandfather and her son. And it was in no way an attraction of opposites. Worth and courage recognized worth and courage, and felt at home with them. Ellen Muir and young Wu were both indomitable, naturally upright, proud, clannish. They had twenty qualities and several prejudices in common.

They talked together gravely for hours. He helped her often as she moved keenly about her housework, and Muir rocked with silent laughter at the sight, knowing that those delicate yellow hands had never performed anything menial before, and in all human probability never would again.

Wu watched his hostess with lynx eyes, and the more he watched the more be respected and admired. Late at night, in the hour he invariably spent alone, and had done so from his first coming to England—the hour in which he read and wrote and spoke and thought in Chinese, when in spirit, and bodily too, he made obeisance to his ancestors' tablets across the world—he wrote down carefully much that she had said and that he had learned from her. Among his many sons the gods might send a daughter, and if they did she too should learn of Ellen Muir.

Wu knew, of course, that many of the English ladies he had seen at theaters and had met at aristocratic dinner-tables were respectable, above reproach. But he had never yet escaped a shudder of contempt when he had seen one "dressed" for evening. He had seen the coolie women, in the cocoon sheds on his grandfather's silkworm farms, scantily clad in one brief garment, that by their own chilliness they might be warned if the room grew too cold for the delicate spinners, and that they might easily shelter the hatching worms beneath their breasts, but that semi-nudity was a necessity and had a use, and rarely was the privacy of the shed invaded; but women undressed (as he termed it) collectively, voluntarily, and interspersed among men, he thought abominable. Ellen Muir did not dine in décolletage.

The eminent scholar—for as such the scholar world now recognized Wu's once tutor—she commanded, and even at times reprimanded, sharply, exacting and receiving the docile obedience of a tractable child. And that appealed to Wu as inevitably as did the high-necked stuff gowns. Mother ruled sons so in China. And in China sons showed their mothers just such meek obedience. The keeper of many of the most valuable treasures at the British Museum spilled marmalade on her best tablecloth one day, and she scolded him roundly, and Wu saw nothing funny in it, and would not, had he known that the son had bought the cloth and kept up the home.

The little house stood on one of the loveliest of Scotland's hillsides. A brown burn rushed by the door. Great birds wheeled and whirred above the eaves. This woman almost worshiped the beauty of her homeland, and it touched her to see how much their strange guest saw and felt it. He saw even more of it than she did—though, fortunately for their mutual liking, she could not suspect that—and he felt it very much indeed. It reminded him of the country beside the Yangtze in the neighborhood of the Falls of Chung Shui.

One long vacation Wu and Muir climbed the Alps and the London papers reported Wu killed. But it was another Chinese, an undergraduate at

Cambridge whose name was Ku, who had misstepped and slid down into the engulfing ice. But the mistake reached Oxford, and several there were sorry to hear it. And Florence Grey, who had been married the week before, heard it on her honeymoon, and felt a little saddened for a few moments. He had always seemed a nice boy, and he was so far from home.

Once he lived for three months in Tours, alone with the people and the language.

After Oxford he traveled carefully, as he had done everything so far, sometimes alone, sometimes with Muir, searching Europe for every experience that might serve his grandfather's desire and plan.

When Wu was twenty-four he went home. James Muir had half expected to be asked to go also, but Wu did not suggest it.

His European phase was over, and he wished to be alone with his own people in his own land.

Bland and courteous to all, yet he spoke little on the long voyage, but sat looking out across the waters towards China. And he did not trouble to leave the boat either at Malta or at Colombo.

But he was not dreaming as he sat brooding, looking out to sea. He was planning, for himself and for his race.

There were international clouds ahead. Wu saw them.

A week in Hong Kong—he had much to do there—and then he pushed across the mainland that was still China, where feet of Europe rarely trod, and journeyed to his home.

When he had paid his long respects to the graves and the tablets, he set his house in order, and the estate. But indeed all had been well kept in his absence. It seemed as if the old mandarin's spirit still brooded there and his adamant will still ruled.

To visit all he owned took Wu some months, though he went swiftly, by boat, by horse, and in chairs with which the coolies ran, for there were several wide estates and a score of smaller holdings.

All seen at last and ordered to his mind, he took the old winding road to Pekin and knocked at Li's yamén gate.

CHAPTER IX
WU LI LU

WU did not see his wife in Pekin. He stayed with Li several days, and long and earnest was their talk, many and deep their interchanged kot'ows, and the cups of boiling tea and tiny bowls of hot spiced wine they drank together innumerable. Mrs. Wu was well, they assured him, and utterly inconsolable at her approaching departure from her parents. She wept and wailed continuously, and would not be comforted. Wu bowed and smiled. For this was as it should be. No Chinese maiden would do otherwise, and his bride's high estate predicated an utmost excess of grief. And once he caught through a wide courtyard the noisy storm of her grief. Evidently she had been well brought up, and Wu was highly satisfied.

He took profoundly respectful farewells of Mr. and Mrs. Li and hurried home.

And while he waited for the coming of his bride, some days thinking of it a good deal, some days thinking of it not at all, he had twofold and strenuous occupation. He divided his time between preparation for the reception and the housing of his wife, and laying the foundations of his own relations with the innumerable "tongs" or secret societies that in China play so powerful and so indescribable a part in all things of great pith and moment, and more particularly in everything touching international affairs and the treatment of aliens in China.

Sociology and political economy had been no small part of Wu's studies in Europe; there he had observed and gleaned much on those lines that he planned to graft upon the sociological and political methods of his own people.

While studying Europe he had kept in passionate touch with China. He knew that the mighty current of her being ran underground. He was permeated by things European now, for the time at least, but was in no way enmeshed by them. He did not make the mistake that some highly intelligent Chinese have made after years of European study and travel—the mistake of underestimating the quality, the power, and the permanence of the "tongs," of which so comparatively little is heard, so much felt, in every part of China.

He knew that who ruled China in deed must rule through the secret societies of that tong-ridden and yet tong-buttressed land; he knew that who would influence and serve China greatly must work through the tongs, or work but half effectually.

He intended to rule in China, to be one of the supreme powers behind and beneath her throne; for he was loyal to the Imperial Manchu, in his heart held no traffic with republicanism or rebellion, and meant to hold none with his hands. He intended to rule because dominance was his nature and his delight, and equally because he believed it to be his duty—his duty to China and to the house of Wu. Even more than he intended to rule he intended to serve. He was his country's servant. He had dedicated his life to China, and sworn her his fealty on almost every day of his exile.

He determined to rule and to serve with and through the established tongs, and himself to establish others, because he saw clearly that so he could serve best, and with the surest, tightest grip.

While he waited for the girl to come with noise and cavalcade, he stayed at home and in the neighborhood of home; but every day odd messengers came and went, quiet, unobtrusive men. Often Wu was closeted for hours with some shabby-looking coolie, footsore and travel-torn. Wu was seeking and making affiliation with tong after tong. He was sowing seed all over vast China.

But he found time, or took it, to oversee every item of the bridal preparation. So lavish had been his orders on his first home-coming, and so well had they been obeyed, that further preparation might have been dispensed with—only a Chinese mind could have detected blemish or contrived improvement or addition. Wu's mind was very Chinese. Thirteen years in banishment had not discolored it in the least. Everything that Lu would touch, every place that she would see, was in some way or detail given additional beauty or comfort. In her garden he lavished a wealth of care. The very flowers seemed to respond to his urging, as things much more inanimate than flowers do respond to such a master will as that of Wu. Wu Lu's garden foamed and glowed with bud, perfume and flower, until even in China there could scarcely have been another spot so roseate or so full of rapture.

There was a pagoda of course, a bridge, a lotus lake, a sun-dial and a forest of tiny dwarf trees.

The pagoda had eleven storeys. Each storey's projecting roof had eight corners, and from each corner Wu had hung a bell of precious blue porcelain, silver lined, silver clappered. The slightest breeze that came must set one or more of the delicate things a-ringing, and by a costly and ingenious device each motion of a bell threw down on the garden not only music, but sweet, aromatic smell—a different odor, as a different note, from each bell.

That was the last thing Wu could find to do.

And then they gave him his wife. They brought her to him through the gloaming one balmy autumn eve, sitting hidden in her flowery chair, carried through the paifang which he had regilded and newly crimsoned in her honor and in that of his never-to-be-forgotten great-grandmother.

She came in greatest state, and much of the glittering ceremonial they had enacted fourteen years ago they re-enacted now; and all that necessarily had been omitted before because of her tender days, and of the marriage having been (irregularly) celebrated at her home in lieu of his, was scrupulously performed now.

At the house door he bent and lifted her from her chair, which the bearers had put down on the ground. She shrank back on her cushions into the farthest corner when he drew the curtains aside, and when he reached to touch her she panted delicately like some frightened pigeon. He could not see her, even when he held her in his arms, for she was shrouded from crown to toe in her voluminous veil of crimson gauze. There had been no difficulty about her wearing it this time. She knew all the niceties of her important rôle, of which she had been so outrageously ignorant before, and performed them to a Chinese perfection. He saw only a red-wrapped bundle—it felt soft and tender to his gentle grip—with an under-gleam of jewels and gold, and the iridescent glitter of the strings of many-colored beads hanging from her crown thickly over her face. And no one else saw even that much, for when the chair had been laid at his feet the bearers and all her retinue and his had turned away and stood backs to the chair.

He carried her in, holding her over a dish of smoking charcoal at the threshold, that all ill-luck might be for ever fumed away from her.

In the great hall he sat her high up upon her chair of state and took his seat on his. For more than an hour they sat so, and neither spoke. But when the wild goose which the medicine-man flung from a lacquered cage circled about her head and not about his own, indicating that she would rule, not he, Wu laughed aloud, and under her red veil the girl looked down at her half-inch embroidered shoe and smiled well pleased.

They drank from one cup. The crimson cord was tied about her wrist and his, fastening them together now for weal or woe.

At length he rose and led her to the tablets of his ancestors—hers too now, for Li was no longer her father—and there they bent together and paid homage again and again.

Then came the marriage feast.

And through all the incense burned, the tom-toms bleated brazenly, a hundred instruments gave out their unchorded melodies, and the slave-girls shrilled Chinese love-songs in their sweet falsetto voices and a marriage hymn that is four thousand years old.

And all this time he had not seen her face, and she but dimly his.

But at last they were left alone. One by one the horde of people who had witnessed and served them made repeated obeisance and withdrew.

They were alone.

Gently, carefully, slowly he led her into an inner room, and there he lifted the red veil and looked at her face. After a long moment she raised her pretty almond eyes and looked in his—two gorgeous, bedizened figures, standing very still, with a cloud of red silk gauze heaped at their feet.

Wu made a sudden sound that was almost a sob, and held out his arms.

"My flower," he said.

All night long the perfume of the flowers, the sweet, shrill voices of the sing-song girls, and the soundings of the guitar and the flutes stole softly in through the chamber casements; all night long they heard the throb, throb of the drums and of old barbaric love-songs; and all night long each felt the beating of the other's heart.

After that Wu Li Lu forgot that she had had a father and a mother, brothers, girl-friends and a home in Pekin. And Wu let all the days slip by, forgetting business of his own, affairs of China, life-plans, life-schemes, almost forgetting his grandfather; scarcely remembering, his wife's soft hand in his, to make obeisance before the old, old tablet in front of which their children would bow and worship them in far-off years to come, when he and Wu Lu should be dead.

For a year they lived in paradise, the pretty paradise that comes but once and does not come to all.

Mrs. Wu was as sweet, as delicate, as the graceful pet names he called her. She had no great strength of character, and little distinction of mind. How long it would have taken the infatuated man to learn this is impossible to guess. Whether, when learned, it would have diminished her fascination in the least is as difficult to determine, but, on the whole, probably not, Wu being Wu in China China.

When their first year closed in she bore him a daughter, and in bearing died.

CHAPTER X
NANG PING

THE years passed, and Wu took no other wife. Time enough, he reasoned; and while he devoted himself, body and soul and seething, subtle intellect, to the big tasks he had set himself and had had set him by the old mandarin long ago, the bachelor habit grew upon him and encrusted him with its self-sufficient and not unselfish little customs, as it does so many men of Europe. Perhaps in this and in some other things Europe had marked and tinged him more than he knew.

Except for his wifelessness, he kept all such establishment as a Chinese gentleman should; there were flower-girls in his retinue and much in his life of which Ellen Muir would have disapproved violently.

He had felt no disappointment at the sex of his firstborn. Perhaps his grief (it was very great) at Wu Lu's death made him indifferent to the great sex-blemish in the child. Or possibly his descent from Queen Yenfi and from a score of ladies little less able or less famed gave him an unconscious estimate of the woman-sex strangely un-Chinese—unless China be misreported.

Mrs. Li had petitioned for the custody of the babe, but Wu had refused sternly. "She is a Wu. She stays with Wu." But he conceded a point—a minor point. A younger sister of Mrs. Li was widowed at about the time of Wu Lu's death, widowed while still a bride and childless. She begged to come and be foster-mother and servant to the motherless babe; and Wu had consented to her coming, for a time at least, partly because he had known and liked her husband, partly in pity for her widowhood—the most uncomfortable condition in Chinese life, and abjectly deplorable when the indignity of childlessness is added—partly because he had no kinswoman of his own to fill a post which he instinctively hesitated to confer on any hireling. Sing Kung Yah came; Wu found her amiable and tractable, and, he thought, fairly efficient. Of her fondness for the child or the child's fondness for her there could be no doubt, and her place in their household soon came to be one of established permanency. From the first Wu exacted for her treatment from his retainers such as Eastern widows rarely enjoy, and gradually he gave her some real authority, as well as much show of it, in addition to the lavish courtesy he paid and enforced for her. Sing Kung Yah was pathetically grateful. She never heard of Ellen Muir, and little thought that she owed her unprecedented ease of widowhood to the dignity and firm despotism with which an Aryan woman had worn her weeds in Fife.

When Nang Ping was three her father brought her to Kowloon, and when she was thirteen established her as mistress of the tiny and very charming estate he had bought and perfected there, just beyond the English holding, and where he made his home when his business lay, as it did more often than not, in Hong Kong.

He knew now that he should take no wife. He had no wish to, and he saw no necessity. For he could adopt a son—presently. There was time enough. A wife was neither here nor there, but certainly a son was indispensable. He could not die without a son. Without a son he could not be properly buried, or mourned and worshiped.

Upon the great wealth his grandfather had left him he piled wealth far greater. But far beyond the riches he amassed he amassed power and influence. The ramifications of his influence were endless and tortuous. Tze-Shi felt Wu's influence as she decreed policies, signed edicts and enacted laws of tremendous reach, weaving and fraying out the destiny of China, and there was not a coolie in Hong Kong but felt and obeyed it. No one in China—unless it was Tze-Shi herself—wielded more power than Wu.

He held the Chinese in Shanghai, in Penang and in Rangoon, in Bentick Street and in Yokohoma, in the hollow of his hand.

Wu wore a mandarin's button now. And he had presented himself at one of the great national examinations in the first year of his fatherhood. To be enrolled among the literati served him and his purposes, as it did to wear the coveted peacock feather. But he did not overvalue either of the showy distinctions, or often wear them conspicuously. Chinese to the core, superficially he was no little cosmopolitan. All that he had found good in English life and in English ways he adopted frankly, but always for a Chinese purpose, with a Chinese heart. At home he usually wore the dress and ate the food of his country, but not always. Out of his home, at least in the treaty ports, he was usually dressed as Englishmen dress, but not always.

Nang Ping had more apparent freedom than other Chinese girls of fair birth have; and some of it was real. She had English governesses from time to time. She spoke English almost as purely as her father did, but with less vocabulary and far less command of idiom, and French quite as well as he; she played Grieg and Chopin better than Hilda Gregory—the rich steamship magnate's only daughter, and not a contemptible pianist—so the German music master who taught them both had told the Governor's wife.

The Gregorys had been in Hong Kong for a year—the mother, the son and daughter, as well as Mr. Gregory himself. But the two girls had never met. Hilda Gregory went everywhere, but Nang Ping did not often leave Kowloon.

CHAPTER XI
IN THE LOTUS GARDEN

KOWLOON was drenched with sunlight, and the lotus garden was drenched with music. A minstrel paused a moment to drink in the beauty of the great lilies, white, yellow, pink, amber and mauve, one that had cost a fortune, clear pale blue, one that had cost more, a delicate jade green.

The strolling singer retuned his lute and moved across the garden, singing as he went.

It was the typical garden of a rich Chinese home—so repeatedly caricatured on the "willow-tree-pattern" crockery of cheap European commerce—caricatured but also somewhat accurately portrayed. But the gardens on the plates for sale in half the pawnshops in outer London (the aristocracy of the pawnbrokers will not look at them any more), in every household furnisher's in Marylebone and Camberwell, in Battersea and Shoreditch, and on the business streets of every British town and village, are of one uniform Chinese blue—the blue the sampsan women wear when their clothes are new—and background of white, Chinese white, appropriately enough. This living garden in Kowloon was of every vivid hue on nature's prodigal palette, and its background was of blue hills and purple haze and blue, white and limpid golden sky.

A twisted camel's back bridge of carved stonework, like coarse lace in its pierced tracery, dragons squatting and guarding its corners, and flowers hung from it everywhere in baskets of bamboo, of crystal, of painted porcelain and of lacquer, spanned one corner of the lake, above which a crooked flight of steps at each bridge-end lifted it high. Dwarf trees in glazed pots, some on the ground, rarer specimens on carved stands of teak wood and of ebony, stood here and there. And in the artificial water, half river, half lake, which the miniature bridge crossed, the priceless lotus grew and glowed. Most of the great lily cups were pink, others were deeply red.

Some distance from the house there was a pagoda open to the garden, its plaid floor strewn with cushions, a book or two, a woman's scarf, and from every outer point and eave hung a pot or a basket in which flowers of every brilliant hue grew and bloomed.

A sinuous gravel path turned from the dwelling-house to the outer wall, twisting and turning ingeniously all over the garden, passing close to the cypress bush at the foot of the steps that led to the bridge, skirting the baby grove of dwarf orange and lemon trees, and encircling the gnarled old cherry tree.

Whatever we may think of China, the sun thinks well, and shines so gloriously nowhere else. It made the flowers in Nang Ping's garden glow with a vivid brilliance that was part their own, part his; it touched the summits of the hills seen in the distance with a light blue haze which deepened to purple at their base. Against that dark purple background the sumptuous little garden foreground glowed with a riot of color, and quivered with pulsing, scent-breathing flowers.

A servant squatted on his yellow heels, picking up dead leaves and broken flowers heads, gathering them into his tidy basket. Another gardener was sweeping the gravel path as carefully as if it had been the velvet carpet than which it was no less soft.

Four girls tripped down the bridge, chattering and laughing as they came, and the gardeners took up basket and broom and moved away.

Hearing the singer (he had left the garden now), the girls rushed with one accord, and climbed and clambered up until they could peer at him over the wall. One poised like a fat balloon-shaped butterfly on the high edge of a great flower-pot, two jostled together tip-toe on a majolica bench, and one (the smallest footed of the lot) climbed squirrel-nimble up a tulip tree. They pelted him with flowers, tearing blossoms ruthlessly from shrub and vase and vine and tree, and each commanded him shrilly to sing to her her favorite song.

"Chong-chong er-ti" (professional singer), "sing on," one cried; "Yao won chong" (let us play with him), another; and the girl in the tree tore the jasmine from her hair and tossed it into his hands.

He leaned against the wall and sang:

"Over green fields and meadows Tiny Rill ran

(The little precocious coquette!);

She was pretty, she knew, and thus early began

Gayly flirting with all that she met.

Her favors on both sides she'd gracefully shower;

One moment she'd kiss the sweet lips of a flower,

The next lave the root of a tree;"

and as he sang, Nang Ping, with Low Soong, her cousin, in her wake, came slowly from the house, and stood listening too, one finger on her lips, her eyes far on the fading hills.

They did not see their mistress—they were her play-girls, in attendance on rich Wu's child—until the man had done and gone. But when they did they rushed to her, laughing and pelting her with speech. "Nang Ping! Nang Ping! Come, play with us! Come, play!" But she beat them off, saying, "Go away. I do not want you now. Go away."

But they clustered the closer and girdled her with their arms, but again she shook them off, repeating impatiently, "Pa choopa, pa choopa;" and realizing that she meant it, they went, tumbling against each other as they ran laughing and singing, and turning as they went, and hurling flowers at her, and crying, "Pu yao choopa," that they did not wish to go away.

When they had gone the cousins went to the pagoda, looked in it, and then about it, carefully. Then they beat the garden as some careful watchman might some treasure-place of price.

It was growing dusk.

The girls went together to the lotus basin, and stood a long time looking down into its darkling glass. But neither spoke. The brilliant lilies were softer-colored now, turning to pink and blue-greys, and the red few almost to ruddy black.

A long, low whistle pierced through the gloaming from beyond the wall.

Nang Ping's tiny hand clutched excitedly at her sash. "Soetzo"—"go and watch over the bridge," she told her cousin quickly. But Low Soong had already gone.

The blackbird whistle came again, nearer, but very soft.

Nang Ping answered it with a high falsetto crooning, and in a moment more a man cautiously parted the bamboos that grew clumped beyond the wall, vaulted it, and stood within the garden. Nang Ping ran to him with a little gurgling cry, and he caught her in his arms.

No Chinese lover this, in Oriental gala dress, with glancing amber eyes and coarse threads of strong red silk prolonging his long braid of straight hair, but a Saxon, wide gray-eyed, a distinct wave in his fair short hair, trim and British in his well-cut suit of white duck, with the crimson cummerbund wound about his waist.

He looked down with laughing tenderness at the picturesque little creature in his clasp, half-affectionate, half-amused, and she looked up at him with all a woman's soul—soul aflame—and all a nation's passion in her eyes, adoring and perfect trustfulness.

"Oh! my celestial little angel," he murmured at her flushing cheek.

The girl nestled closely and sighed with content, and he held her, and played with the dangling jewel in her fantastic hair.

"You have been so cruel long, Basil," the girl told him gently, but moving not at all.

Basil Gregory laughed lightly. "So? I could not come before. You're an impatient puss."

Nang Ping shook her sheeny head, and the red flower in her wonderfully dressed hair shook and quivered, and all the jade stick-pins and the hanging emeralds and turquoise jangled against the tassel of small pearls that she wore pendant from her comb. "No. I am never impatient. But the sun-dial tells not lies. You came not soon, and I did miss you hard."

"Well, I've brought you news. Guess."

"Thy honorable mother———"

"Good girl! You've guessed it first go. My mother and Hilda are coming to-morrow to make the acquaintance of pretty Miss Wu and to see her very honorable garden."

"Your mother and your sister," the girl said under her breath softly. "Ah!"

"They were no end pleased to come, especially the mater. She'd come quick enough anywhere I told her to. We've been the greatest chums always, the mater and I. Hilda pals with the governor, but she's no end keen on China, the motherkin—goes into all sorts of smelly dives and dens after blue plates and shaky ivory balls, and—and all that sort of thing, you know; reads the rummiest books, knows all about spotted dragons and crinkly gods. She bought one yesterday, a rum, fat fellow made out of some sort of crockery stuff; he sits squatted on the floor this minute in her own room, and if you pat him on his noddle the old chap nods it, and goes on nodding it, too, for a blessed hour by the clock"—Nang Ping understood less than half of this truly British ramble, and listened to it with a puzzled smile—"and she is no end keen to come, to see how things are done in real China. I wouldn't wonder if she wrote an article for one of the picture papers at home—'The Chinese at Home,' or some such stuff. I say, you'll be sure to give her tea Chinese fashion. No borrowed European tricks, you know; just pucka Chinaman way!"

Nang Ping understood the drift, if not quite all his words. "It shall be as you wish: Chinese reception, Chinese delicacies, offered Chinese way."

"That will be ripping then."

"How strange it will be to talk with thy honorable mother!" the girl said wistfully. "And thy sister! Is she like me, or more beautiful?" she asked most seriously. And that he might judge his answer the more nicely and adjust his answer to exact truth, she went from him a few paces, opened her fan wide, spread out her arms, and stood very still, a pathetic figure of Chinese girlhood on view, waiting, anxious but meek, an Englishman's verdict. And then, remembering that the light was somewhat dim, she came a little nearer, but not too close, and repeated her grave question, "Is thy honorable sister like Nang Ping, or even more beautiful?"

Basil laughed with kindly patronage. "Hilda?" Strolling to the wide stone bench he threw his hat on to it and sat down. "All nice girls are like each other, Nang Ping. Hilda's so-so. But Tom Carruthers thinks she's 'top-side' nice. Carruthers, the governor's secretary, and I rather think he's going to be my honorable brother-in-law. The governor won't object. Tom's right enough, and old Carruthers got any amount of tin. The Right Reverend John B. thinks Sis nice too, or I'm greatly mistaken. It's a queer freak for a parson, for Hilda isn't exactly churchified, but Bradley finds her nice all right."

"And my lord finds me nice?"

The gray eyes narrowed. "Very nice," the man answered, and held out his arms.

She went at once and sat down on the other end of the bench. Gregory bent and kissed her, and presently she kissed him in return. And the sudden darkness thickened, creeping closer, for there is no true gloaming, no lingering dusk, in the Orient. It is day there, or else it is night.

The glow-worms came out then and speckled the garden with tiny points of fire. Nang Ping called them by a prettier name: kwang yin têng, lamps of mercy, as her father had called them when, as a boy of ten, he crossed Sze-chuan to wed her baby mother in Pekin.

They kissed again, the man and the girl. Kissing is not a Chinese art. Basil Gregory had taught Wu Nang Ping to kiss.

"Oh! if only I could!" the girl said impulsively, and then broke off as suddenly as she had begun.

"Could what, Nang Ping?" He asked it a little uneasily—uneasy at a something in her voice.

"Tell them all about us," she replied simply, but her voice aglow with ecstasy at the thought.

Gregory was aghast. "Tell them all about us!" he cried hoarsely.

"Oh! not all things," she whispered, creeping a little closer in his arms. "There are some things one would not tell, even to the birds."

Basil Gregory's conscience, to its credit, shuddered sickly then, and his arm trembled, not in tenderness, but in shame.

But self-preservation is indeed the first law of much man-nature, and he said quickly, "I don't mind what you tell to the birds, but you must be extremely careful not to let my mother or sister know. *Extremely careful*," he repeated with dictatorial emphasis.

"Why?"

"They would not understand."

"Why?"

He made no answer, and after a little she questioned on, "They would not like to know that *you* are happy?"

"Of course they would, but——"

"And that it is I that make you happy?" the light young voice pestered on wistfully.

The Englishman shifted uneasily on his seat. "Oh, no! nothing of that sort, to them, Nang Ping," he said petulantly. "Don't try to understand. Just leave it all to me."

"But," the girl persisted, "do they not understand love?" She put her arms about him.

"Oh! well," he parried, "you see, they are English—very English."

"But they are women." The Chinese girl shook her head, smiling unconvinced, and all its jeweled filigree twinkled and winked in the opalescent half light. "They are women. All women understand love, even before the man comes to teach them. We are born so. Your honorable mother and the honorable Hilda, they understand; Nang Ping is sure they do, the wise and virtuous ladies."

"Not—not altogether. You see, things are different with us. Secret love is not looked upon like—like married love."

The girl laughed softly. "Then let it be no longer secret!" she purred contentedly, warmly willing to make his people hers, their ways her ways. "You shall tell them!" she said brightly, laying her little hands palm down on his.

"Oh! but, Nang Ping," Basil began miserably. But Nang would have none of that. She nestled to him closer still. "Basil," she interrupted, "if our love were not secret, but married love, and I flew away with you before my honorable father came back, then would thy honorable mother like me in her house?— if I did that—for love make brave for everything?"

Gregory was almost choking. But he controlled himself: that was the least he could do for her now. "Dear child!" he said huskily, and then he kissed her. There was tenderness in his kiss, and passion and bitter remorse. She felt the passion and the tenderness. He broke from her gently and moved away, standing looking down moodily at the darkening lotus flowers, distressed, all his light-hearted happiness of idle, selfish weeks gone, gone forever. "Oh, Nang Ping!" presently he said ruefully, "it would be better if you had never met me," and he moved restlessly still a little farther away.

But still she would not understand. She rose and went to him, and put her little arms about him again. "No," she said with tender, caressing emphasis, "because I am happy." And then she added—for it was growing dark, something that lay warm on her heart to say—that must be said soon now, "Basil's honorable mother would like me then, if—if I gave a son to worship at the grave of thy ancestors!"

Gregory recoiled a little from the girl's gentle, clinging arms—recoiled with a startled cry: the world-old cry of man confronted for the first time with very self; the cry of man hoist at last with his own petard. But pity, too, for her, as yet so free from pity for herself, welled up in him (he was not all bad—who is?), and he controlled himself again for her sake. It was difficult, but even so it was not much to do in return for what she had done for him. And it was the only return that he could make, or would, the giving her some gentleness of treatment even in the crash of his own dismay. He came back, and caught her elbows in his hands, and held her from him so—at arm's length. "Nang Ping," he tried to say it lightly, "what amazing ideas you get into your head!"

"No," she said stoutly, "not so! Listen! All the women in China make one big prayer in the temples to the goddess Kwan-Yin"—he released her arms, letting his fall at his sides helplessly, his fingers clenched in his palms—"a prayer to her to bring them a son!"

Her lover turned away, distressed, tormented.

"Oh!" he said brokenly, "what a fool I've been!" It is almost the oldest of the man-cries, almost as old as "I love you" and "I take you for my own."

Nang Ping ran to him, crying, "Oh! how I love you, Basil! I want to fill my hands with happiness to pour it at *your* feet. Do you know how my mother died? She died when she bore me to her lord my father. And I would gladly die so, only the child must be a son, to worship at your grave and to teach his sons and his sons' sons to worship so." The pretty, delicate creature clung to him in an ecstasy of devotion, all her fresh womanhood dedicated to him, and then she laughed softly, pressed her hands together in a lightened mood. "Oh! I would gather the dew from the cherry blossoms to bathe me in its scent, to make me more beautiful to thee!" And this, too, was an old, old cry, as old as woman-sex.

"You see me, Lord Bassanio, where I stand,

Such as I am: though for myself alone

I would not be ambitious in my wish,

To wish myself much better; yet, for you

I would be trebled twenty times myself."

A girl in Belmont put it so, in a dream a man dreamed beneath an English mulberry tree. And girls have said it countless times, each girl after her own sweet fashion, and men have accepted it, some in manhood splendidly, some in dastardy cravenly. Basil accepted it in shame, drinking the bitter cup of his selfish brewing.

"But," he said, bending over her tenderly as she clung to him, "you are as beautiful as the cherry blossom itself, Nang Ping."

She bent back and looked up searchingly into his face, and then she broke away and danced a little from him, as if too quick with her own joy to stand longer still. "And as happy as heaven!" she cried. "Ah! and when they see me, will they not guess?"

"Oh! but you mustn't let them; you must not," his answer came quickly.

She shook her head slowly. "But I am all happiness that I cannot hide." Then a new thought caught and frightened her, and she turned back to him anxiously. "If they guessed, would they take you from me?"

"Why, yes," he told her quickly, snatching at her idea; "they might—yes—yes—certainly they would."

"Oh, no, no! That would kill me." She shuddered as she spoke.

He went to her now, and standing behind her put his arms about her again. "Oh!" he said contritely, "you mustn't think so much of me, Nang Ping. You were happy before—before you met me——"

"But I was only waiting for you to come," she said.

At that he kissed her. How could he help doing it?

"I was really only two moons old. I was only sleeping and waiting, like those lotus flowers, waiting for you to come and wake me. You are my summer and my sun."

"That's all very poetical, Nang Ping," he said, fondling at her elaborate and stiffened hair, "but you must not take all this too seriously, you know."

She broke away from him at that, speaking wistfully as she moved. "I do not understand you. You are the poem of my life and the song that sings in my heart!"

The man's face darkened with trouble. He was indeed troubled. But still he spoke kindly, and he went to her and caressed her lightly, soothingly, as he said, "Listen, Celeste."

"Ah!" the girl cried, "you gave me that name. That makes me yours. I am Nang Ping no more."

"Listen, Celeste"—at a change, a chilliness in his tone, she stiffened a little; it is so most women face a blow—"my people are going home—father, mother, my sister Hilda——"

"So soon!" But her face brightened, in spite of herself, as she said it; it was not such very bad news after all. "How can they bear to leave you?" she added wonderingly.

"They can't," Gregory said desperately. She did indeed stiffen then. And there was piteous accusation in her eyes. But she said nothing; and presently he went on lamely enough, "and that is what I had to tell you."

"You—you are leaving me?" the girl said very quietly.

"I must."

"But," she said intensely, "you will not go. You will tell them that you cannot go—*now*!"

He must have understood her then, if he had failed, as he had tried to fail, to do so before. "I couldn't tell them about you, dear." Poor wretch! it was the best that he could find to say. "With us, things like that are not so easy," he added weakly.

"But you could tell them that you cannot leave me," Nang Ping pleaded. "You *must* tell them that," she whispered desperately.

"But I am not leaving you forever, little one," the man faltered. "England is not many weeks from here."

"Yes, but I cannot follow you!"

Follow him! The heavens forbid! "No, of course not," he said quickly, "of course not, you silly little Celeste. But I shall come back. Some day, when you least expect me, I shall be here in the lotus garden or in the pagoda."

"The pagoda!" she moaned.

"The pagoda," he hurried on, "where we learned to love." He tried to draw her to him, but she recoiled. "No, no!" she cried hotly. "If the bird of love once leaves its nest, the nest grows cold." And then she broke quite down and threw herself sobbing on the steps of the bridge.

"Oh, Celeste!" Basil Gregory said wretchedly, humbly—he was humbled, for the hour at least, and wretchedly uncomfortable—"I—I didn't know your love could mean so much, but—but—oh! well, don't you see?—won't you see?—even if I didn't go it could not last forever, this." That was bad and crude enough; but he went on and made it worse (such men usually do). "I— I am not a mandarin in my own country, not even the son of one; and you know *you* are to marry a mandarin here in your—your own country." (He had heard that more than once in Hong Kong; and really he had supposed she knew he knew. It was commonly known. And many wondered why Wu Li Chang had let it wait so long.)

Nang Ping looked up at him, her narrow eyes wide with horror. "Not now!" she said tensely. "And when I tell my august father why, he will kill me," she added as quietly.

"You—tell him why?" the man cried in consternation.

"Yes, because now I do not wish to live."

"You must not tell him!" he said roughly.

"Only when you are gone, or he would kill you too!" Nang said, simply and without bitterness. The Englishman winced. "He will ask me why I disobey him, and I shall tell him."

"Don't do that—not that! I couldn't have it on my conscience!" And indeed he tried to believe that he said it for her sake. "Keep our secret, Celeste," he begged. "Think of the perils we have run whilst he was here"—the Chinese girl smiled a little at that wanly—"of the happiness we have had when he has been away, as he is now. Tell him nothing, for fear, for fear, dear, that when I came back we should never again be able to meet."

"You will never come back."

"I will, Celeste—I swear it! I swear it now! I see things differently."

"You will never come back." She turned slowly, and without looking back went on into the house.

"Celeste, come back! Nang Ping! Nang Ping!" he called, and she knew that he was calling her to say at least good night, as was their custom, in the pagoda. But she neither slowed her quiet step nor turned her head. The pagoda had sheltered her happiness; it should not be soiled by her despair. She went on and left him standing alone by the lotus lake.

He waited there a while, confident that she would come back to him; but presently, convinced that she would not come that night, or perhaps could not, he went stealthily away, very sorry for himself and not a little vexed with Nang Ping: the offender is easily vexed.

Low Soong came from the coign of watch, looking after him curiously, and wondering what had happened. She had seen little and heard nothing, but she sensed trouble in the air. Basil did not turn or speak to her, and when he had gone she passed slowly into the house.

There was not a sound in the garden. The darkness had come. Nothing was visible except the gay lanterns and many lamps lit on the walls and at the house-door, and in the deserted garden itself the vivid pulse of the glow-worms poised on shrubs and trees or winging brilliantly through the purple night.

CHAPTER XII
O CURSE OF ASIA!

DO you know Hong Kong? If not, you are poor with poverty indeed. Except in China earth has no lovelier spot, and heaven itself needs none. The interior of the island is almost bleak, not beautiful, but its edge is paradise.

Other unknown wonder-places you may a little learn from books, from travelers and from pictures, but not Hong Kong. No words can in the least describe it. The attempt is an impertinence. Canvas and camera are useless too. "Hong Kong," the gazetteers say, means "Fragrant Streams" or "Place of Sweet Lagoons." But they are absurd. "Hong Kong" means "superbly beautiful." If you know it, your eyes have been enriched forever. Climb the Peak, feathered with fern and bamboos, you are enwalled in beauty. Go far along the island by-ways, beauty leans toward you from every side, and beckons you on and still on. Pause on the bamboo-outlined path that bisects the great amphitheater of Happy Valley, and you may bathe your spirit and your sight in beauty, whether you look to the right, where the graves of European dead in China rest beneath their sumptuous coverlets of flowers, or to the left, where the Chinese jockeys, with their blue petticoats tucked up above their brown hips, and their bright satin jackets showing up their dancing cues, and English boys in regimental colors—gentlemen riders—canter neck to neck on the race-course, rehearsing the ponies for to-morrow's race.

It is a unique juxtaposition, that sweet and perfumed bit of God's acreage, and the lurid, teeming race-course, the dead men's bones (and women's, too, and babes') just under the grass, and the betting, straining, champagne-drinking, well-dressed crowd, with only a narrow strip of yellow, bamboo-fringed path between; unique as is the old juxtaposition of life and death, and, too, strangely eloquent and appropriate of Anglo-Chinese life.

Hong Kong! Heaven and Hell in one. Hong Kong a gem of lovely, laughing China given to Britain—or, perhaps, loaned for a century or two. Wu often wondered which.

Every light in Victoria seemed twinkling hard as Basil Gregory's boat gained the shore, a lamp in every window, a thousand painted paper lanterns, no two shaped or colored alike, swaying ambiently in the hands of coolies who trotted along the bund and up the hill paths, along the Bowen Road and peak-climbing streets, carrying chairs, pulling rickshaws, or running errands, uninterested but faithful, the most reliable hirelings on earth, and often, when the European employer gives himself half a chance with them, the most devoted.

Basil walked some distance from the spot where he had landed before he hailed a rickshaw. The naked coolie grunted a little at the address the Englishman gave him, but said grimly, "Can do." For Gregory had named a bungalow that nestled in a tiny grove of persimmon and loquat trees, nearly halfway up the Peak—and Hong Kong Peak is steep.

It was not his home address that he had given, nor that of any club respectable or otherwise, or tree-hidden wayside tea-house, but the bungalow of a man he had treated none too well, and to call upon whom this was an odd hour.

In our moments of greatest personal dilemma and peril we seek the strangest confidants: sometimes in half-crazed desperation, sometimes in shame and fear of our nearer and dearer, sometimes instinctively, and *then* oddly often it proves well done. But whatever the most general explanation, most of us are prone at such tremulous times to lean upon some one not of our constant or closest entourage.

Basil Gregory had little estimate of Wu's position and power, and none at all of Chinese character. But he had heard something of Wu, of course, and had read unconsciously something of her father between the pretty lines of Nang Ping's gilded home life, and the young fellow realized that he was in personal peril, though he had not the least impression of how much.

He knew that he needed advice and a sounder judgment than his own.

His mother was his chum, and had been from his birth—they had stood together and pulled together always; but he could not take this to his mother. And he hoped to goodness it need not reach his father's ear. He feared his father's anger far less than he did his mother's sorrow, and he divined that the paternal anger would be nine-tenths financial and not more than one-tenth moral. But such an escapade as his was calculated to injure a business that depended considerably upon a nice balance of British interests and Chinese industriousness and acquiescence. And the elder Gregory could be nasty at times, and disconcertingly close-fisted too. Certainly he could turn to neither parent now. He was not brave, but he certainly would have thrown himself into Hong Kong harbor or into the deadlier foaming rapid of Tsin-Tan rather than have had his mother know the truth about Nang Ping.

In his schooldays he had made half friends, half foes with a boy a few years his senior, whose influence, the little way it had gone, had all been to the good for Basil.

Basil had not done well at school or at 'Varsity. But 'Varsities are fairly used to that, and are built of long-suffering stuff, and young Gregory's shortcomings had not over-mattered at Queen's. But at school—a nice school, strictly run—he had been in serious trouble more than once, and once had been saved from expulsion by Jack Bradley, and at some sacrifices on Bradley's part.

Both the school and the 'Varsity had been rather inappropriately selected. Basil came of commercial stock and was dedicated to a commercial life, and commercial life of a sort for which a few years' business training in Chicago would have been more useful preparation than any amount of term-keeping at Oxford. But Gregory the father, who had had a very limited education, was, as is usual with such men of means, obsessed that his son should have the public-school and 'Varsity hallmark that he himself lacked. And Mrs. Gregory had wished it no less ardently. She had Oxford associations in her blood and of her girlhood, and her own father had worn an Oxford hood and held a modest incumbency near the town.

Basil Gregory learned some of the prescribed lessons at public school: he had to. And he might have learned something of books and other erudite lore at Oxford, for they do teach at the 'Varsities any one who insists upon being taught. But Basil had not insisted, and left Oxford knowing a little less than when he went.

Bradley had been at Queen's, but had worked while Basil played, and such intimacy as had been between them died away, naturally enough, in the wider life and the greater individual freedom and scope of 'Varsity. But they had met sometimes; and once Bradley had been of great service to Gregory.

When Basil had reached Hong Kong a year ago, John Bradley had been serving there for some time as a curate in the Cathedral Church of St. John.

The young priest had held out an eager, friendly hand at once, but Basil had almost ignored it. It was shabby of him, and he knew it at the time. He knew that the other's overtures were not in the least to the rich ship-owner's son, but altogether to an old schoolmate newly come to a foreign country.

The priest—he lived quite alone—was just sitting down to his solitary dinner when Basil's rickshaw came through the gate, ran up the path between the tall lychee trees, and stopped at the door.

The older man gave the younger the cordial greeting of their old days, and added, "Come and eat. Oh! but you must. I'm famished."

And Basil sat down, both glad and sorry to postpone even by half an hour the unpleasant tale he had come to tell.

The priest was no anchorite, and his simple food was good, his wine sound. Both had their flattering tonic effect upon the easily influenced peccant, and as he ate and drank his misdemeanor dwindled away in his own eyes, until almost it seemed to him that he had been more sinned against than sinner.

But it seemed nothing of the sort to John Bradley, and it was soon evident as Gregory unfolded his errand while they smoked on the tiny balcony that jutted out into the begonias and laburnums of the little garden. The priest was sorrowful, but the man was furious. With some effort he heard the other through, and then he ripped out an ugly oath.

The visitor was astonished. Old John had always been a bit particular, of course—had to, don't you know, and all that—but a man of the world and a thorough good sort. And this was not the first confession his schoolfellow had made to him.

"I say, easy all," Gregory protested. "I wish it hadn't happened"—you nearly always do—"but you needn't play Peter Prigg. It isn't one of your flock. The girl's a nice little girl. I'm fond of her, I tell you. But she isn't one of your reserved flock. She's Chinese——"

"Oh, hell and damnation!" interrupted Bradley, striking the well-built railing with a fist so angry that the interlaced bamboos quivered and shook, "that's the infamy of it. If you had to be a beast, don't you see how much less loathsome you'd have been if you had seduced some girl of your own race?"

The other was too dumbfounded to reply, and the priest pounded on: "O curse of Europe! That such men as you pour into Asia and do this damnable thing! You'll boil in oil for this. You insufferable ass! Don't you realize in the least who and what her father is? You might better have affronted Tze-Shi herself. Boil in oil, I tell you, and, by God, so you ought! If it were not for your mother, I'd help Wu to heat it. How would you like some Chinese man to do to your sister what you have done to this girl? Oh! you needn't spring up like that. You'll not put a finger to me. I could pitch you over there, down to the road a thousand feet below, and for half a string of counterfeit cash I'd do it too. Oh! Basil, old chap, how could you, how could you——"

"Well," sulkily, "I'm not the first."

"No," brokenly, "and you'll not be the last. And where will it end, where will it end!"

"I thought you——"

"Oh! I don't mean where will this special case end—for you and for that poor child I know how it will end—but how will it all end?—the putrid inter-racial welter and tangle that we Christians have made! And we—misunderstanding China, spoiling China, insulting her people, fattening on her industry—we, we English call ourselves men! We push our way into China. We laugh at everything she holds sacred, mock what we should admire, condemn what we lack the brain to understand, spit on a culture four thousand years older and in a good deal as much deeper and more sincere than ours, we steal what we want—oh, yes! it's just that, most of it—we teach her boys to smoke opium, we show her a dozen new corruptions, teach her twenty new sins, we seize and spill her thimbleful of saki and give her a tumbler of brandy, and her women—her women——" he broke off.

The other man winced now. He knew there were tears in Bradley's eyes, perhaps on his face. Just once before he had known John in tears, and he thought of it now, a never-to-be-forgotten radiant summer day when a young boy, an only child, had been publicly expelled from school for the saddest of young crimes—the one crime that even the laxest of our public schools neither forgive nor condone—and sent broken home to his mother, a widow.

"You'd like to throttle me when I dare say, 'How would you like it, what would you think of it then, if a Chinese man treated your sister as you have treated this Chinese girl?' Well, I say it again—and I hold your sister very dear—I say it again. And I say more: I say, '*Why not?* You have set the example—you and some generations of Christian gentlemen! And I tell you the day of reckoning will come." With a gesture of despair he picked up his discarded pipe and filled it with nice men's opium—tobacco.

When he had lit his pipe, Bradley sat and pulled at it moodily, and for a while Basil, thrashed and sore, sat and watched him. But the prick of personal dilemma could not give way long to, or even be dwarfed by, any thought of a general tragedy, be it as great and terrible even as Bradley averred.

"You said you knew how this was going to end for me——"

"And for her! Yes. It began in selfishness. It will go on, forever, in misery. It will end in misery. But there is just one thing now. A crime can never be so damned black that it can't be made blacker. Yours is black enough, and it is going to stop right there. You must marry her."

"I say——"

"You needn't. There is nothing for you to say; you have come to me for help, and I am going to help you, as far as I can."

"But——"

"Oh! there'll be trouble—plenty of trouble. Wu will never forgive you or the poor child; though it's he himself he ought not to forgive for having let a Chinese girl out and unwatched so *with us English about.* He'll punish you both, and what Wu does he does well. There'll be no escaping him. No boat will take you beyond his reach, no spot on earth hide you. You can't stay in China with her. Her position would be too intolerable, even for one of us to inflict on a woman. You must take her to England—if you can get there. And even if Wu lets you do the best you can with the monstrous mess you've made of life for yourself and for her, you'll both be miserable there, but not quite so miserable as you'd be in China. England is the one country on earth where the Eurasian, the poor innocent mongrel result of such conduct as yours, is treated a little better than contagion and vermin. Think what chance your children would have here! You have seen such children here, and how they fare!"

Little as he, in common with most of his race, had troubled to observe in Asia, Basil Gregory knew well enough how those half-European, half-Chinese were despised and treated in Hong Kong, and how much more despised by the Chinese than by the Europeans. And he knew too—though not so thoroughly as Bradley did—that to the Chinese at least such Eurasians were doubly despised when born in wedlock. The Chinese mind has some contemptuous shrug of "n'importe" for such racial misdemeanor that is unaffectedly wanton, but to that mind marriage makes the gross miscarriage ten times more putrid. Such few attempts at European-Chinese marriage as are braved in China are between, almost always, European men and Chinese women. Exiled, the Chinese will marry and treat well and honorably the women of the race of the place in which he lives—he does it in Singapore, in Chicago and in Rio—but never for him such mixed marriage in China.

Basil had no intention of making the experiment in China or otherwise. Escape, not atonement, was his intention.

"Yes," he said presently, "and if only for that reason, the children, don't you see that it would better end here and now? At the worst—now—one. But if—if I did marry Nang and take her to England, there might be others."

Bradley groaned. "It is all very difficult. The consequences of wrong always are. I don't see my way. You must let me think a bit; perhaps to-morrow I'll see what's best, least bad!" He groaned again, but he did not tell Gregory that it had just occurred to him that legal marriage without Wu's consent might prove impossible. Wu's consent would never be had, he thought. They solve such problems differently in China. They cut them.

CHAPTER XIII
Mrs. Gregory

ON one point, and on just one, John and Basil had agreed last night: Mrs. Gregory was to be spared as much as possible. She and Hilda were to remain happily ignorant of what had happened—ignorant of it in its worst form, if that could be compassed.

Basil had carefully omitted telling the clergyman of the proposed visit of the morrow. He would have cancelled it if he could have thought of any way. But he had not a devisive brain. His mother had quite set her heart on the excursion. He felt safe that he could trust to Nang Ping's pride. Her pride would carry her through, and save and screen him, as such outraged womanly pride has saved and screened such men ever since Eve gave an apple to a man in Eden.

In this episode of Nang Ping (a little nefarious episode of his life; the soul-crux, the supreme tragedy of the girl) Basil Gregory cut the sorriest figure, for he had but toyed with her, he had indulged passion, passion had not mastered him, she was his toy, he her god; he felt tenderness for her, but not love; he had not the great excuse of a great love. His lingering by the sun-drenched lotus pond and in the scented dark of the old pagoda had been mere dalliance, not obsession. And yet the young Englishman was not all bad—far from that. To no one do the wise lines of the Western genius apply more closely:

"In men, whom men proclaim divine,

I find so much of sin and blot;

In men, whom men condemn as ill,

I find so much of goodness still—

I hesitate to draw the line

Between the two where God has not."

There is a streak, at least, of angel in most women and in all men. Basil had a rich vein of angel. All that was best in him leapt to his mother. They had been sweethearts from the first. Such love as he had loved as yet was hers. It was a chivalrous love, and passionate. The other primal love, the love of man for his mate, might come to him: probably it would; it comes to most, but it would never equal the love he bore his mother. No other woman would ever be to him half that his mother was, or have from him half that he gave her.

Mothers that are loved so can face most sorrows with some buoyancy. This mother had sorrow, and she fronted it almost blithely.

Between these two, in a very beautiful sense, the spiritual umbilical cord had never been cut, and never would or could be cut.

She appealed to him in a dozen ways. She was gifted with youth. She laughed at the years, and they laughed back at her and caressed her. She looked his own age, scarcely more, and some days, in some moods and in some lights, she looked his junior. And, too, hers was a radiant personality. Her son joyed in her. He was proud of her, and proud to be seen with her. And she gave him love for love. But her love for him needs no explanation, nor merits one; he was her boy and her firstborn.

The night before, after Bradley had cried, "I don't see my way. You must let me think," the two men had sat silent for a time, and then the clergyman had re-begun, trying again to thrash it out, breaking nervously the silence he himself had enjoined. And he had referred again to the hideous discomfort of mixed marriages.

The waters of the Tigris do not mingle with the salt water of the sea until they have flowed through it a long, long way from the river-mouth. And so, it seemed to him, many suffering generations must pass before, if ever, any marriage could in truth unite races of East and West, or result in descendants less than sorely unhappy and bitterly resentful.

But marriages that tie the bloods of alien races are not the only mixed marriages. There are mixed marriages of another sort that bring as much, perhaps more, discomfort to the two most directly concerned, although they entail no social inconvenience: marriages of alien individualities. Such his mother's marriage had proved, and Basil sensed it, and that she winced daily. He had never definitely realized it. He had never thought about it clearly. But he felt it. And this had roused all the angel in him to her defense, and made him very true and knightly to her.

The daughter of a poor Oxford cleric, Florence Grey had married "surprisingly well." Robert Gregory was rich even then, good-looking, jovial, and to his young and pretty wife indulgent. He was indulgent to her still.

She had married him quite gladly, and for a time been well enough content. But after a year or two the sag had come and the disillusion. What in him had seemed once tonic and individuality came to seem brusque, and even boorish at times. She grew used to silken raiment and spiced meats, used and a little indifferent, though doubtless she would have missed them had she lost them, a tinge contemptuous of them. And often in the whirl of life—in Manchester, in Paris, in Calcutta, and now in gay Hong Kong—she longed a little for the Oxford quiet and Oxford ways, cool, green lanes, a dim old church, a shabby old library, dim too, full of well-worn books, simple usual things—roast mutton, milk pudding, and soft English rain, gray English skies.

But, too, she enjoyed life, and reaped from it with both hands. And her husband had been and was well content. He had married her for love, and he loved her still. But he had had no exultation and no opalescent anticipations. And so, reasonably enough, he had suffered no relapse. Such extremes of feeling, such quiver and ardor as he had ever known, had come to him in office and shipping yard. Business was his cult. And so far he had proved an excellent business man. He was perfectly satisfied with himself; and it never occurred to him that any one else was not. That would be preposterous, and certainly Florence was not preposterous. He was magnificently satisfied with himself, and in a suitably smaller way he was satisfied with his wife.

She had given him no cause to be dissatisfied. And they got on well together. They always had. She wore well. She dressed well. She never tried to understand his business, or to talk to him when he was reading the market reports or the shipping news. She was a handsome creature. People liked her. And she had borne him two children. He would have resented a third; to have had none would have enraged him as much as if he'd been a "Chinaman."

Yes, Florence had done him very well, and he acknowledged it to himself, and boasted of it to all his cronies. And he had done her well too, by Jove! He was always kind to her. He let her have her own way absolutely when her way did not cross his, and their ways too rarely met (in any soul-sense) to cross often. And he was generous to her. He began that way, and, it is no little to the credit of so busy and business-bound a man, he had always kept it up. They had been married twenty-five years, and he bought flowers for her still. And jewelry he gave her constantly. No woman, unless she was the wife of a rich noble or a millionaire, had more good jewelry.

Mr. Gregory had given his wife some good jewelry for a wedding present. But the handsomest gifts she had received then had been sent her by an acquaintance he had never seen: a Chinese undergrad who had left Oxford the year before—"damned rich Chink," as Robert Gregory expressed it, when he did not put it even more chastely, "a Rothschild of a nigger."

The Chinese gift, a bracelet of emeralds and turquoise and jacinths and pearls, still was the most beautiful and the most valuable jewel Basil Gregory's mother had, and she wore it on every occasion that justified such splendor. And Hilda, watching its green fire and blue softness on their mother's fine white arm, could but wonder hungrily whether it would become ultimately the possession of herself or of Basil's wife.

"It is the most beautiful jewel I have ever seen," John Bradley said when he first saw it.

"Yes, isn't it?" its owner acquiesced; "but when I have it on, I always feel as if I were wearing a bit of Revelation."

"More like a bit of the Koran," the priest had reassured her with an odd smile.

She was greatly puzzled. She had always supposed the Koran was a somewhat indecent book, quite the sort of book a clergyman would not mention to a lady. She resolved to get a cheap copy—she believed there were cheap editions; there were of almost everything now—the next time she sent to Kelly and Walsh's.

And this resolve was not born of any wish to sample a questionable classic, but of a wish to repair an injustice she was regretful to have done even to a book or a heathen faith. Mrs. Gregory was a thoroughly nice woman.

CHAPTER XIV
NANG'S VIGIL

SING KUNG YAH was away temporarily from her important post as Wu Nang Ping's chaperone-guard, spending a few weeks of semi-religious villeggiatura in a Taoist nunnery with a kinswoman who was its abbess.

So powerful was Wu's personality and his wealth that he had been able to command for his widowed kinswoman and for her participation in the gala things of life, even from the most conventional of his countrymen, considerable courteous toleration. But it was toleration only, and never approval. His influence was enormous. Every tong in China would have torn at the vitals of any one rash enough to exercise against Sing Kung Yah a social ostracism contrary to his wish. And so the unprecedented festivity of the kinswoman's widowhood was tolerated even by the Chinese whom it both shocked and affronted.

But anything more, or kindlier, than tolerance, even the great Wu was powerless to win for her—at least from the Chinese. And both he and she knew this, and it was the one fly in her very nice amber. She would have been ostracized fiercely if those of their own caste had dared; but, they not daring, she was tolerated coldly. And feeling it (approving it even in her thoroughly Chinese heart) she was often glad to steal away into the quiet, and behind the screen, of the Taoist nunnery on the cool, far-off hillside.

She had quite a number of English friends in Hong Kong and at Sha-mien. The English thought her great fun, and she was eagerly sociable. And English merchants, anxious to conciliate the powerful Wu, encouraged their womenkind to friendliness with his kinswoman. But she longed for friends of her own race; and except Nang and Wu she had none. She longed for cronies, and she had not one, except the Taoist abbess.

Strange that a people so implacable to comforted and comfortable widowhood should be ruled by a widow! But so it is. And, after all, the Chinese race has a right to its share of human inconsistency. Tze-Shi was an Empress, the mother of a son, and had a great personality. Sing Kung Yah had been born a long way from the imperial yellow, was childless, and had little personality of her own. And so Nang Ping, in the sweetest way, had run a little wild, as roses and honeysuckle do, and so the frequent visits—that were something of a skurrying too—to the Taoist convent on the hills.

The Wus were not Taoists, strictly. Like most Chinese of their class, they mingled a loyal observance of the rites of all three of the great Chinese sects and an anxious acceptance of their tripled superstitions, with an easy and respectful contempt for them all—certainly for all except the Confucianism that has made and welded China for twenty-five centuries, but that every Chinese of half Wu's intelligence knows is, in fact, a magnificent irreligion, a philosophy, a patriotism, but no God-cult.

In her aunt's absence, as well as her father's, Nang Ping was absolutely mistress of herself and of all in her father's house. When she left Basil Gregory she had closed the door panel of her own room, hanging a purple scarf in its outer carving, and no one, not even Low Soong, dared disregard the imperative silken signal that she would be alone and unmolested. Even when the gong brayed out the call of evening rice she made no sign. Wu Low Soong brought a tray of food and laid it gently on the floor, with a timid supplicatory clatter, beneath the purple scarf, and, after listening a moment as she knelt with her hands still on the tray, crept ruefully away. She had shared in the outer edges of all Nang Ping's love raptures, shared the dangers of the forbidden sweetnesses, and it was very hard to be shut out from the newer excitement of what was evidently a jagged love-rift.

Nang Ping lay very still all night, uncushioned and uncovered on her polished floor. Her frightened eyes were closed, but she was wide awake—wider awake than she had ever been before.

She felt Basil linger. She heard him go. She heard each night-sound all the night long. She heard her household's every stir, and heard it hush.

In the morning, before any but the night-watchman stirred, she stole out into the garden and wandered about it aimlessly. But she did not enter the pagoda.

While it was still very early she went back to her own room, beat on her own gong, a little burnished steel disk, summoning her women. And when they hurried to her, surprised and heavy with sleep, she bathed and put on fresh garments. It was her habit to chatter gayly with her women while they dressed her, but to-day she scarcely spoke and they scarcely dared speak. She sat quite motionless in her ivory chair while Tieng Po dressed her hair. Tieng Po was one of the cleverest tire maids in China, and wonderfully quick. It rarely took her more than three hours to do her lady's hair, and to-day she did it in even a little less. But she had never done it more elaborately, and all the time her mistress watched her with cold, critical eyes. For Nang Ping had a glass, a very lovely one that Wu had bought in Venice. It had been her mother's, and reflected more clearly and with less strain on the eyes than the mirrors that most Chinese women consult.

When Nang was dressed—she was very fine—she sent for Low Soong and ordered food.

The two girls breakfasted together in silence, and were silent afterwards as they paced the Peacock Terrace together until the sun was high and cruel. But Low Soong began to understand, and as each moment passed understood more and more. The women and the peasants of no other race chatter so much or so incessantly as the Chinese do; only the gentlemen and the children are often still. But no other race has so little need of words. The Chinese is the psychic of all the races. Even the women have wizard minds. They are all sensitives. And as the girls paced silently, but arm in arm, Low Soong learned it all.

In the early afternoon Basil contrived to send a note to Miss Wu, and it reached her safely. Indeed, it ill needed the subterfuge he spent upon its delivery, for its few formal lines, saying that he would, as promised, have the honor to wait upon her presently, and have the pleasure of begging her acquaintance for his mother and sister, might have been cried aloud from the Kowloon housetops, or published in the *Pekin Gazette* and the *Shanghai Mercury* or the *Hong Kong Telegraph*. Written words could not have been less compromising; such a love-letter could not have compromised a nun or a female fly. And it was the last that he would write her. (It was almost the first.) Nang's little lip quivered as she read it, and she made to tear it into bits; then the little painted lip quivered more piteously, and she thrust the paper inside her robe. He had had no need to warn her. She should play her part. He might have trusted her in that, and in all.

She began to think that Englishmen were timid. And she wondered too if they might not be dense, some of them, sometimes.

CHAPTER XV
THE MEETING OF THE MOTHERS

BASIL GREGORY had written his formally couched note of warning in a fidget. Nang Ping had no experience of masculine fidgets. She had seen her countrywomen fidget, but never her countrymen.

And Basil was in a fidget still when he came to her presently, not by stealth this time, no whistle heralding him, but walking swiftly from beyond the bridge.

She greeted him placidly, too proud to show the hauteur she felt now; but Low Soong knew that Nang Ping's heart was fluttering sickly under her jade and coral girdle.

Low returned his greeting with a placid face, but her narrow eyes were yellow with hate, and she turned at once and went to her old place of watch on the bridge.

"They will come soon?" Nang asked.

"Yes, they are lingering by the big lake, in the outer garden, and that gave me the chance to speak to you a moment. Oh! my darling." He had been near to hating her as he had been coming to her across the rippling water—hating her because he had wronged her, and now feared that he might not escape quite all share in her punishment; but now, as she stood there in all her pretty feminine trappings among her flowers, he longed to take her into his arms. She had never looked so altogether desirable to him before—probably because he had made up his mind to leave her, to snap his life and his years from hers. "Have you missed me? Why did you leave me so? How are you, dear?"

Nang Ping smiled oddly. She said nothing.

And Low Soong called from the bridge, "Chillee! Chillee!"

Women's voices, deeper throated than Nang's and Low's, European voices, could be heard coming that way, and Basil said nervously, "Yes," adding in English what Low had just said, "They are coming. I shall leave them when they are going—make some excuse, and I shall go and hide in the pagoda by the lake——"

"Oh, that pagoda—by the lake!" Nang Ping interjected softly, but her voice was grim.

"I shall see them pass, and when they have quite gone I will come back. Wait for me when they are gone. I must speak to you. Remember!" He moved away from her, and went and stood beside an old stone lantern, as if examining and admiring it for the first time.

"Low Soong!" Nang Ping said breathlessly, and Low hurried to her from the bridge and put her arms about her. And they stood so for a moment.

But the voices and the footsteps were close now, and Nang Ping released herself from Low's comforting arms, and stood gracious and alone.

This was one of Florence Gregory's young days—one of her very youngest. Still in her early forties, she looked a radiant twenty-five as she stood an instant on the bridge, and then came gayly down it. And her radiant English beauty—blue eyes, golden hair, cream and rose face—looked all the more radiant because of the delicate gray of her gown—a dress of artificial simplicity, Paris-made. It had not cost as much as Chinese Nang's fantastic clothes had, but it had cost a great deal, and it was the more perishable.

Hilda Gregory, walking beside her mother, quite a pretty girl seen by herself, seemed in the mother's wake rather than side by side, though far the more brightly clad, and was a dim afterglow of the matron's glory—as Low Soong, for all her gay apparel and own high coloring, standing a little apart, seemed too of Nang Ping's. And Florence Gregory looked as much Basil's sister as Hilda, who was a few years his junior.

A Chinese serving woman followed the Gregory ladies. She was palpably Mrs. Gregory's maid, and not Hilda's; why, it is impossible to say, unless because the mother was unmistakably of the woman-type to which servants and dogs attach themselves, that claims them, and to which they belong. Hilda Gregory probably played tennis and golf better than her mother, and plied a more useful needle; but she buttoned her own boots as naturally as it came to the mother to lean well back at ease against down cushions and have her hair brushed by a servant. Ah Wong, the amah, carried a closed parasol, a costly European thing of lace and mother-o'-pearl, that would have suited Miss Gregory's rose crêpe quite as well as it did Mrs. Gregory's silver ninon; but the sturdy Chinese figure, plainly clad in dark blue cotton, was unmistakably in attendance on the mother.

There were six here now, not counting the Wu servants moving on the outskirts of the group, silent and busied. But Mrs. Gregory and Wu Nang Ping held the stage: English womanhood and Chinese something at their best.

They made a great contrast than which the old beauty-packed garden had seen nothing prettier: two living, sentient expressions of womanhood, greatly different, greatly alike.

Each was natural, each was artificial—sweet, elaborate, decorated, highly bred.

Nang Ping's face and lips were painted; Mrs. Gregory's were not. But her nails were slightly, beneath her gloves, and so were Nang's that had never worn a glove. Mrs. Gregory's eyebrows were lightly penciled. Nang Ping's were not. Nang Ping's hair had taken the longer to dress, but the dressing of the other's had cost an hour. The black hair was stiffened into shape with thick scented gum; the blonde hair was marcelled into shape by hot tongs. And Mrs. Gregory had the slightly smaller feet, and far less comfortably shod. For Wu had set his face against one custom of his country, and braved the anger of his ancestors. Nang smoked a pipe—Basil Gregory could not insert his smallest finger-tip into its tiny bowl—Florence Gregory smoked cigarettes; and they both inhaled sometimes. And each considered the other of inferior race.

They looked at each other curiously—Mrs. Gregory frankly so. Nang veiled her keen interest. But her interest was the more. The English woman was keenly interested in China and in things Chinese. The country had fascinated her powerfully, its odd people considerably. But she did not take Chinese womanhood very seriously. Every one of intelligence knew by now that many Chinese men were clever, almost hideously so, but equally every one knew that Chinese women were limited—very. Of course, the terrible old woman who ruled at Pekin was shrewd, unless her ministers, Li Hung Chang and the rest, did it all for her, which was probable; and then, too, she wasn't Chinese really, Tartar not Mongol. And Mrs. Gregory had no suspicion of what must have interested her in Nang Ping indeed. She was keener to see the garden, and, if possible, the house—it was said to be very wonderful—than to exploit little Miss Wu. But she thought the girl pretty after a grotesque Chinese fashion, "cute" and not unattractive, and she looked at her with sincerely friendly eyes.

The young eyes that looked back at her were mingled adoration and resentment. This was Basil's mother, and she was like him. This was the honorable mother who had given him life and nursed him at her breast. And this was the woman because of whom he was going to forsake her, and shut her out forever from peace, honor and paradise. Because of this woman standing smiling at her here he forbade her Europe and joyful motherhood. And he had shut her forever out of China! Why? Oh! why?

There are three supreme moments in the life of every Chinese girl to whom the gods are not hideously unkind: the moment when her unknown bridegroom lifts up her red veil and looks upon her face—perhaps to love and cherish, perhaps to loathe and punish; the moment when the midwife says, "Hail, Lady, it is an honorable *son*," and lays the funny little red, squirming firstborn on her breast to be adored, and always to adore her; and the moment when she meets eyes with her husband's mother, and they look a little into each other's souls. And this last is *the* supreme moment of her fate. In all the small ways that make up the most of every woman's life, her comfort and happiness will depend upon this mother-in-law even more than upon her husband—and mothers-in-law live long in China. Women are the pampered class in China, as they are almost everywhere, and will be until "new" hermaphrodite "movements" have pulled nature from her throne. And in the quiet ways, the ways that count, the supremacy of the Chinese mother is even greater than the autocratic supremacy of the Chinese father. Occidental readers may believe this or disbelieve it as they like; superficial travelers, ill-equipped for Asian sojourn, may see or miss it, but the fact remains. Motherhood has ruled China for thousands of years. It is not the fair young wife or the favorite daughter who rules a Chinese, but his mother, old, wrinkled, toothless, bent. From the thraldom of his father, from the thraldom of his gods, he *may* escape; from the thraldom of his mother, never! Nang Ping knew now that she would never wear the soft red veil. That great moment had been, and passed, for her when Basil had kissed her first in the pagoda. The child that even now just fluttered beneath her breast—a son, she thought, and surely blue-eyed—must die unborn; she knew that now. He would never purl and pull and purr at her exultant breast. But this was Basil's mother, the honorable grandmother to whom she had given a first grandson! What this moment might have been! Something of the agony of the disappointment gnawing at her baffled heart crept into her narrow eyes, and turned her faint and sick, and almost she swayed an instant standing proud and gracious among her flowers—and the child leapt.

Basil Gregory stood irresolute, embarrassed, looking from his mother to Nang Ping, from Nang Ping to his mother.

Mrs. Gregory turned to him with a happy smile. "Ah! Basil, there you are."

"Yes, Mother, I missed you," he said as lightly as he could, "and found my way here to make the acquaintance of Miss Wu."

He gestured courteously toward Nang as he spoke, and Mrs. Gregory moved to the girl and held out her hand. Nang Ping moved too, a little towards her guest, and made the elaborate gesture, hands clasped, of Eastern greeting. Mrs. Gregory still held out her hand, and wondered, when she gained the girl's, which was the softer or the better kept, Nang's or her own. Basil had wondered it often.

"This visit to your beautiful garden is the greatest treat I've had since I arrived in China, Miss Wu," she began.

Wu Nang Ping bowed. "I am pleased to receive you in my honorable father's absence. He has had much kindness in England. It is his command that always English friends have most honorable welcome here, and it gives me happiness. My cousin, Low Soong."

"How do you do?" Mrs. Gregory said cordially. "And this is my daughter." The three girls bowed, the two Chinese with grave formality, a gesture of the arms more than a bending.

"Such a perfectly beautiful place!" Mrs. Gregory said it sincerely, her beauty-loving eyes here, there and everywhere gloating.

"This is my own garden, where I walk with my women," Nang Ping told her.

"It beats our poor little garden, Hilda," the mother said gayly.

"Into fits." Just a trifle of the surface vulgarity which, with its hard coating of adamant varnish, covered and hid Robert Gregory's soul side—even from his wife—and wronged him, had caught and scorched, slightly, the delicacy of Hilda's breeding. Even Florence Gregory, some rare times, used a slight word of slang: "As the husband is, the wife is."

Low Soong listened to Hilda with polite indifference. Low Soong had no English. But Nang Ping wondered dully how a garden could have a fit; she thought an epileptic garden must be very horrid. But she said smoothly, "Ah! in London you have only walls and roofs, I think."

"You have been there, Miss Wu, of course?" Mrs. Gregory asked.

"I have never been to any country."

"Really? But—you must excuse me—but your excellent English."

"My honorable teacher was English. My honorable father knows it like you; he has been there—to Oxford."

"Really! I was born at Oxford. And my son"—she turned to him a little, meaning to coax him into the talk, and wondering to see him stand so awkwardly and wordless—he was not often so socially inept, and never gauche—"my son was there."

"And my honorable father has taught me to esteem English people because they are all"—she paused an instant, but she did not glance towards Basil, and added with a grave, deferential smile—"all honorable men."

"Well"—Basil's mother smiled too, a prettily pathetic smile which was half good manners and half sincere—"I am afraid there are a few exceptions, sometimes." She went up to her boy and laid her hand fondly on his arm. "But"—not speaking to him, but still to Nang—"it is the duty of all Englishmen to live up to such a high reputation."

"I must be off, Mother," the man said hurriedly, releasing himself gently, "if Miss Wu will excuse me. I thought Father was coming."

"He has. We left them down by the fish-pond, him and Tom, talking to a quaint old gardener."

"Oh! Well, I'm afraid I ought to be off—to the office. I'll go straight to the hotel afterwards—dinner usual time?"

"Of course, dear, unless you'd like it earlier or later. Do you know, Basil, you haven't dined with us for days?"—Nang Ping knew it. "I'm getting quite anxious about your health, dear. Bother that fusty office! You don't seem a bit yourself."

Her boy laughed at her and put his hand under her chin. (And Nang Ping watched them curiously.) "You dear—why—I—I'm as right as rain."

"Then prove it, my son—a big man's dinner at eight. Now, if Miss Wu will excuse you"—for evidently he was uncomfortable here—and why not, the dear English child? How should he be anything else in this funny Chinese nook with these Chinese girls? Probably he could not even see how pretty this smaller one was, for all her narrow eyes and absurd, grotesque clothes and paint, and it was plain that he could not find a word to say to either of them, not even to this one who was playing hostess so nicely, and who understood English and spoke it surprisingly. His silence towards the plump dumpling of a cousin, who was showing Hilda about the garden with quaint bobbings and solemn pantomime, was excusable enough. She didn't know a word of English, it seemed; though you never could tell what a Chinese did or didn't know, John Bradley said, and Ah Wong said so too. But really, Basil might have made an effort, and said a little something civil to the English-knowing hostess; he was not often so shy—he *had* been at Oxford, and he was her son. Robert had no *savoir faire*, but, as a rule, the boy had some.

When he was free from his mother, Basil moved to Nang Ping to take leave of her. She received him with a quiet dignity that seemed perfectly natural. "Chinese, but quite the grande dame," the mother thought.

He uncovered and looked down at Nang. "Good-day, Miss Wu." She shook her hands at him in Chinese-salutation way, and straightening up looked at him with just the edge of a courteous smile—not an eyelash quivered. He turned and looked towards the other girls, but Low Soong had turned her back and was bending and gesticulating over a peony bed.

"By the way, Basil," his mother said as he passed her, but paused to give her one more smile, "the gardener was telling your father that he knew you." She wished him to go, and yet she stayed him.

Basil shot Nang a look—of consternation—taken aback and off his guard. Mrs. Gregory did not catch it, but both Hilda and Low Soong did. Nang Ping held herself impassive, but distress flickered for a moment in her eyes. Then he turned back to his mother, trying to seem unconcerned.

"Knew me? Why, I—he's never seen me here in his life."

"He didn't say he had, silly," Hilda Gregory said, strolling towards them, Low Soong tottering deftly beside her—Low's feet were bound—"he said he'd seen you in Hong Kong."

"Oh!" her brother laughed feebly, "in Hong Kong—that's quite possible. Well, now, I really am off. Good-by, Miss Wu." And Nang Ping bowed to him once more, in the prescribed ceremonial way, her face perfectly emotionless, dismissing him suavely, turning from him before he had quite gone.

"Will you not be seated?" she asked Mrs. Gregory, with a deferential gesture pointing to the old stone seat.

Hilda and Low Soong still strolled about among the treasures of the garden.

Ah Sing and perhaps half a dozen other servants moved about on padded, noiseless feet, preparing Miss Wu's tea-table with all its picturesque paraphernalia of elaborate teakwood stools and benches, lacquer sweetmeat-cabinets, glazed porcelain tea-bowls as thin as gauze and painted by master craftsmen, trays of candied fruit, and several delicacies of which Florence Gregory did not know the name and could not guess the nature.

"So," she said, surprised to find how comfortable a stone bench could be, "Mr. Wu was at Oxford. How interesting! I wonder when. I knew a Chinese gentleman—a student there—when I was quite a girl. We lived at Oxford, my father and I. I forget his name. I have the saddest memory, especially for names, and it could not have been your father whom I knew, for I distinctly remember hearing, the year after I was married—or some time about then—that my friend was dead, killed in a climbing accident somewhere on the Alps. He was a fine sportsman."

"Many Chinese gentlemen are sent to Oxford, I have heard my honorable father say," Nang Ping rejoined. "The Japanese go more to Cambridge."

"Yes—and yet," Mrs. Gregory said musingly, but more interested in watching the servants than she was in her talk with this rather wooden and very painted-faced child of the East, "your name—'Wu,' I mean—has seemed familiar to me from the first, and now I seem to remember that the man I knew at Oxford had a surname rather like that—or even that. How odd!"

"There are many Wus in China," the girl said. "It is a most large clan. All our clans are very large. We are, you know, so old."

"Wu." The English woman said it slowly, as if trying to send, on the sound of it, her peccant memory back to some forgotten hour.

"Oh! it is a most general name. It means Military. I do not know why, for," she added almost hastily, "we have had no soldiers in our family—everything almost but that. All Chinese names mean something, but of most of them— they are so old—the meaning is lost in the mists of far, far back, uncounted years before history was written or kept in record. And perhaps I ought to have remembered that one Wu was a soldier once. Wu Sankwei defended Ningyuan against T'ientsung when the Manchus first overran China. But that was, oh! so many years ago, and since then none of my honorable ancestors have been soldiers—or at least very few," she added, with a sudden blush beneath her paint, too honest to conceal from Basil's mother, who was also her guest, her military forbears, descent from whom she felt to be a bitter disgrace, though she knew, as every educated Chinese must, that in all China's long history there are few greater names than that of Wu Sankwei, the defender of Ningyuan. "'Li' is the name in China the most common and perhaps the most proud. It is our 'Smith' name. And we are very proud of it, because many of its men have been great and noble, and because their honorable wives have borne them many children. Scarcely the census-takers can count the Lis. My honorable mother was a Li before my honorable father married her to be Mrs. Wu. They were cousins, but more than a century away—'twenty times removed,' as you would call it in your English. The honorable Li Hung Chang's our distant kinsman, my honorable kinsman on both sides. My own honorable father has 'Li' blood on the side of distaff; his honorable name is Wu Li Chang. We are Chinese, we of our house, but now in some of our blood we are Manchu too."

Mrs. Gregory smiled up at the girl. "Will you not sit here too?" And Nang Ping bowed and curled up on the other end of the big seat.

Ah Wong opened her mistress's parasol and brought it, and Mrs. Gregory took it with a grateful "Ah!" "We have enjoyed ourselves so much in your wonderful country, Miss Wu," she went on; "we are quite sorry our time here is drawing to a close. You know—but I forgot, you know nothing of us, of course—well, we are going soon, going home."

"All of you go?" Nang Ping knew that they all were to go, but she could not resist the self-inflicted pain of hearing it again.

"Yes, all four of us—we are just the four—and I think my son will be glad to get home again, after a year in the East."

"I doubt that not," the girl replied, in an odd, quiet voice. "But," she added, reaching up one ring-heavy hand to pull down a flower, only to pitch it aside when she had smelt it once—the Chinese rarely do that—"but he said he liked the East."

"Oh! yes, indeed he does. We all do. Who could help it? But, after all, it is not quite the same thing as home, you know, especially to a man; and, besides, Basil has many friends whom he longs to see again. And"—adding this good-naturedly, anxious to interest the girl and smiling significantly—"we don't want an old bachelor in our family, you know; we have but the one son."

"'Bachelor'—that is one English word I do not know."

"Well, what I mean is that Basil must return home before all the eligible young ladies of his acquaintance forget him."

"That means"—the girl's voice hurt her throat—"he is going home to marry?"

"Well," his mother admitted, "there is a young lady at home, I believe, who will be very glad to see him again, so I hope it will eventually come to that."

Nang Ping laughed. And Mrs. Gregory thought, "How very oddly the Chinese laugh! It's anything but gay."

"And he will never come back?"—the strange creature said it with a smile.

"Oh, yes!" Hilda said, joining them, "some day, perhaps, when he has settled down, to take charge of this branch."

"I'm afraid Basil is the sort of son who never settles down," his mother said lightly. Nang Ping thought it most strange, and not nice, that the mother should say it at all, but she quite believed—now—that it was true. She rose, and clapped her hands for Ah Sing.

"If you will honor me by taking tea," she said, and led the way to the highly decorated table where the ornate meal was elaborately laid, the blue-clad servants standing about it in a circle, as still as stones. At their young mistress's approach they bowed almost to the ground—so low that their cues swept the grass, and one caught and tangled in a verbena bed. Mrs. Gregory suppressed a smile, but Hilda could not suppress a low giggle. But she tried to, and that much is to her credit.

"How jolly!" she cried, as they sat down to an accompaniment of many bows from the cousins. "How perfectly jolly!"

"Delightful!" agreed her mother. And Nang Ping, in spite of the choking misery in her throat and smarting in her breast, was pleased at their pleasure.

She thought it sincere, and both Low Soong and Ah Wong, watching lynx-eyed and imperturbable, knew that it was. Low Soong was but an obliging mannequin this afternoon, Ah Wong but a lay figure, expressionless and almost motionless, but neither had missed a word, a look, or a meaning from the first, although Ah Wong had little English and Low Soong had none.

CHAPTER XVI
GRIT

MRS. GREGORY bore her part in the pretty little function with creditable imitation of Chinese propriety. She had been coached by a woman at Government House. She blessed her own foresight that she had, and reproached herself that Hilda had not.

Nang Ping raised her bowl of scalding tea almost to her forehead, and then held it out first towards Mrs. Gregory and then towards Hilda, and waited for them to drink—and so did Low Soong; and when they drank, the two girls bowed several times and then drained their tiny bowls.

When the sweetmeats were pressed upon them Mrs. Gregory took one candied rose petal, and then—after much urging—took, with a fine display of reluctance, the smallest crystallized violet on the dish. But when Miss Wu entreated Hilda, "I beg you to condescend to accept and pardon my abominable food," Hilda helped herself generously to five or six of the glittering dainties. A guest at a London dinner-table who had seized in her own hands a roast fowl by its stark legs, conveyed it to her own plate, and then began to gnaw it, without even wrenching it into portions as Tudor Elizabeth would have wrenched it, would not have committed a more outrageous act. Nang Ping immediately helped herself even more generously than Hilda had, and Low Soong, after one startled instant, did the same. Mrs. Gregory saw it all, and wondered, with a social conscience abashed and chastened, if she would have had the fine courage, had the situation been reversed, to seize the second chicken and chew at it noisily. And she looked at her little hostess with new respect, convinced again that Nang Ping was exquisitely "grande dame," and beginning to suspect that the pretty, painted doll-thing had something in her after all, if only one knew how to get at it. She wondered what a girl living so, amid such a riot of fantastic ornament and seemingly meaningless petty ceremony, thought and felt. Did she think? Did she feel? Or was her mind as blank, her soul as impassive as her face? What did motherhood itself mean to such dolls, and could wifehood mean anything? Ah! well, if marriage was but a gilded mirage on the horizon of such opera-bouffe existence—as, for all she could see, the existence of well-to-do Chinese women was—that unreality might lessen pain more than it dwarfed happiness. The English woman sighed a little. But they must love their babies, these funny little creatures. Every mother loved her baby. And there was something gentle and loving, she thought, in this girl's face, beneath the paint and the conventional mask. She looked up and searched the younger face with kindly, motherly eyes. Yes; it would be pretty to see a baby cuddled in those gay silken sleeves. She smiled at the thought and at the girl, and Nang Ping smiled back at her. Something cried and fluttered at

Nang's heart, and flashed softly from her eyes, and found a moment's nesting in the older woman's heart. And for an instant the Chinese girl and the English woman were in close touch; and, if they had been alone, perhaps— who knows—

But before the tea-bowls had been replenished four times they heard the truants, Mr. Gregory and Tom Carruthers, coming.

Carruthers was speaking. "There, Mr. Gregory, there's a pond full of goldfish—and such goldfish! By Jove!"

"My dear Tom," an older voice said impatiently, "there's more sense in a bowl of herrings than a pondful of silly goldfish."

"Ah!—still," the younger persisted, as the two men came in sight, "you must admit this is another lovely spot."

"H'm, yes," Robert Gregory allowed, pursing up his lips deprecatingly in a way he often had when bartering in boats or rates. "Rather reminds me of Kew Gardens, but inferior—too gimcrack!"

But Carruthers saw the others then. "Ah! There they are! Taking tea under rather better conditions than Kew, I fancy."

Nang Ping rose and went towards Gregory hospitably. He lifted his hat perfunctorily and spoke to her crisply, not waiting for the welcome she had risen to accord. "How do you do? Miss Wu, I presume? It's awfully good of you to let us have a look around."

Mrs. Gregory rose too, and came up to Nang Ping, feeling the girl's resentment at a tone to which she was unaccustomed—a resentment she in no way showed.

"My husband, Miss Wu," the English lady said, presenting him to the girl, and speaking to her with pointed respect, and the man took the hint a little, and bowed pleasantly enough as Nang Ping almost ko'towed.

So this was the father—Basil's honorable father! She liked him least of the three—the three who might have been her relatives—more to her than her own father, whom she had known so long and loved so well. He was not like Basil, but like the daughter. Of the three she liked the honorable mother best—much. "You are just in time to take tea, if you will honor me," she said.

"May I present Mr. Carruthers to you, Miss Wu?" Mrs. Gregory asked.

Nang Ping greeted the additional guest with the widest outpush of her joined hands and the most stiffly formal bow she had made yet. But she liked this face; he looked, she thought, indeed an "honorable man."

"Tea! By all means," Mr. Gregory said briskly, steering for the richly laden toy tea-table in a businesslike way. He thought there'd been bowing and arm-shaking enough for a month o' Sundays.

Low Soong giggled a little when Tom Carruthers lifted his hat to her—Nang shot her cousin a severe look—and then, to Mr. Gregory's disgust, all the bowing and arm-waving was to do again.

"I am sorry not to serve tea in the English way," Nang Ping said, as she returned to her seat. (Gregory had already taken his.)

"Why!" Mrs. Gregory protested, "what can be more delightful than to serve China tea in the Chinese way in China? And this is such a real treat to me! I can have my tea in our stupid home way—half cold and quite insipid—any day."

"Well," Gregory commented, leaning back negligently in his chair and stretching out his legs in comfortable abandon, "perhaps I've not been here long enough to appreciate Chinese customs. That's the worst of being a real Englishman, Miss Wu—one misses English comforts."

Tom Carruthers saw a tiny shadow of disgust cloud across Nang Ping's painted mouth, and he knew, without looking, the distress on Florence Gregory's face. "Mr. Gregory," he interposed, "your tea," and pointed to Gregory's waiting cup.

They all were waiting to drink together; not to have done so would have been a rudeness.

"Oh!" Gregory vouchsafed, lifting the tiny piece of porcelain critically and tasting the brew gingerly when he had discarded the covering saucer a little roughly. And when he drank, the others drank with him.

He tasted the delicate tea superciliously, and disapproved it frankly. "Here, boy," he called to one of the Wu servants, and holding out the cup with a disgusted grimace, "take it away." The servant with the Wu crest embroidered on his back bowed low, stepped forward, bowed lower, and then took the offending handleless cup and gravely bore it away. And the four women looked on, Hilda amused, his wife distressed, the two Chinese girls smilingly imperturbable. It is difficult to decide which owes China the more apology—English missionaries or English manners.

"By the way, Miss Wu," Gregory said, speaking staccato between sugared mouthfuls—he had appropriated the nearest dish of sweetmeats to his sole use, and evidently approved its candied contents as much as he had disapproved the tea—"I'm very dissatisfied with your father."

Nang Ping smiled a little haughtily, rising as she spoke. "I am sorry my honorable father should offend."

"Yes, so am I. Of course, business is business. I admit I live up to that myself, and I must expect others to. But I have heard that he has just bought over my head—over my head, mind you—a dock site which is indispensable for my new line of ships to Australia. I wrote him about it, and reply seemed, I must admit—well, a trifle vindictive."

The girl sat down again quietly, but Tom Carruthers, who had risen when she had, stood still leaning a little on his chair and watching her closely.

"But you have not seen my honorable father for a long time," Nang told the financier.

"Oh!" he returned, "I, personally, have never seen your father, Miss Wu; but my manager, Holman, saw him a couple of hours ago."

Nang Ping's fingers tangled quickly in her girdle. Only Ah Wong saw it, but several of them noticed Low Soong's start—it was noticeable. "It cannot be so," Nang said.

"Eh? Of course it is so. Old Holman's got both his eyes; he sees all right."

"But"—and, in spite of her, a little of the concern she felt crept into her voice—"but he has been in Canton for twenty days."

"Oh! well," Mr. Gregory returned indifferently, "then he must have come back. It's scarcely two hours since Holman met him and told him we were visiting Kowloon. And your father particularly requested that we should visit his garden. He said any member of my family would be made very welcome. Holman said those were Wu's exact words—exact old josser, Holman, always. Any member of my family would be made very welcome. And, you know, that's all very well when you've just done a man down in business—any one can afford to be polite then." He got up and dragged his chair a few feet and reseated himself beside his wife.

"Robert," she greeted him, "you can scarcely expect Miss Wu to be interested in your business disappointments." She turned then to the girl. "It will be a pleasant surprise for you; you did not know your father had returned?"

Nang shook her head a little. "No. It is strange, for he is never unkind to me."

"Oh! I know what brought him back," Gregory persisted bellicosely, "and it's a dog-in-a-manger business, and I wrote and told him so, because the dock site isn't any earthly good to him."

Florence Gregory sighed. "Robert," she said severely, "I am sure Mr. Wu does not trouble his daughter with his business worries."

"My dear," her husband snapped irritably, "it is not his worries we are discussing, but mine. By the way, Miss Wu, has your right honorable father by any chance a brother?"

"Alas!" the girl replied sorrowfully—she had missed the slur in that "right honorable" (no one else had missed it, not even Low)—"alas! His honorable mother was unfortunate in only having one son."

"Well," almost grunted the Englishman, "I could have sworn she'd had twins."

"Robert!"—his wife's voice was coldly angry. But Hilda giggled.

"Twins!" Carruthers said, a little fatuously. He was puzzled, and he liked to understand things as he went along.

Gregory answered his wife's expostulation with expostulation. "My dear, it's scarcely two hours ago since Holman saw him in Hong Kong. And yet, as soon as we get this side of the water, your gardener, Miss Wu, tells me that your father has just arrived here in Kowloon, and that he was here for a while yesterday, and yet I don't see him about anywhere, and I particularly want to see him."

"In that San Fong make a mistake," Nang Ping said quietly. But she had risen to her feet in evident distress, though she controlled it bravely, and the others had all risen too, as if her sudden motion was a one that prompted them. Even Gregory saw that he had made a *faux pas*, and looked awkwardly towards his wife, saying, "Oh! well, maybe he did, but I don't believe it. I'm not educated up to green tea and chop-sticks, but I've lived in China off and on some good few years now, and I understand your lingo right enough, at least the 'pigeon' variety of it, and that's what the gardener said, and if you ask me, he savvied what he was talking about."

Low Soong had slipped round to Nang's side, and stood very close to it.

"Robert," his wife said bitterly, "I really don't know which is worse, a bull in a china-shop or you in a Chinese lady's garden. You make one understand why they call us foreign devils." He shrugged his big shoulders sulkily in reply, and moved off to the pond, whistling unconcernedly.

Mrs. Gregory followed him, and he turned towards Nang and said patronizingly (but that was unintentional—he couldn't help it), "It's really quite a charming place, Miss Wu, 'pon my word it is—charming. Quite Oriental, isn't it?" He paused at that to let them all appreciate his unique discovery, and wondered impatiently why the dickens Carruthers grinned. "I suppose every country has the landscape that suits it best, but there are some little bits of England that take a lot of beating."

"The light is failing now," Florence said—she had quite relinquished her hope of seeing the interior of the house—"and I am afraid we are keeping Miss Wu long after her tea-time."

"Oh, no!" Nang Ping said, "not at the least; but"—for she knew her strength was ebbing fast, and she felt very ill—"I—I am not strong to-day. And—I must seek my apartments early, as my honorable father has returned." She turned to Ah Sing, who had not moved from his sentinel place in front of the pagoda, and said to him, "Tsu tang yang ur!" And he bowed and went to summon the lantern-bearers.

Florence Gregory took both the Chinese girl's little hands in hers. "How cold they feel, even through my gloves!" she thought. "Good-by," she said very gently. "Good-by, Miss Wu, and let me thank you for the great treat you have given us."

Nang Ping made no reply—she couldn't—but she looked up at her going guest with something so pathetic in her odd eyes and something so nearly a-tremble on her mouth that the older woman almost bent and kissed her.

"Where's Basil?" Tom Carruthers asked. "Has he cleared off, Hilda?"

"Yes," she told him, "he had a conscientious fit and has gone to the office to work. Good-by, Miss Wu," she said to Nang Ping, "and thanks awfully. It's been quite too ripping."

Nang felt too faint by now to wonder what the odd English words the other girl used meant. But she smiled up at Basil's sister very kindly.

"You shall be attended to the gates," she said to her, and added to Carruthers, as he came to take leave, "My own garden is locked at sunset."

Carruthers said something brief, and then looked about to take his leave of the cousin, and wondered to see her slipping stealthily away and out of sight. She was a funny little bunch, he thought.

"Father hardly brought his garden-party manners with him, did he?" Hilda said unconcernedly to her mother, as they and Carruthers passed from the garden, four blue-robed Chinese, with great lanterns swinging from their hands, in close attendance, and Ah Wong just behind them.

"No," his wife said wearily. "And I'm afraid he didn't leave many behind, either."

Except for a group of silent, motionless serving-men, Robert Gregory and Wu Nang Ping were alone in the darkening garden now.

He held out his hand to her. "Good-by, Miss Wu."

She did not take it, but she bowed to him deeply, and because he was Basil's father and she thought that she should not see him again she gave him the utmost obeisance of Chinese ceremony, sinking quite down to the ground. That extremest collapse of leg and knee, the ko'tow of utmost reverence, is reserved, as a rule, for an Emperor, an imperial mother or first wife, the grave of Confucius in the Kung cemetery, outside K'iuh-fu (where only the crystal tree will grow) and for the tablets of one's own ancestral dead.

"Oh! To be sure," he said good-naturedly enough, letting his extended hand drop to his side. "Well, good-by and good luck. I had hoped to meet our interesting friend. I had quite a lot to say to him. But I'm pleased to have met you, even if I don't think much of your tea. You must come up to our hotel one day, and Mrs. Gregory and Hilda'll give you the prime stuff. Good-by." He added to himself only half under his breath, as he marched off, "And I hope my visit isn't going to be wasted!"

Nang Ping stood motionless and watched him till he was out of sight.

CHAPTER XVII
The Signal of the Gong

AND then the breakdown came, and she sank down, weeping and distracted, on the long stone seat. Her father in Kowloon! Her father who was almost omniscient! How long had he been there? What had he learned?

Somewhere in the house a great gong sounded—seven slow beats, deep throated as the braying of some bloodhound, but low and soft at first, growing louder, then soft again, all musical, but almost uncannily significant. As the second note beat into the garden, Nang Ping roused herself, and sat up against the seat's back, clutching at it desperately. She listened in fear that grew to anguish as note followed note. Only one hand ever struck that gong! As the brazened signal died away in the scented evening air, she sprang up and ran distracted on to the bridge, calling, "Basil! Basil!" thinking no longer of herself but only to save the lover who had spoiled her life. Women are like that in China—and in England.

He came at once, and she bent over the bridge to him and said, as he stood on the path he had come by, "You must go. My father! Go quickly!"

"Your father!"

"Go—go now! Quick!"

"But we're safe here—for the moment." He was glad of an excuse to leave her, and yet he wanted too to stay, to toy, if but for a moment, by the lotus lake where he had found the dalliance sweet that had proved fatal to poor Nang Ping.

"No, no!" she told him frantically. "Not safe. Safe nowhere. Never safe again. But most dangerous here. Go! Fly, Basil, fly! Before my father's wrath falls on you, fly! Take the path by the Peacock Terrace and go."

She had infected him now with her own breathless fear, but even so he hesitated an instant longer, for she had urged him to go; and when is not the man reluctant to go whom a woman forbids to stay?

"Celeste"—he called her by the name with which he had wooed her and never wooed in vain—"little flower, our happiness has been too great, too perfect. There must be some other way: there shall!"

"None! None!" the girl said solemnly.

"I love you, dear," he whispered passionately.

"No," Nang Ping said gently, "your love has flown away from me, and the nest of my heart is cold for always now."

"It isn't true," he protested hotly. "It is not true."

"Go!"

"I will come back to you."

"No!" Nang Ping's voice was soft and clear and tender as a flute. "Go. Go, and forget."

"Then"—he lifted his hat and came towards her uncovered, his arms outstretched—"farewell, Celeste."

But she turned and moved a little away, not even facing him again. She was afraid to trust those arms, a thousand times afraid to trust herself. "Farewell to life and love," she said under her breath, smiling wanly but moving steadily towards the house.

With a cry—half remorse, half passion, and something too, just a little, of the brute, grim and primal, not to be baulked of his prey—Basil Gregory sprang after her to catch her in his arms. But before he reached her, just before, other arms caught him and held him in a vice.

Ah Sing had glided like some upright indigo-colored snake from the pagoda—"the pagoda by the lake"—and, springing seemingly from space, one from one direction, one from another, two of the gardeners, almost as quick as he, reached the Englishman almost as soon. Six arms pinioned him, without a word, without a sound. And there was no expression on the Chinese faces of the three—no hatred, no determination, not even interest.

But another man, a dark-robed figure, stood on the bridge, above them all, and slowly he smiled—a terrible smile.

Nang Ping had not heard the four Chinese—no one could have heard them. But she caught the slight sound of Basil's desperate struggles—he was struggling too frantically to waste any of his strength on voluntary noise. She turned and ran to him, crying, "Oh, Basil!"—no matter who heard her now. The end had come, and Nang Ping knew it. She threw herself in front of him, thrust herself into the seething coil, to protect his body with hers, as far as she could.

With a supreme effort—or did that still figure on the bridge give a slight signal that Ah Sing caught?—perhaps both—for a moment Basil's right arm was free. He whipped out his revolver. But with a touch of Ah Sing's finger-tips—it looked an indifferent touch, and the servant's eyes had not turned even for the smallest space of time from that quiet figure on the bridge—the English arm fell helpless at Gregory's side, the revolver clattered down the stone step, and Basil, turning his head up in pain, saw the motionless looker-on.

"My God!" the boy cried. "Mr. Wu!"

Nang Ping turned slowly round, looked at her father as if entranced and dazed, then with a scream that cut through the hot air like the voice of a child that had been knifed and was dying, fell prostrate at the foot of the bridge, and lay moaning with her face on Basil Gregory's shoe, her hands, with some last instinct to protect him, clasped about his silk-clad ankle.

CHAPTER XVIII
AT THE FEET OF <u>KWANYIN</u> KO

NANG PING sat crouched at the feet of Kwanyin Ko, the Goddess of Mercy, on the floor of her own room. She had been alone all night.

She remembered seeing her father on the bridge. She remembered falling at Basil's feet. She remembered nothing more—clearly. She thought she recalled, as from a dream, being carried from the garden and laid here. She thought it had been gently done. Whose arms had lifted and borne her? She thought that she had been laid on her bed; across the room her sleeping-mats were unrolled, and a light down coverlet was tossed across the hard little cylinder which was her pillow. Some one had laid her down to sleep. Who? And some one had brought her food and drink, for on a tray near the mats there were fresh fruit and a dish of wine.

Had she been awake when she crawled here to lay her sorrow at Kwanyin's feet? Or had she thrown off the coverlet and crept across the floor in her sleep?

A nightlight burned dimly in an opalescent cup, and across the garden she could hear a cricket call and some big insect buzzing in the dark.

She tried to think, but she was too tired. She turned her face to the floor and laid so, prone before the painted graven figure which was the only succor left, the only semblance of woman's companionship within her reach. Where was Low Soong? Had Low been caught too in the coil? If not, surely Low would come to her presently, if she could. What had they done to Basil? She clenched her hands together in supplication so frenzied that her nails cut into her palms and her rings tore her flesh. What would come now? Or, rather, when would it come, and how? She knew what was to come.

But she could think no more. She could suffer. That faculty was left her, but she could neither reason nor plan. And why should she? The end was absolute, and absolute the uselessness of thought.

Towards morning she found the little tinder-box, stuffed her pipe, and began to smoke. It was innocuous enough a drugging, but gave her growing nervousness something to do. Three or four whiffs empty those tiny pipes. To throw out the ash took a moment, to refill the bowl took another; the drawing on the stem killed a third—over and over again, and one of the terrible night hours had gone. And still the Chinese girl lay on her hard wood floor smoking mechanically, as in Europe a girl so placed might have crocheted, or a woman older but no less desperate have played patience, or tried to play.

When the first streaks of day came to sharpen the familiar outlines of the room and of its furnishings, and sharpen her sense of pain and peril, she threw the tiny silver pipe across the floor. It fell with a clatter on the arabesque of the hard inlaying.

This Kowloon house of Wu was a veritable treasure-house. Not an apartment in it (for the servants lived, and cooked even, outside) but held much that was priceless. And no other room had been plenished with such lavish tenderness as had this room of his one child.

The old bronze table that pedestalled and throned Kwanyin Ko had not its match in Europe, neither in palace nor museum, and Kwanyin Ko, herself looted from a palace six hundred years ago, was worth something fabulous: no dealer would have sold her for sixty thousand yen.

The lapis-lazuli peacock, so exquisitely carved that its feathers were fine and delicate as those of the big birds that strutted in the sunshine on the terrace beyond the lotus pond (and the emerald points that studded each feather thickly and the threads of gold and silver that just showed their threads of burnishing here and there were real) was worth its weight in rubies.

In all the room—and it was large—there was not one thing that of its own kind was not the best. Wu had skimmed China relentlessly, and much of its cream was embowled here: Nang Ping's. And China is wide and rich. Every inlaid instrument of music that strewed the cushions and the floor, every classic book, the picture on the wall (there was only one picture, of course—a landscape by Ma Yuan—heavily framed in carved and inlaid camphor-wood) was a masterpiece, the culmination of some imperial art of an imperial people, art begotten of a spiritual and indomitable race's genius, and nursed and perfected by centuries of unfatigued patience. Cedar and sandal-wood and ivory hung and jutted from walls and painted ceiling in cornice and lambrequins cut into lace-work, as fine (though thicker) and as beautiful as any ever made on a Belgian pillow. Three hundred robes, each in its scented bag of silk, each costlier than the others, were piled on the next room's shelves of camphor-wood, and the lacquer chests of drawers and the carved coffers that stood beyond the sleeping mats were crammed with jewels. Nang Ping had sapphires that Maria Theresa had worn and a ruby that had been Josephine's, a pearl that had blinked on the hand of England's Elizabeth. She had, and often wore, a diamond that Hwangti's Queen Yenfi had worn four thousand years before. And the girl's best gems had been her mother's.

And in this toyed temple of Chinese maidenhood and her father's devotion Nang Ping lay huddled on the floor, "by Love's simplicity betrayed, all soiled, low i' the dust."

Remember Nang Ping so long as you live, English Basil—while you live and after!

The day came in, a lovely, laughing day of perfect Chinese summer, and Kwanyin Ko blinked and grinned in the early radiance.

Nang Ping rose up a little and knelt before the joss, praying, as she had never prayed before, the old, old prayer of tortured womanhood, Magdalene's petition, echoing, moaning in every corner of earth, girdling the world with a hymn of shame and with terrible entreaty, the saddest—save one other—of all prayers; never to be answered on earth, never to be disregarded or coldly heard in heaven.

And in another room, ko'towed before an uglier, sterner joss—the God of Justice—Wu the mandarin was praying too.

And in the pagoda—for it was there that it had been Wu's humor to prison him—Basil Gregory was praying, trying to remember words of simple, tender supplication that his mother had taught him in England when he was a little child.

CHAPTER XIX
PREPARATION

A BIRD was singing rapturously in a honagko tree as Nang Ping rose from her knees. She stood awhile at her open casement—it had been flung wide all night—listening to the little feathered flutist, saying good-by to her garden. The pagoda gleamed like rose-stained snow in the rosy sunrise, and the girl smiled wanly, thinking how like a bride's cake it looked—the high tapering towers, white-sugared and fantastic, that English brides have. She had seen several at a confectioner's in Hong Kong, and she had seen an English bride cut one with her husband's sword at a bridal in Pekin. It was far prettier, Nang had thought, than the little cakes, gray and heavy, that Chinese brides have, but not so nice to the taste—flat and dry. The lotus flowers were waking now, slowly opening their painted cups of carmine, white, rose and amethyst; the peacocks were preening to the day, the king-bird of them all flinging out his jewels to the sun, and the shabbily-garbed hens, in the red kissing of the sunrise refulgence, looking to wear breasts of rose. A lark swayed and tuned on the yellow tassel of a laburnum, and a bullfinch see-sawed and throated on the acacia tree. And every gorgeous tulip was a chalice filled with dew.

"Good-by," the girl said gently, and turned away.

She still wore the rich festive robes of yesterday. She began to take them off, slowly, drawing strings from their knottings, slipping hooks from their silver eyes, pushing jewel-buttons out of their holes, letting the loosened garments fall one by one in a rainbow heap of silk upon the floor (as Wu, when a boy, had shed furs and gems upon a floor in Sze-chuan). Her women would find and fold them presently. But it mattered nothing. Nothing mattered now.

She still was wearing her nail-protectors, two on each hand—necessary adjuncts to the toilet and to the comfort of many Chinese ladies, whose long spiral nails would be a torture if unprotected. But it had been Wu's pleasure to have Nang Ping taught the piano, and so, of course, she had to wear her nails short. But whenever she was "dressed" she wore the fantastic ornaments, to indicate that Wu's daughter did not work. She discarded them now, and listlessly let them fall upon the silks heaped at her feet: two were of green jade (one finely carved, one studded with diamonds), one was silver set with rubies, the fourth was gold set with pearls and moonstones.

When all the finery—such finery as Europe never sees, except burlesqued on the stage—had been cast off, she began to re-dress herself, steadily and very carefully.

From the silver ewer she poured water into the silver basin. It needed both her hands and much of her strength to lift the ewer; it was heavy with the precious metal's weight, and she had never lifted it before. In all her life she had never once dressed or undressed herself. When the attar and the sweet vinegars had creamed in the basin she bathed her face again and again until all the paint was gone. She only wore rouge and thick-crusted white paint on days of function and of festival. On days of homely ease and unceremonied home-keeping her skin was as clean and unprofaned as a baby's.

It is a canon of Chinese womanhood never quite to undress unnecessarily. Modesty at her toilet, even when performing it alone, is enjoined the Manchu girl as it is the Catholic girl of Europe. And this Manchu niceness has permeated the other Chinese races. And in China a maid would be held not chary, but prodigal indeed, did "she unmask her beauty to the moon." A land of several peoples sharply distinct in much, China is in much else the land of great racial amalgamation. And it is impossible to trace back to their source many of this wonderful people's most salient qualities. Tartar has infected Mongol, Mongol inoculated Tartar, Taoist taught Mohammedan, Confucianism and Buddhism have mixed and fused, Teng-Shui tinged all, sometimes tainting and degrading, occasionally idealizing and lifting up to poetry. And modesty of body is simple instinct with Chinese girls of every blend and caste. Nor is it lost—as so many of youth's sweetnesses always must be everywhere—in the gray slough of old age. Nowhere in China will you encounter the unique exhibitions of antique female nudity that occasionally startle one so extraordinarily in Japan. The old women of China, even the poorest, are always clad, and a Chinese girl slips from the screening of her smock into the screening of her bubbling bath without an instant's flash of interim.

The early daylight showed Nang Ping very lovely, as she stood there in her one last garment. Chinese women of the mandarin class are often exquisitely lovely, especially those of mingled Manchu and Mongol bloods. Nang's sorrow was too new to have bleared or blowsed her yet; it had but thrown a gracious, pathetic delicacy about her as a veil. And even the charming coloring of her was not impaired.

There is no greater beauty of coloring than the coloring of such girls—not in England, not in Spain. Nang Ping's skin was no darker than the liquor of the finest Chinese tea, and not unlike it in hue, not green, not buff, but white, just hinting of each, and in her cheeks the delicate pink of a tea rose told how red the blood at her heart was, and how thin the patrician skin that masked and yet revealed it. The little figure, tall for a Chinese, was tenderly drawn and perfectly proportioned; the young presence, for all its gentleness, was queenly; the firmly modeled head was well set on the straight shoulders. Hair could not be blacker or arched jet brows more beautifully drawn. The girl's mobile mouth was large, but exquisitely shaped, and her red lips parted and closed over teeth that could not have been whiter, more faultless or more prettily set. There was a dimple in the obstinate chin, and one beneath the tiny mole on her right cheek; and her black, velvet eyes (soft now, and almost purple with unshed tears) were as straight set in the small head as the eyes of any Venus in Vatican or Louvre.

She stood a moment, gazing into space, clad only in her delicate smock, and then slowly she redressed herself in her simplest robes—soft, loose and gray. She had many such gowns, and wore them often. The Chinese are too greatly, too finely artist to let the gorgeousness in which they gloat degenerate by over-use into a commonplace. The blare of their brazen music has its long reliefs of slow, soft minor passages; their gayest gardens have prominent heaps of dull, barren stone, long stretches of cold, gray walls; each sumptuous room has its empty, restful corner. Nang Ping had fifty pictures of great price, and more ivories, each a gem, but all the pictures save one, all the ivories save one, were stowed away always, and just one at a time placed where it might joy her sight; and most often she moved softly about her home habited in plain raiment of neutral tints as gentle as a dove's.

Her hair took her longest. She had never brushed it before, and the unguent took time to remove. But at last even that was done, the jeweled pins heaped away, the long black strands braided about her head.

And then she sat down on the floor again, her cold, ringless hands clasped at her knees, and waited and listened until her father's gong should strike.

She knew that she should hear it presently.

Once she started, and caught up from the floor a little scented bead. She held it to her face, and then laid it away in her bosom. It was her father's, one of a string he often wore, and in her bitter misery she was pathetically a little happier for the proof it gave her that his own hands had carried her here. She would keep it in her bosom always—while she lived.

Twice servants came in with trays of food and drink; blanc-mange, soup, tea and wine. They made deep obeisance to her when they came and when they went. But she did not speak to them, nor they to her.

And no message came until the message of the great gong's soft boom.

CHAPTER XX
WHAT WU DID IN PROOF OF LOVE

WU, when he had laid Nang Ping on her mats and covered her, went to his library, and sat thinking through the night.

When he had lifted her, he had not glanced at the Englishman, nor had he even looked in the direction of prison or prisoner since. The servants had their orders. Those orders would be obeyed. With Basil Gregory, Wu had nothing more to do—yet.

All night long he scarcely moved by so much as the drumming of finger or toe, by so much as the quiver of a lash. None of Nang Ping's restlessness was shared by him. He was beyond restlessness. His agony was absolute. Mothers suffer acutely when daughters "fall"—good mothers and bad. But such mothers' sorrow can never equal the red torment of fatherhood so punished. Nature holds stricter justice between sex and sex than she is credited. And such partiality and unfair favoritism as he does show now and then is given, as is the gross favoritism of man-made laws constantly (in Europe and in Asia), to women.

Analyze what law of life you will, and the resultant conclusion will have something to testify of Chinese wiseness. The punishment of a crime never falls solely upon the direct miscreant. Blood and love must pay their debt. And the Chinese legal code which allows and decrees that kindred shall suffer (even to capital punishment) for a kinsman's crime is less fantastic and less fatuous than it seems to Western minds.

Basil Gregory and Nang Ping had sinned. Wu and Florence Gregory were to be punished with them. And because Nature forgives man less than she forgives woman, the sharper, surer punishment was to fall on the father and the son.

Compared with one year in Wu's life, the joy Nang Ping had stolen in the garden was but "as water unto wine." And, suffering now to her sharp young utmost, she was suffering less than he.

When day came he rose, as Nang Ping did, and went to the window. Her room was on the one higher floor; his looked almost level with the garden—his own garden. For he too had his own private pleasance, taboo to all, unless expressly bidden there. And Wu rarely gave that permission, even to Nang Ping. That bit of garden was his outer solitude, and this room was his indoor privacy. It was here and there he kept alone.

No race prizes privacy more, more realizes its value, conserves and guards it with more dignity and skill, or with so much. A people of interminable clans, knit together and interdependent as is no other people, yet it is with the

Chinese people, both Mongol and Tartar, that individuality has its fullest rights, its surest safety.

Towards noon he bathed, put on again his plain dark robes, went into the great hall and ate a little rice. He had work ahead, much work, and he intended to do it well. He had no more time for thought, nor need. His thinking was done. His years of selfishness were past. He no longer saw or felt "a divided duty." He was China's now—Wu the mandarin. Each hour should be full. He would serve assiduously and relentlessly, not with brooding thought, but with action piled on action.

At dusk he smote upon the gong hanging in the smaller audience hall, an apartment half of state and half of intimacy.

Nang Ping heard the deep notes reverberate through the house—she had been listening for the sound all day—and rose to her feet before they died away. She was standing ready at her door when her father's message came, and she followed the servant, for herself relieved that her waiting was done, for herself feeling little else, but miserable for Wu. He had been tender to her always, and she had loved him with an absorbing love, until the Englishman had come to kiss her face, dislocate her life and change her soul.

She went in steadily and alone, bent in obeisance three times, and then stood before her father quietly, her hands folded meekly at her breast, her eyes patient and sorrowful, but not afraid.

And she was not afraid. Basil was dead by now—she made no doubt of that; the spoiler of Wu's daughter could not have lived in Wu's vengeance for a day. There was no more to fear for Basil. For him the worst had come, and was done. For herself fear had no place in her now. Her father would not torture her—that she knew. But she thought that she should scarcely have winced if he had. A slight, slip of a girl, slim as willow in her scant dull robe, she came of a race whose women had hung themselves more than once to honor a husband's obsequies; and one—a queen—had burned to her death, lighting beside the imperial grave her own funeral pile of teak- and sandal-woods, oil-and-perfume drenched, Nang Ping was not afraid.

Wu met her eyes, and she met his; and his were not unkind.

"Will you tell me all?" Wu did not speak unkindly. And this was the first time he had couched command to her in interrogative.

"My honorable father," the girl said sadly, "I will tell you nothing."

The mandarin smiled. This was too grave a time for anger. And he had a bribe that he knew could be trusted to buy from her what he would, let the telling cost her what it might.

He had never bribed his child, not even with sugar-plums for her smiles when she was a babe. But he would bribe her now. Their old days were done, and with them some old principles of conduct. And their old relationship—spoiled now—was drawing to its close.

"You fear to injure the Englishman!" But even that he did not say roughly.

"My honorable father, not that. He is past beyond injury now; Nang Ping knows that."

Again he smiled. But he only said, "You fear to implicate Low Soong?"

At that Nang Ping raised her eyes to his in entreaty.

"Have no fear. No punishment shall fall on her. She is not worth it. She shall be well dowered and honorably wed soon. She has dealt ill by me, and by you, her kinswoman, foully; but even so, I will not do her an injustice to you. She never betrayed you. In her first panic the slight, silly frog-thing fled—to save her own dishonest skin—but she came back but now, creeping to share your lot, and begging to speak with you. Do you care to see her?"

"I wish to see no one, O honorable sir."

"I thought you would answer so. Be at rest for her. She shall fare well." He did not add that he would keep his word. There was no need: Nang Ping knew it.

He called for lights, and when the red candles were lit and the sweet torches in their sconces until all the room flamed with light, and the noiseless servants had withdrawn to await his next command, whether it came in a moment or in a year, he began to speak again. And because he was Chinese, and because he still loved her well, his words were long.

"Sit. Listen. I am not blameless. I shall be blameless from this hour. My venerable, honorable grandfather, the sainted Wu Ching Yu, dedicated me to a great task. I have obeyed him for the most, fulfilled it in the main, but not with the single purpose such high duty claims. I loved your mother. That was most right. Less would have wronged her; and she was fragrant as the yellow musk, holy as the queen-star. But for one celestial year, at her plum-blossom side, I forgot my task; at least I let it wait, and sometimes I have let it wait for you. Not again shall I do so. Scarcely time for suitable penance will I allow myself. I am Wu, and the house of Wu shall be avenged. I shall live for that and for China. My venerable grandfather, three thousand times wise, did well to send me to England. And he bade me study Englishmen closely. But I did ill to take to myself too much of their custom. We have learned too much of Europe. It is well to learn of every nation, but to accept too much from inferior peoples is a hideous crime; and in that crime I have shared to China's hurt—and yours. You are undone. China is threatened with the loss of all that has made her for thousands of years paramount and exquisite. Sometimes, alone at night, I have thought that I have heard the wind cry, and Heaven sob, and the parting knell of China toll. And I have thrown myself prostrate before our gods, and entreated that China—our China—may prove stronger than her enemies, stronger than her fools. But my soul aches. For I realize that change is in our air, from Canton to Pekin, from Ningpo to Tibet, and that any hour revolution may strike our mighty empire to the heart. The rebel, the missionary, the fanatic and the adventurer, the foe without and the dolt within, press her hard. Her plight is sore to-day. But China has held together longer than any other empire in history. We Chinese never forget, and we do not meekly forgive. Again and again we have seemed to accept innovations, have tried them, have found them unacceptable, and then we have discarded them once and forever. We are in peril now; but the end is not yet. Already the word passes over China, as a breath of summer over the head-heavy poppy fields, 'Back to Confucius'! And I—I descended from that great sage—I, too, who love China as I did not love your mother—I, too, have betrayed China—and you! I have given you a freedom that was in itself a soil to a maiden. I ask your pardon. All night long I have asked your honorable mother's, and the forgiveness of my most noble ancestors. You have been to me both son and daughter; the women of the Wus have often been so, and endowed in it with great merit. But in me it was a sin. But from this I shall be wholly China's. This moon I perform a duty to our house— my last selfish rite. It done, I am my country's, my people's. I shall wed now, and give my honorable ancestors other sons, China men-Wus to be her rulers and her servants. That I have not done so before is my crime. I thought to adopt your husband, or if that might not be, he too highly ranked in his own great clan, one of your younger sons, that all I had might go to you and to one you had borne. I sinned to think it. Adoption is honorable, decreed of our sages, countenanced of our gods, but only for those to whom sons of their bodies are denied. A man should beget men, father his own heir."

He said much more. It was his last indulgence of self, for even his stern resolve yearned over her, and his tortured heart delayed the parting with the girl. He spoke of her childhood and of his own. But of the high traditions of the women of its blood, upon which their great house was built as on an impregnable rock, he did not speak again. He spared her that—his only child, the first woman of her name to err in the degree that is not forgiven Chinese gentlewomen.

Presently he commanded again—and no question now—that she should tell him all, and commanding turned his screw.

"He is not dead," he said. "He lives. He is unharmed." Nang Ping swayed a little on her stool and caught at her knees with her hands. "Tell me all."

"O honorable sir," she sobbed, huddling at his feet, "I cannot."

Wu smiled. "All! Omit nothing. You can save him so!"

Nang Ping started up, sitting bolt on her heels, and searched her father's face with narrow eyes widened and piteous.

"All! And he shall live. Even, he shall go free!"

Nang Ping moaned, hung down her head, and began to speak, for she knew that Wu Li Chang would keep his word. And even this price of shame her discarded love would pay to save her man. Her words came with tortured breath—in gasps. But it was for Basil, and she kept her bond. She told of their first meeting and their last. She told it all—all but those utmost things that never have been told, and never can, and in China least of all.

Why Wu exacted it was hard to say. Perhaps he could not have told himself. If it tortured her, more it tortured him an hundred fold. And there was little of it in detail, nothing of it in essential, that he did not already know. Much of it he knew better and deeper than she did. Perhaps to hear it from her lips was no small part of a self-inflicted punishment he had decreed his scourge since he had been so lax a father—lax a father, and he Chinese! And she motherless!

He heard her in silence—without once a word of prompting or of interruption. And not once did she raise her head or look at him. If she had looked, her faltering words must have died. For his face twitched with convulsive pain again and again, and foam beaded white on his clenched lips.

There was a long silence when she had done, and neither moved.

At last he said, "Is there something you would ask of me, some message you would give?"

Nang Ping trembled violently. But the message her soul cried out to send she dared not speak; and if she had dared, surely she must have spared him it, for she was gentle, and he had always loved her well and shown her tenderness. When she could command herself a little, she said, falteringly, "If Low Soong might have a jewel or a robe—one, from me."

"Of all that was not your mother's or my mother's, or any mothers' of theirs, Low Soong shall choose all that she will. And I promise you that I will bear that frail no ill-will. It was not for her to guard what I, your father, failed to guard."

Nang Ping tried to thank him, but she could only bow her head and lay it near his shoe. She dared not touch that shoe. It was an old, easy shoe. She had embroidered it when a child.

"The day grows warm," Wu said presently, rising and bidding her rise. And when she stood before him, he laid his hand a moment on her shoulder and said softly, "Nang Ping!" for she was motherless, and very young, and he loved her still.

"The day grows warm. Go to the easement and tell me if the sun is on the tulip tree." And as she moved away, without a sound he seized the great sword hanging beside the shrine and struck her once.

It was enough.

She scarcely moaned—just a soft quick sigh—and one smothered word.

Wu Li Chang caught the sigh but not the word. Surely Kwanyin Ko had granted something of Nang Ping's prayer, and was merciful to Wu in that. For the Chinese girl had died speaking an English name.

He did not catch the word; but he saw something fall from her dress and roll towards the altar, and he rose and found it—a little scented bead.

And all night long, until the day broke over China, Wu sat motionless and alone in the room where he had played with her often in her baby days, taught her as a child, decorated her fresh young womanhood with gems and love: sat immovable and alone, while the heart's blood of his only child clotted and crusted at his feet.

CHAPTER XXI
A CONFERENCE

LORD MELBOURNE once said that "nobody has ever done a very foolish thing except for some great principle." Well, it would be difficult to find the great principle underlying most of the very foolish things the average European does in Asia. As a nation we British are very wise in our conduct there. As a race we deal honorably with the Oriental peoples—when once we've conquered them—and honorable conduct is a high wisdom in itself, and from it we reap a fine reward—the respect of the Eastern races. But as individuals we perpetrate a long series of crass blunders, of petty daily idiocies, whose sum total is tragedy and sometimes threatens international holocaust. And it is the Englishwoman, not the Englishman, who is the worst offender. Our security in Asia is built up on Oriental respect and liking, and Mrs. Montmorency-Jones can do more in a day to undermine it than a Sir Harry Parkes can do in a month to build it. Insolence is her method; fair dealing is his.

The average British man in Asia learns little enough, Heaven knows! of the natives among whom he lives; the average British woman learns nothing. She does not decline to know the natives; no, indeed—she simply ignores them. Woman rules in Asia—and especially in China—as (if a woman may be allowed to hint it) she does almost everywhere. And Englishwomen living in Calcutta or Shanghai do English interests grave injury, by courting, winning (and meriting) the dislike of Indian and Chinese women. The Englishwoman does it not by any overt act or series of acts, but by a consistent supercilious contemptuousness of attitude. I am a memsahib. You do not exist. The secret societies—the tongs and the brotherhoods—are responsible for much of our Asiatic difficulties; our own women are responsible for more. If the Boxers made Pekin run red with European blood, some women of the European Legations did even more to bring down the trouble and to foment it.

And the pity of it is its absolute unnecessariness: just a cup of cold water now and then, just a little human kindliness now and then, and the liking and sympathy of Oriental womanhood were ours. Some one has written of "the heart that must beat somewhere beneath the impenetrable Oriental mask." The mask is not impenetrable. An honest, friendly smile will pierce it. The Oriental is nine-tenths heart. A typical Asiatic can be won by moderate kindness to great loyalty and devotion. Page after page of the history of the Indian mutiny proves it.

And of the Chinese people this is even truer.

Florence Gregory was a kindly, likeable woman, and during her year in Hong Kong she had not thought it necessary to make herself detestable to the Chinese with whom she came in contact.

On her part this was neither tact nor studied policy. They interested her and she liked them, and in return they liked her. She gave them courtesy and decent treatment, and sometimes a sunny word or two, and in return they gave her of their best and served her loyally. Ah Wong, her amah, adored her.

There was nothing that Ah Wong would not have done for her English mistress. And the story of it is this: Mrs. Gregory had never saved Ah Wong's life or rescued her son from slavery. She had just been quietly and decently kind to her in the little daily ways. Oh! those little ways, the little things—too small to chronicle, almost too small to sense sometimes—but to women they are *everything!* The big things scarcely count to women; but the little things—they count.

When Basil Gregory did not keep his promise to dine at their hotel his mother was disappointed, but not inordinately surprised, and only moderately hurt. It had happened before.

They waited dinner half an hour. Robert Gregory would not allow a longer waiting. And even the mother dined with an unruffled appetite. Even when midnight came without him it occurred to no one to be in the least alarmed—to no one but Ah Wong.

Ah Wong had seen the impalpable intrinsic stalking in the garden at Kowloon. And what she saw alarmed her then. Basil's continued absence alarmed her more and more. She was alarmed for her mistress's peace of mind. Basil himself she neither liked nor disliked. She thought Robert Gregory a funny old chap. The son did not interest her.

When Basil did not appear at the office the next day his father was angry. When three days passed, and no word came of the truant, they were alarmed—all of them. And in a week the island rang with hue and cry for him.

Mrs. Gregory was distraught.

Perhaps the son's disappearance might have worried the father even more if there had been no other pressing anxieties. But there were—several.

There was the very deuce to pay at the Hong Kong branch of the Gregory Steamship Company, and a good deal of inadequacy with which to pay it.

It was a bright, hot day—a blue and gold day, without a trace of Hong Kong mist and murk—and the windows in the manager's room were open wide.

The furniture was sparse but rich; it was Robert Gregory's own room, and he was of the type of business man who likes to do himself well in the format of his office routine, more in a sincere pride in his business cult than in personal vanity or any pampering of self, and also in a well-defined theory of advertisement: Persian carpets and Spanish mahogany desks indicate a firm's prosperity clearly. Gregory's furniture was very expensive, but sensible, solid and untrimmed. He earned and amassed money in big ways and in small, but, in the main, he left the spending of it on fripperies to Hilda and his wife. A photograph of Hilda—the one ornament the office confessed to—stood on her father's desk, in a splendid wide frame that might have been Chinese, so costly and so barbaric was it, had only the design and the workmanship been better. But if the picture was somewhat over-framed, its girl-subject was not over-dressed, for English Hilda, who from her father's office table smiled up at all the world, was several inches more décolleté than even the moon had ever seen Nang Ping.

But modesty and even decency are as much virtues of the eye that looks as of the creatures of its glance; and John Bradley, sitting in Robert Gregory's chair, saw only maidenhood delectable and flawless in the picture his eyes sought again and again. And any man who, to Robert Gregory's knowledge, had seen anything coarser, Robert Gregory would have shot cheerfully.

Holman, Gregory's head clerk, sat moodily opposite the priest, looking out into the quay. The long window he faced was the apartment's most conspicuous feature, and through it outrolled a teeming panorama of steamships and shipping industries. Docks and shipping in the near distance looked even nearer in the clear magnifying atmosphere, and close at hand smoke curled up from the funnels of a large steamer, flying the house flag of the company—a noticeable pennant even in that harbor, where noticeable objects jostle each other by the hundreds. The big lettering—"G. S. S. Co."—was as bright and blue as the sky against whose brilliant background the smoke belched forth from the fat funnels, and the bunting that backgrounded the letters was yellow—impertinently yellow, for it was of the precise shade that in Pekin would have spelled death to any other who wore it or showed it on his chair, so sacred was it to reigning Emperor and Empress. But Robert Gregory did not know that, nor did Holman. But they should have known it—certainly Holman should, for he had lived in China many years now, and was far from being so crassly stupid concerning the Chinese as his chief was.

Between the big ship and the office building a constant procession of coolies passed up and down the dock, and the hum of their incessant intoned chatter filled the room with a noisy sing-song that rose and fell but never rested or drew breath.

On a rostrum behind the *Fee Chow's* side, Simpson, an old and trusted clerk, was watching the coolies load, and a Chinese clerk perched near him on a high stool, checking each bale and box. A compradore sat at his desk on the wharf, wrangling with a knot of loin-clothed coolies who were gesticulating wildly with arms and poles and chattering like angry chimpanzees.

"And that is all you can tell me?" Holman said, as Bradley rose to go.

"All I care to say. I've strained a point to say that much."

"And you will not tell me where you got your information? Is that quite fair?"

John Bradley shook his head. "Not information. I have no information— none. But I have my suspicion, and I believe it is well based."

"Built on Chinese rock!"

"Well—yes—in part. And I have a great deal of respect for Chinese rock. As for being unfair, that is the last thing I'd be willingly. And I have tried to look at this from every side. A man likes to respect confidence; with a priest it is a duty, solemn and imperative. But if I chose to blab, I have not one concrete fact to state. A Chinese woman, I will not tell you her name—if I know it— comes to me in the middle of the night, getting into the grounds somehow over the wall or up the hill, certainly not through the gate, and begs me to find some way of getting Basil Gregory's people out of China. She urges me to let them lose no time in searching for him, because no searching will find him; and they, she insists, are in danger that will grow deadlier every hour they stay on here. I did not know that Basil was missing until she told me; it's two nights ago. I had been expecting him to call—to complete some talk we'd begun———"

"About a girl?"

"But I was not particularly surprised that he delayed keeping an appointment that was not very definite. Basil was always a procrastinator. The woman does not know where he is or what has happened to him. Take that from me. She said so, and she was speaking the truth. It is part of my business to know when people are telling the truth and when they are lying to me. She had some suspicion—what it was I have no idea, or whether it was right or wrong—but she would tell me nothing, except that she risked her life to warn me that at all costs the Gregorys must go from China, and go now."

"And leave poor Mr. Basil to his fate?"

Bradley made a gesture of baffled helplessness.

The clerk's lip curled. "You have a poor idea of my intelligence. I know it all now—all that you know—and what you suspect."

"Then you do not know much," the other retorted hotly.

"No," Holman admitted grimly. "Not much to chew on, and nothing at all to go upon. Ah Wong comes to you in the middle of the night—it *was* Ah Wong; she is devoted to Mrs. Gregory, and quite indifferent to Mr. Basil, dead or alive. You learn from her, or from some one else, the next morning, of the visit three days ago to Wu's garden at Kowloon, and off you go to Kowloon to dig it all out. You said you went to Kowloon to try to interest your friend Wu in the case, because he is the one man who can do anything that can be done in China. Now, you did not go—excuse me, Mr. Bradley— to Kowloon to try to interest Wu in the case; you went to find Mr. Basil."

Bradley threw down the hat he had taken up and sat down again. "You are wrong there," he said. "For I too believe that Basil Gregory will not be found. But I did go to try to interest Wu Li Chang in what is very urgent to me— for—for several reasons—because I know him to be, humanly speaking, almost omnipotent, and because I trust and like him."

"Trust and like Wu Li Chang!"

"Emphatically," was the quiet answer. "I've seen a great deal of Mandarin Wu since I first came out. He's a gentleman, and every inch a man. There is no one I respect more, and very, very few of my own race I respect as much. We are friends, I tell you. And I think he likes me. I went to beg a great favor of him."

"H'm!" the clerk mused aloud. "And he wouldn't see you?"

"And I couldn't get in. I have never been refused 'come in and welcome' at Wu's before, and I must have been there fifty times. But I couldn't get past the outer gate yesterday. The mandarin didn't refuse to see me; I just couldn't get in."

"Much the same thing——"

"Not at all! I was met at the gate and turned away from it with every courtesy. If Wu had wished to avoid me, I might still have been made free of the grounds, as I have been a dozen times when he has been away or too busy to chat. But I was driven—with the utmost politeness—from the gate. Why? Because there was something in there I was not to see—I believe, Basil. And if Basil, Basil alive. A dead Englishman would have been obliterated."

"But could not a living one be hidden beyond your suspicion, even by so astute a Chinaman as Wu Li Chang?"

The clergyman looked puzzled. "Yes—yes—undoubtedly, most probably, but such men as Wu take no chance, and there is always just one chance that any living prisoner may make himself heard or seen. But dead men tell no tales."

Holman shook his head. He was unconvinced.

And Holman was right. Wu Li Chang would, had he chosen to do so, have let all Anglo-Hong Kong stroll through his gardens, and have kept twenty prisoners there undiscovered at the same time. He had had Bradley denied entrance at his gate because his home was the home of mourning, and in it there was no room or welcome for any Englishman, except the one grimly guarded guest in the pagoda by the lake.

"Well," Bradley said, rising again, "I can only repeat, as you value Basil's life, let Mr. Gregory do nothing to rasp Wu Li Chang. See him, I must and will. But it will have to be at his convenience and consent, not at mine. I don't know why I should hope to influence him. But I can only try." He picked up his hat, and continued looking at the girl in the frame. "Wu may be coaxed; he cannot be coerced. There is no force to which we could appeal, even if we had anything to go upon, and we have nothing. The Tsungli yamên itself, at Pekin, could neither coerce nor punish Wu Li Chang if it were minded to——"

"You know that Mr. Basil was seen here on the island after they had all returned from their visit to Wu's daughter?"

John Bradley waved that aside contemptuously. "Rubbish!"

"Precisely what I think," Holman acquiesced tersely.

At the door the priest turned to say earnestly, "Remember, Mr. Gregory must do nothing to annoy Wu now—absolutely nothing. Basil's very life may depend on that."

"I'll do my best," Holman said, none too confidently, rising wearily and taking a step towards the other.

"And, Holman, not one word about Ah Wong—that you think she has been to me. It would serve no purpose, and it might cause her trouble—so—I expressly ask you, not one word."

"Not one word, then," the other man said, taking Bradley's outheld hand.

And they parted with a grip long and strong. They were brother Masons.

CHAPTER XXII
SING KUNG YAH'S FLOWERS

THAT afternoon Florence Gregory, coming in with Hilda and Ah Wong from a weary, distracted searching—searching here, there, everywhere—found in her sitting-room such a basket of flowers as she had never seen before, and a red Chinese visiting card, three inches wide and fully eight inches long. Ah Wong eyed it dismayed, and at her lady's command translated the ideographic characters reluctantly. "No like," she added. "Chlinese lady no make vlisit so way—Chlinese lady no have vlisitling clard chit. No like."

"But who is Sing Kung Yah?" Mrs. Gregory asked wearily, not interested to know, except that any straw might prove a clew to the only thing on earth that mattered now, and so must be clutched.

"Lido wuman," the amah said contemptuously, her fine, acrid Mongolian disgust in no way softened by the unhappy fact that she herself was a widow also.

"Whose widow is she?" Mrs. Gregory was puzzled.

"Not know."

"Who is she? Why has she called?"

"Not know—whly she clome—or send slweet blossoms. Not know if she clome itself."

"Find out."

"Madam, can do," the woman said, running off on her errand reluctantly.

"Did," she reported presently. "Top-side chair. Plenty coolie."

"Who is she?"—the English voice implied that the English mistress intended to be answered explicitly this time.

And Ah Wong answered desperately, "Her all same klinsloman Wu Li Chang. Live Kowloon yamên. Be mock mother lonorable miss-child we dlink tea."

"Great Scot!" Hilda exclaimed. "What a time to choose to force her acquaintance on us—a Chinawoman! Even they must have heard of Basil's disappearance, with every wall and corner in Hong Kong placarded with his description and his picture."

"Oh! be quiet," the mother told her. Florence was thinking—thinking hard.

Ah Wong was thinking too, and on the Chinese face, usually so inscrutable, there was an unmistakable pinch of anxiety, and her dog-like, devoted eyes were growing haggard.

"Take them away—where Mr. Gregory will not see them. But take care of them. Let the hotel servants see that we are treating them with the greatest respect. Do you understand?"

"Ah Wong understland," the woman said. "Can do." And she did do; but she only just could, for the great gilded bamboo basket of flowers was so heavy and so huge that she could scarcely lift it; she staggered a little as she carried it from the room.

And Basil Gregory's mother went on thinking—on and on.

The mandarin Wu was said to be the most powerful man in China—at least in this part of China. Surely he could help them to find Basil. And he was a kind man—his girl had said so. And his near kinswoman—the aunt who had been on a visit at a Taoist nunnery or something when they were in Kowloon—had called and brought a garden full of flowers. That call should be returned, post-haste. Perhaps she could help, the woman who had left the flowers and the absurd red card; and the girl, the little girl who had given them tea, she could help, too, to persuade the all-powerful mandarin, if it needed much to persuade him; of course she could and she would; of course she would—she had had the kindest eyes and a soft, girlish mouth. How she, his mother, wished that Basil might have shown little Miss Wu just a little more attention—not too much, of course; that might have alarmed or even offended a Chinese girl—you never could tell about such oddities; but if only he'd shown a little less—yes—a good deal less cold indifference— indifference so cold that it had been almost a rudeness—and girls felt such things, and resented them too—even Chinese girls, probably. Of course, she, his mother, rejoiced in the niceness of her boy, and that he was not as other young Englishmen were in China—some of them—but manly Aryan self-respect was one thing, and an almost brutal display of racial superiority and masculine indifference was quite another. She wished indeed, that he had treated the only child of the great Wu less cavalierly, for his manner to the pretty Chinese creature had been very cavalier—Chinese, but a girl for all that. Still, his fault was in his favor, and it was no part of a mother's office to forget that. Basil was innately and intrinsically—and she believed irradicately—nice. Thank God for it! He had been a little wild at school— the best boys always were (repeating to herself the foolish old threadbare paternal fallacy); a trifle lax at Oxford too—but, her son and always nice!

There was nothing cavalier about the way in which Ah Wong carried her fragrant burden through the hotel corridors. Her manner to the honorable flowers grown in the garden of the jade-like mandarin, and gathered by noble, jeweled hands, was conspicuously obsequious.

But when she had placed them in a cool, dark room, sacred to an adjunct of her lady's toilet, and into which Robert Gregory never came, nor the hotel servants, her manner changed. She put them down abruptly, fastened the doors (there were two) feverishly and securely, and gestured angrily towards the gleaming golden basket of bloom, with a use of arms and fingers strangely identical with the motions with which the Neapolitan peasant averts the evil eye. Then she ran one matting-blind up, letting such breeze as there was blow across the flowers and out of the room through the window.

She even knelt down by the big basket, and with a guttural groan sniffed—not at the blossoms, but at the stems, and at the gilded wicker-work. But if there was some insidious poison hidden in the gift, to kill or disfigure whoever smelt or touched, Ah Wong could not detect it.

But how could she? Why should she hope to pit her wit against the wit of Wu?

Next, the woman got a sharp bamboo, and, kneeling down again, prodded cautiously but thoroughly among the leaves and stems and the depths of moss. She trembled as she worked, for she was prodding for some small poison-snake or asp, and was terribly afraid; but because another woman had treated her decently for a whole year, and kindly more than once, she worked on until convinced that nothing that crawled or stung was hidden in the glowing gift.

Then she unlocked one door and made several hurried journeys into the adjacent sleeping-room, carrying a small tub, a spirit-lamp, a box, a manicure set, a dozen sundries, and arranging them as best she could, first locking the dressing-room door from the bedroom side and hiding the key in her bosom.

The flowers seemed innocent enough, but Ah Wong would die before her English lady should touch them or inhale their breath.

Ah Wong was absurdly wrong—if devotion can ever be absurd; the flowers were exactly what they seemed. Wu Li Chang was no crude bungler. When he unsheathed his knife the knife would cut, but it would leave no trace of Wu.

Of the tragedy that had been enacted at Kowloon Ah Wong knew exactly nothing; but she suspected almost all, and the details of her suspicion were uncannily accurate. She was Chinese.

CHAPTER XXIII
AH WONG

THAT same night, at midnight, Tom Carruthers and Hilda Gregory sat hand in hand on a verandah that looked down the Peak on to the city and the water beyond. The midnight sky was thick with stars, and up and down the Peak's town-side thin snakes of light crept now and then—the lantern lights of late-sojourning natives, or of those pulling and pushing the rickshaws, and carrying the chairs of European merry-makers returning to the Peak to sleep in its comparative cool—a party that had dined at Government House, a dozen who had made moonlight picnic in the grounds of Douglas' Folly or at Wong-ma-kok, a man who had worked late at the bank, three who had played late at the club, several who had been at a dance, and perhaps fifty who had been yawning over the Richelieu of a very scratch Australian company. In Hong Kong—the town itself—the lights were still many, for Hong Kong both works and revels late o' nights, and on the nearer water dimmer lights blinked sleepily. And from the mastheads of many a ship larger lights hung bright and clear—red, green, blue, orange. There were half a dozen that Carruthers could identify as theirs—lanterns slung from craft of the Gregory Steamship Company—and he pointed them out to Hilda.

They spoke to each other but fitfully. Each was trying to think of some worth-while suggestion to make about poor Basil, and neither could.

A window that led from the balcony to the room beyond was open, and Robert Gregory and his wife were sitting in there, not silent like the two on the verandah, but going together over and over again a dozen sorry theories of their son's disappearance, a dozen feverish plans for his rescue.

The island and the mainland beyond had been well beaten by now. All the Europeans, the Government House, the Civil Service, residents, officials big and small, had tried to help in the search. For Robert Gregory was a power in Hong Kong, and Mrs. Gregory was well liked. And many of the natives were trying, too, to help in the search, or seemed to be.

In the Company's offices on the bund, a light still burned in the manager's room, and Holman and William Simpson sat there in earnest, anxious conclave.

"Nothing could look much blacker," Simpson was saying.

"Nothing."

"The bottom seems about out!"

Holman nodded grimly.

And indeed the affairs of the great Company seemed desperate, and all in the last few weeks, chiefly in the last few days! Strike had followed strike among the dock hands, inexcusably, inexplicably. Demands for increased wages, made when some important contract, already overdelayed, must be fulfilled quickly, or lost, were scarcely acceded to when they were renewed. It looked as if their hands were determined to ruin and shut down the Company by which they all lived and that had treated and paid them well for years. It was one of Robert Gregory's boasts that he believed in keeping his tools bright and his machinery well oiled. The *Fee Chow* must not miss the next morning's tide, and yet her loading had been hindered and bungled consistently. A dozen mishaps and a dozen odd financial backsets had followed each other, and it looked as if disaster had come to the Gregory Steamship Company, and come to stay.

Too anxious for the house they had served long and staunchly to rest, and anxious for their own salt too, the two men had returned after office hours to talk it over—to find a way out, if they could.

And the deeper they went into their canvass of affairs, the more difficult and bad it all seemed. And certainly the strange disappearance of young Gregory was far and away the worst feature of the entire complication. The Gregory purse was long, the Gregory credit enormous; both would stand a great deal of strain. But the accident (or whatever it was) to his boy was beginning to tell upon the father—that had been evident all day; and when Robert Gregory's nerve went, the greatest asset of the firm went.

And for this reason, rather than for any keen feeling for the young man who had shown but little for the business at which they toiled loyally early, and late, while he neglected it or played at it flippantly, and from which, as a rule, he drew in a day rather more in the way of cash than they together did in a week, it was of his disappearance and of the chance of his return that they spoke and planned, much more than of the ledger that lay between them, or the more immediate affairs of the office.

And while the six—two here, four in the hotel on the Peak—were trying to think and to contrive, two others, but quite separately, were doing something more active.

John Bradley, just at midnight, came out of a tiny house in Po Yan Street, not far from the Tung Wah Hospital, in the heart of Tai-pingshan, the poorest part of the Chinese quarter—a malodorous hovel in which a native miscreant, whom Bradley had befriended more than once, and whom, rightly or wrongly, the clergyman thought he could trust, lived. Sung Fo would have come to the Englishman on receipt of a message, but Bradley had thought it best to manage otherwise. And he feared nothing in Hong Kong, and indeed had nothing to fear, not even here in its worst quarter of slime and dirt and worse, tucked away behind the cobblers' lanes.

He had found Sung Fo at home, and had made the bargain he had come to make. Sung Fo had promised to "look-see" and "try-find," and for the rest Bradley thought he could do nothing but wait and watch and pray.

Like Ah Wong, he knew nothing but suspected everything, but with much less accuracy than she.

Unlike Ah Wong, all John Bradley's sympathies were with Wu Li Chang.

He would do anything that a man might do to find Basil Gregory.

He would do anything that a man might to avoid injuring Wu Li Chang.

And to spare Wu he would have gone even a little farther than he was prepared to go for Basil's sake, had not Basil been Hilda's brother.

But if his sympathy was all Wu Li Chang's, his anxiety was not. He had a firm conviction that nothing he could do, by purpose or by accident, could harm or imperil Wu Li Chang.

When he had been walking away from Sung's—perhaps for ten minutes—picking his way over garbage heaps and broken side-paths, he paused to look curiously at a house of which he had heard a great deal but had never entered—a well-kept brick edifice, taller and better built than many houses in that quarter, painted a dull light blue, and owned and inhabited by a Chinese apothecary who was infamously famous throughout the Empire.

It looked an innocent house, clean and law-abiding. It was lightless, and each of its shutters was tightly closed; but at midnight—a quarter-past midnight now—that it was darkened and closed but added to its air of trim respectability. And yet, to this quiet blue house half the poisoning crimes in China were attributed by the native and the European authorities alike—attributed, but not one ever traced.

The authorities had raided the place again and again, but always uselessly. Nothing incriminating was ever found—nothing but the ordinary wares of a well-stocked apothecary: glass bowls of Korean ginseng-plant roots (one, five inches long, was worth ten pounds, and a little of its dust would give vigor to the old, hair to the bald), skins of black cats and dogs (stewed, they prevent disease, and are the best hot-weather diet), musk, rhubarb and silk-covered packets of dragons' blood (invaluable medicinally, but not what it sounds—a dry resinous powder scraped from Sumatra rattan), cups of rhinoceros' horn, skins and horns ground into powdered doses, antidotes to poison, or guaranteed to impart the qualities of the animal which it had protected or adorned. Horns of cornigerous animals hung in tidy rows, and formed a conspicuous part of the stock-in-trade, for they give the human partaker strength and courage, still silly nerves, quell fearfulness. A pyramid of the hoofs of young deer, specific to inculcate fleet gait, half-screened the chief treasure of the place: a lacquer cabinet of hearts. There were three hearts, each in its own well-sealed jar: a lion's heart, and two that were human—a pirate's and a young girl's. The criminal's was preserved in alcohol, the maiden's in honey; and each was of fabulous value. There was no secret about their being here. They had been honorably bought: one from the criminal himself just as he bent down smilingly on the Kowloon execution ground, the other from a widowed grandmother who was a holy woman and very poor. The girl had been very lovely, and some rich man would buy her heart one day, no doubt, to enhance the marriage chances of a plain but favorite daughter. The pirate had been a monster of ferocity, and to eat his heart would be to become forever brave. Chinese warriors have eaten the hearts of their bravest foes. They can pay no greater compliment, none more sincere. Two alabaster boxes were stowed carefully beneath the counter: one held charms; the other held smaller boxes of p'ingan tan (pills of peace and tranquillity), the choicest drug in China. Tze-Shi sent boxes of p'ingan tan to troops sorely pressed or whom she wished greatly to reward. There were ointments here made from the gums of trees that surrounded the tomb of Confucius, and precious medicines brewed or pounded beside the Elephant's Pool, where Pusien washed his elephant after crossing the great mountain from the west; some in Pootoo, the sacred isle of Nan Hai, and still others in a garden that Marco Polo knew. There were simples here that would cure women of vanity, and one (but this the apothecary would by no means guarantee) that healed them from overtalkativeness. But all this was as it should be, and the police had never been able to find here anything nefarious or even objectionable.

Something about the building fascinated Bradley—probably the contrast between its docile and pleasant seeming and its sinister reputation—and he stood some time gazing at it, scrutinizing each closely shuttered window—there was not a balcony; it was unique in that—and the tight-shut door with the apothecary sign hanging from the lintel.

"It looks a peaceful place, innocently asleep after a day of honest industry," he said to himself; and then some old words that were great favorites of his, from a book he never tired of reading, came to his memory, and he bespoke them aloud softly to the star-emblazoned Chinese night: "He it is who ordaineth the night as a garment, and sleep for rest, and ordaineth the day for waking up to life."

But the apothecary's house was not quite asleep. A thin line of light trickled out from below the door, and then the door opened narrowly and a woman, shrouded from crown to shoe in humble blue, came into the street.

He did not see her face, although, as by law obliged, she carried a lantern, but she saw his, clear-cut in the white moonlight, a late, just-rising moon, and for an instant she turned as if to speak to him; but she thought better of it, and walked quietly but quickly away.

Bradley wondered who she was—up to no special harm, he hoped. It did not occur to him that her gait was familiar, at least not individually so—thousands of amahs walk so. But he noticed that her coarse blue clothes looked very clean—as clean and as blue as the blue house of Yat Jung How.

He went home then, and Ah Wong went too, back to the hotel, slipping out of the Chinese quarter stealthily, but going along the Praya unconcernedly and through Queen's Road and Ice House Street, and up the long climb to the Peak, and past the night watchman at the hotel door. She had a night-police pass; and her mistress had given her leave to spend the evening on some errand of her own.

It's a long climb up Hong Kong Peak. Ah Wong was very strong, but her indefatigable little feet ached when she slipped into the room where she had locked the flowers almost twelve hours ago, and day was slipping rosy up the sky.

Day was coming, but she did not lift a blind. She lit a candle. And when she had laid off the long blue cloth in which she had veiled herself, closely in the Chinese quarter, carelessly in English-town, she took from her dress the spoil of her visit to Yat Jung How's blue house: three bottles.

The smallest of the three was filled (it was very small) with a few drops of opalescent green liquid. Ah Wong studied it grimly awhile, and then she knotted the phial in some corner of her garments, and tucked it securely back inside her dress.

The second bottle held about a dram of something that smelt disagreeably when she uncorked it; but she kept it well away from her own face and nose, and turned it instantly into the moss in the basket. It was deadly poison this, and would destroy any reptile or scorpion thing that came within a yard of it, and so potent was it that being near it would render any other poison quite innocuous—Yat had told her so. And she trusted Yat Jung How. She had known a way to make him trustworthy.

The third bottle was a generous, roomy receptacle, squat but wide. It held nearly a pint. And this was disinfectant, warranted to purify a poisoned room, and smelt of an acceptable cool pungence as Ah Wong threw it lavishly about the room, until she had spilled the last drop.

Then she lit several handfuls of joss-sticks and pulled up the blinds. But she did not unlock the doors, or leave one unlocked when at last she left the room, to sit outside it till her lady called. She intended that no one but she should pass into that room until the Kowloon flowers were all dead, and she had won Mrs. Gregory's permission to burn them herself, basket and all.

The sweet pungence of the joss-sticks came to her from under the door. From under the room's other door no doubt it was filling her mistress's chamber with thick sweetness—but that was well, for the English lady loved the smell. Mr. Gregory did not especially. Quite possibly he might swear a little in his sleep. But he often swore in his sleep. Ah Wong had heard him.

She leaned back her head against the cool corridor wall, anxious and tired, but well content with her night's work.

And she had left her three jade bangles (and they were good) and her seven silver ones and her stick-pin of seed pearls and coral with Yat Jung How. And almost she had pawned her soul to him, and had quite pawned all she would earn for years.

Heathen Chinee!

CHAPTER XXIV
IN THE CLUTCH OF THE TONGS

THE next day there was still no word of Basil, and at the Steamship Company's hong the tangle was steadily tightening.

Holman sat glowering at a telegram he was reading for the third or fourth time, but looked up impatiently as a Chinese clerk came in and stood waiting to speak.

"What now?"

"Coolie men talkee muchee. No plenty money, no can do plenty work."

"Fetch the compradore here," Holman snapped, thrusting the telegram into his waistcoat.

"Can do," the clerk said, and went out.

Tom Carruthers stood by the window, doing nothing in particular, but watching with a rueful, puzzled face the seething, jabbering coolies outside. He swung round as the clerk went. "I say, Holman, what is all this? A third demand to-day for more wages!"

Holman pushed a ledger aside abruptly. "That's what I am trying to find out, young man," he said—"just exactly what it all means."

The compradore came in a moment—a middle-aged Chinese, as capable looking in his way as Holman was in his. He stood waiting stolidly for the manager to speak, but Holman delayed a little, measuring the Mongol with his shrewd blue eyes before he said: "Look here, compradore, what the devil is the matter with your coolies now? Why have they struck work again, and why the blue blazes have you let them, when you know how late we're with the loading of the *Fee Chow* already, that she'll miss the tide if there's more delay, and that she *must not miss* the tide? Eh?"

"Coolie men talkee muchee"—the compradore said it sadly. "They talkee stlikee."

"Strike!" Tom Carruthers cried. "Strike! That's the limit! A strike halfway through loading. You damn well tell them———"

But Holman interrupted sharply, "Hush, Mr. Carruthers, please. Leave this to me. Now, compradore, what's the grievance? Come, out with it, chop, chop!"

"Coolie man likee work," the compradore replied gently, "no likee money. No plenty money, no can catchee plenty Chow-chow. They talkee me they wantee more money."

"All right, then——" Holman began crisply.

"What?" Carruthers broke in excitedly. Holman paid no attention to that, but continued to the Chinese, "Tell them double pay if she's loaded up to time."

"Can do," the other answered, and went slowly out.

"Well, I'm blowed!" Tom gasped.

Holman went wearily to the window, and stood watching moodily the human yellow kaleidoscope. The compradore was among them now, and gradually the trouble cooled and slacked, and the men began to slouch off to work, but reluctantly, the manager thought. Things looked ugly to him—very ugly.

"I say, Holman," Carruthers persisted impatiently, "isn't that playing rather into those chaps' hands?"

Holman was furious—he had been furious for days now—and he welcomed some human thing upon which he dared to vent his rage. He was "about fed up" with the frets and troubles of the last week. He fixed Tom Carruthers with a vindictive eye. "See here, Mr. Carruthers," he spat out, "if I have any further interference I'll resign instantly—understand? I managed this branch for years, until the governor took a notion to come out. Well—he's a genius at business, and I'm proud to take my orders from him. But somehow, the very devil's in it these last two weeks, and we're up against a bigger proposition than you—or the governor either—have any idea of. I'm doing my best to cope with it, and, by heaven——"

"Sorry to upset you, old chap," the other interrupted regretfully, "but, believe me, this succession of disasters has just about whacked me."

"Oh! all right," the older man said, relieved by his own explosion, and easily mollified after having let slip the snappy little dogs of his badly over-tried temper, "I haven't the heart to show this to Mr. Gregory," he said, taking the wire from his pocket into which he had thrust it, "damned if I have." He spread the flimsy paper out on the desk, and sent Tom a glance that was an invitation. He wanted sympathy, even that of the "somebody's son sent out to learn the business," as he contemptuously said of Carruthers when he did not call him "a flannelled fool." The latter gibe was not quite fair. Tom usually wore ducks, as Holman himself did—you had to in Hong Kong—and though the younger man did squander (if it were squandering) a good deal of time with Hilda Gregory, he only gave a reasonable, wholesome amount to rackets, cricket, and Happy Valley racecourse.

"On top of all else," Holman continued, "look here!"

Tom came and stood at Holman's chair, and read over his shoulder. "Good God, Holman!" he cried, "the *Feima* sent to the bottom!"

"The biggest and finest ship in our fleet," the other said bitterly. "Mutiny of the coolies—they scuttle the ship and bolt with the boats two days out!"

"This will about kill him!"

Holman nodded. "And look here"—he struck the ledger near him with an angry fist—"I say, do you know anything about safes?"

"Not much."

"Well, ours is the finest made. And the one make that *is* 'safe.' There probably aren't a dozen artists that could pick it—all told, Sing Sing, Portland, Joliet—that could pick it in a week. Well, look here; this ledger was taken from the safe—I suppose one night a week or more ago—the page referring to the dock negotiation torn out—and so prettily you can't see that it was ever in, except for the missing number—and the ledger returned to its place and the safe relocked without so much as a scratch being left to show how it was done."

"No wonder we were outbid for the site—*somebody* knew our price!"

"Knew our price!"—he closed the ledger with a bang, and slapped it. "Why, damn it, man, somebody's got us tied in a knot, and it's being drawn tighter every day—every hour."

"It's beyond me, Holman!"

Holman rose and laid his hands on Tom Carruthers' shoulders. "Mr. Carruthers, you don't for one moment believe this awful—simply awful—sequence of disasters to be due to accident, do you? Sunken ships, docks burnt to the water's edge, strikes on shore, mutinies afloat, and—and above all—the disappearance of Mr. Basil?"

"I don't know what to believe—I simply don't. What does it all mean, Holman? I say it looks like some curse, don't you know, come home to roost!"

"You are in the confidence, quite outside of business, of Mr. Gregory," the manager said, sitting down again heavily—"of Mr. Gregory and his family. I want to ask you a straight question."

"Yes?"

"Do you know of any one thing, however slight, that Mr. Gregory may have done to upset Wu Li Chang?"

"Wu Li Chang?"

"Yes, or 'Mr. Wu,' as he's mostly called by the Europeans."

"No," Tom said decidedly, seating himself on the table—that was one of his ways that ruffled Holman—"no, absolutely no. Why, only the other day— Thursday, wasn't it?—we visited at his place—it was there, you know, that the last was seen of Basil, except for his having been seen here, on the island, with two other Europeans later that same evening."

Holman smiled sourly. "Who saw him?"

"Why, those Chinese johnnies who brought the information to Government House."

Holman grunted. "Volunteered the information, didn't they? Went direct to the Governor instead of lodging information with the police in the usual way?"

"Yes."

"Basil Gregory was no more seen by those Chinamen than I possess the Koh-i-noor."

"What?" Carruthers stood up in his surprise.

"Take it from me," the other said emphatically, "in some manner Mr. Gregory has stung Wu Li Chang, and, by Jove, that wound will want some healing."

Tom Carruthers was hopelessly puzzled. "Well," he said slowly, "just who is this chap, Wu Li Chang? And what's his strength?"

"I've been here for twenty years," Holman told him, "and in all that time there's been just one man I've made it a point to steer clear of, in business and out of it—a strong personality, possessed of unlimited wealth, mixed up in every big deal in Hong Kong, swaying a sinister power that we Europeans cannot understand. Mr. Wu is hardly the man to cross swords with. No European can afford to; and there's only one of his own race who ever got the better of him, and that was only momentary, for he was never seen again."

"You mean——"

"The inevitable where Wu is concerned!"

"But how on earth," Carruthers said, "could Mr. Gregory have offended such a man?"

Holman gestured his inability to answer that, but persisted, "There's no doubt about it. To you all Chinamen look alike, but they don't to me. And I've seen men, whom I know to be in Wu's employ, mixing with our coolies for days now. There are two of them down there now—to my knowledge—and probably more. And I know for a fact that several such shipped in the *Feima*; every man jack of 'em is a Highbinder—member of one or other of the rival tongs."

"Tongs?" Tom queried. "That means secret societies, doesn't it?"

"You bet your life it does: secret societies that *are* secret, guilds that are a monster-power—the greatest power in China, the only power that Tze-Shi is afraid of. There are two or three in every province—a heap more in some. And our friend Wu is Past Master of the whole bally lot of 'em. Most of the mandarins hate the tongs, and are in deadly fear of them. But Wu knows a game worth ten of that: he handles them—the 'White Lily' (about the dirtiest of them all), the Triad (that bunch made the T'aiping Rebellion), the Shangti Hui (the Association of the Almighty, if you please), and that prize band of villains, the Hunsing Tzu, and the devil knows how many more. I tell you, Mr. Carruthers, we've got to get to the bottom of this thing, and get there quick, or there won't be a stick left in China belonging to the Company, or a vessel on the high seas flying its flag."

"Well, old chap," the junior said cheerfully, "Mr. Gregory is no schoolboy. He'll give this cursed gentleman of tongs and mystery a run for his money—a damned fine run—I'll have a bet with you, any odds you like—and we'll have a damned lot of fun watching him do it. But, I say, we don't know that you are barking up the right tree; but if you are—and admitting for argument's sake that Mr. Gregory has offended this top-dog Chink or whatever he is—I say, why the deuce should Lord High Pigtail want to take it out of Basil?"

Holman—his mother had been a Scotchwoman—had a tingling suspicion why, but he shrugged his shoulders and evaded, saying didactically, "When you've been in China as long as I have, you'll know as much about their ways and their motives as I do, and that's—*nothing!*"

CHAPTER XXV
WORSE AND WORSE

THE hot day burned on towards its hottest, and the troubles at the Gregory Steamship Company boiled and bubbled like a veritable hell-broth.

At eleven a coolie was caught smuggling paraffin, disguised as a chest of tea, on to the *Fee Chow*. Not a word could be got out of him as to what or who had instigated him; neither threats nor bribes would make him speak, and indeed Holman had little time or nerve to spare to try the application of either coaxing or kicking. He knew that he needed all he had of both to save what was undoubtedly the ugliest situation he had ever faced. The tide *must* be caught at Shanghai: it was vital. And yet the ship must be searched, every inch of her—and the crew. That was even more imperative. One tin of the deadly, dangerous stuff had been detected going aboard—a dozen might be aboard undetected, hidden among the cargo.

It was terribly exasperating; but now that things were at their worst Holman faced them coolly enough, a resolute, resourceful man—strong, crisp and vigorous still after twenty years of seething Hong Kong business life. For several of those years he had, until Robert Gregory's arrival, managed the firm's affairs efficiently. He looked capable of doing so still for quite a number of years.

He gripped the situation hard, and dealt with it briskly, and Tom Carruthers looked on fuming, and Simpson and the other half-dozen European subordinate old hands obeyed him with confident alacrity. Carruthers would have "wrung every dirty yellow neck," "kicked them to blazes," "boiled them in their own paraffin"; but Simpson and the English others thought that old Holman would win through somehow—if he couldn't, no one could—and they were serenely confident that every troubling coolie there would get his drastic deserts to the full—when Holman thought wise and had time, but not before.

But just once Holman forgot himself. When the searching was over (sure enough one tin had been successfully smuggled on and hidden) and the reloading half done, the coolies struck again. And the over-tired manager felt with Tom that that was too much.

Tom was nearly maudlin with rage by now, and when, in reply to Holman's angry, "The men never behaved so like hell before. What the thunder does it mean?" the compradore had said oilily, "Me no savee—no catchee more money—no can do work," Holman lost grip on himself and blurted out thunderously, "They work damn well for Wu Li Chang, don't they?" and regretted it as soon as he had said it.

Murder flashed through the compradore's eyes for an infinitesimal instant, and a venomous hiss snarled through his teeth. Holman had heard and seen a rabid dog snarl so once. But the Chinese commanded himself again instantly, and said meekly, almost sweetly: "Me no savee. Wantee more money, lelse no can do work."

Holman commanded himself as quickly and as well as the native had, and said, speaking as calmly (and almost as slowly), "Get that ship loaded—three days' pay—understand?"

"Savee. Can do."

But Tom Carruthers collapsed upon the window-seat. "If this was lording it over the poor, over-worked, underpaid natives, all he could say was——"

But the bitter and brilliant remark was never made, for as the compradore padded softly out, Murray, a senior clerk and the book-keeper, rushed in excitedly. And European clerks do not rush about much between noon and three in Hong Kong, not even indoors with drenched tatties at the windows and punkahs well manned. There were no tatties in this room—its occupants too often desired to keep an eye on the wharf.

"Out, John," the book-keeper ripped at a Chinese clerk who had come in while Holman was speaking to the compradore, mounted his high stool, and began to write busily. At Murray's order he slid off the stool, closed his book, and went out impassively.

Scarcely waiting until the door had closed, Murray said anxiously, "But, Mr. Holman, I understood you to say that the overdraft for the new dock had been arranged with the Bank—I drew up the exchange accordingly——"

"Quite correct—the transfer is to be made to-day." But Holman's voice was less sanguine than his words. He scented more trouble still, and he eyed askance the letter in Murray's hand.

"There must be some mistake, sir," Murray said desperately. "The Bank has just notified our accountancy department that an overdraft is impossible."

"Why?"

"They write that our security is insufficient and further we must vacate these premises immediately."

"What?" Carruthers sprang up as if some inimical concussion had impelled him.

"The landlord having disposed of the property," Murray continued. And he perched himself dejectedly on one of the Chinese clerks' high stools, as if the accumulated strain of a few morning hours had unnerved his sturdy legs.

"What about the Company's lease?" Tom persisted miserably.

"Expired in March," Holman said doggedly. "We're here on monthly arrangement—I supposed you knew that; every one else does—we expected to move to the new buildings at our own docks. The very roof taken from our own heads!" he concluded bitterly, dropping down heavily into his chair.

Tom looked at him ruefully for a moment, and then went up to Murray. "I say, how much do we need? That'll be all right. I'll cable over to my father——"

"I'm afraid it's no use, sir," the book-keeper said regretfully. "You see, it's this way: the Wang Hi Company refuse to go on with the negotiations; all their principal shareholders are natives, and these threaten to withdraw their capital if any business whatsoever is done with us."

Tom Carruthers gave a long, sharp whistle.

Holman looked up. "Precisely," he said dryly.

"But—but—something's got to be done. We can't sit here and see the ship go down—I'm blowed if we can. And I'm damned if I will. Something's got to be done. But I say, you two, what shall it be? What?"

He spoke to them, but he had picked up Hilda's photograph, and was looking not at them but at it.

They paid his question as little heed as the photograph did in its frame. They had no answer to give him. And he got none—unless he could piece one out from the hubbub that bubbled up from the sweating, teeming wharf, from the screaming, pushing coolie women in the sampans, from the pandemonium of noises and of smells that seethed up from a hundred junks, and from the mighty conglomerate waterside life and boat life that is the Greater Hong Kong. For there are two Hong Kongs—one old and shabby and battered, one smiling and well kept; and the smiling city on the hill-sides is Hong Kong the Little.

CHAPTER XXVI
SUSPENSE

THE three sat brooding in silence for several minutes, until one of the native clerks came in and held the door open respectfully. That meant that the chief was coming, and Murray slid off his perch and slipped quietly out as Gregory came slowly in.

In the unsparing afternoon light he looked a broken lion—an old king-beast with sagging skin and weakened mouth, but with fierce fight still in his tired and anxious eyes.

Hunters know that the smaller breeds of lions are the most dangerous. Robert Gregory was not a large man—he barely reached his wife's good inches. But he was jungle-fierce and jungle-strong. He had fought many a hard fight and had been torn and scarred in fights, but he had never lost one yet. He had pounded his way through the world, butted his way to victory and wealth. He had no finesse and no super-judgment, but he had splendid pluck, lion courage, bulldog pertinacity; and often for his wife, and for his daughter always, he had the charming tenderness that bulldogs show to children.

There was a hint of unscrupulousness in his face, and he had a jaw of iron. He was a very thin man, and it saved him from looking a very common one.

He was scrupulously dressed—now as ever—and, now as ever, just a shade over-dressed. His appearance would have gained had his watch-chain been a trifle slenderer, his cummerbund a less youthful rose, the canary-colored diamond in his ring half its size, or, better still, not worn. But his small, well-kept hands were dark, and unmistakably the hands of a man. He wore a bangle—just a thread of twined gold set with two or three inferior turquoise, and it kept slipping down his arm, almost over his knuckles—a cheap thing that had cost less than his cravat. Hilda had given it to him several years ago.

He came in deliberately—almost as if he too were very tired or beaten by the day's terrific heat—but with a determined air of briskness, and nodded crisply to Carruthers and Holman as he took his own chair at his own desk.

He was at bay. And he was going to fight—to the very end, let the end be what it might. But, in spite of his fierce self-control and genuine grit, he did not look a man "fit" to put up a big fight. For two nights he had had little sleep, and none that was restful. And to Holman's friendly, searching eyes he betrayed several signs of the hideous strain and worry with which he was battling. The business catastrophes that had heaped up about him were bad enough—enough to unnerve any man, and he was palpably unnerved—but the first thought in his mind, the burning object of its ceaseless search, was—

his son. He was holding his head defiantly, but the veins at his temples were twitching.

Holman took the telegram out of his pocket, and, with emotion that he could not quite conceal, leaned across the desk, holding it out to Gregory.

"Mr. Gregory," he said—"the *Feima*——" But he did not have to finish.

"Oh, yes! I know, I know," Gregory said listlessly.

"I'm sorry," Tom Carruthers began; "I'm awfully sorry for this, Mr. Gregory."

Robert Gregory swung round in his chair and banged the desk fiercely with his clenched fist. "Sorry—Tom! By God, I'll make some one pay for this—but *who*? What have we got to fight? Holman, you still think it's this man Wu? Eh?"

"I don't think, governor," Holman said, leaning across the desk in his earnestness, "I'm positive. In some way we've run up against the most powerful man in China."

"Well, I'm testing your theory, Holman. I'm having that cursed Chinaman here."

Tom Carruthers turned in his insecure seat on the window-ledge, so astonished that he very nearly slid off it; and Holman was distinctly perturbed.

"I sent him a chit this morning from the club, telling him I wished to see him here urgently at two o'clock on a matter of the gravest importance."

William Holman shook his head.

"Take it from me, sir, Wu Li Chang is not the man to call upon any one," he said; "they must go to him."

"Indeed!" Gregory snapped.

"And did you see him at two?" Tom said eagerly.

"No, Tom; he sent a coolie with a chit to say that he would call here at three—unless he found it inconvenient—*unless he found it inconvenient!* Look. I've hurried over from the club to see him."

Tom came across the room and picked up the note Gregory had tossed towards him, and stood studying it closely.

The trouble on Holman's face thickened. "If Mr. Wu condescends to answer such a summons," he said earnestly, "why, that very fact strengthens my belief. I tell you he never discusses anything outside his own offices—never!

And if for once he breaks that rule, he has some terrible reason for doing it—some damnably sinister motive."

"Pretty cool sort of johnnie, anyway," Tom commented, still scrutinizing Wu's note. "But I say, what an educated, professional sort of fist he writes."

"Oh!" Holman said impatiently, "he's got us both ways. He has all the advantages of a Western education without having lost a scrap of his Eastern cunning. I came out once with the skipper who took Wu to Europe—Wu and an English tutor he'd had for years—he was only a kid then, but Watson said he played a better game of chess than any white man on board—unless it was the tutor chap—had ever seen played before, bar none. Wu was nine or ten then. He's forty now, and no doubt his chess has been improving every day since."

Gregory smiled nastily. "Well," he said, "you may be perfectly correct in all you say, Holman, but it seems to me that you're all afraid of these Chinamen."

"I am, for one then," Holman muttered. "And I've been here twenty years."

"Unnecessarily afraid. I think you'll find that I'm perfectly capable of dealing with the fellow when he comes—and he'll come all right—oh, yes! he'll come."

"I wonder," Holman said.

"I'm sure I hope so," Tom Carruthers said heartily.

Holman devoutly hoped not, but he did not say it.

"He'll come," Gregory repeated didactically, almost truculently; "he'll come, as full of oil as a pound of butter. What the devil!" he added, with a displeased change of voice, as silk skirts and high-heeled shoes sounded in the hall. "I told you not to leave the hotel," he complained, with affection and dismay mingled in his voice, as his wife and daughter came through the door.

"Of course you did, poor old dear," Hilda told him soothingly, seating herself on the corner of his desk and patting him encouragingly on his shoulder. "But Mother can't rest. How can she? And if she isn't scouring the island— she must know every inch of it by now—she is hunting on the mainland with Ah Wong."

"Oh! I know, I know," Florence Gregory said wearily, subsiding indifferently into the chair Holman placed for her.

"You'll wear yourself out," her husband said roughly, but not unkindly.

The mother smiled, contemptuous of the fatigue from which she was wan and trembling. "It's no use saying anything to me. I can't rest. Have you heard anything? That's all I've come for."

"Not yet, dear. I've seen the Governor again. He was most kind—really very kind. Everything is being done—everything—and will be—and it is foolish to go on wearing yourself out like this."

"I am not wearing myself out," his wife returned petulantly. "The suspense is wearing my heart out—and no one seems to care—no one!"

"Yes, I know how you feel, dear," her husband answered her gently, "and what you must be suffering. But try to spare yourself just a little, for my sake. And believe me—you can—all that is possible is being done—and this—this is man's work."

"Is it?" the mother said dully. "I'm not so sure, I'm not so sure." She closed her eyes and leaned back in the big office chair, burning and shivering with excitement, and terribly, terribly tired.

Ah Wong looked about the office desperately. She wanted cushions, but there were no cushions there, and she went and stood very close behind her mistress; and when Mrs. Gregory moved her head restlessly, the Chinese woman slid her hand between it and the sharp edge of the chair's hard back.

And they might well be tired—the amah too, as well as the frailer, fairer woman. For they had indeed been beating the island and the mainland for days now—searching, searching, and often in quarters of whose existence the English woman could not have suspected, and whose nature she had but dimly grasped—some of them quarters into which no European woman, nice or otherwise, had penetrated before. But Mrs. Gregory had been in no peril. She had not suffered rudeness even. Ah Wong had guarded her well. Ah Wong had known how to do it.

But not one clew, not even the hint of a clew, had they found. Nor had John Bradley, who, in a different and quieter way, had been hunting as indefatigably—and was hunting now.

Robert Gregory sat crouched a little forward now, leaning on the desk, watching his wife miserably, but saying no more—tortured for her (almost forgetting his own pain in hers, or feeling his own only through hers), but pathetically glad to have her rest even this little.

Holman slipped over to the window and stood looking moodily out to the Chinese-and-Mongol-teeming dockside. Tom Carruthers sat quietly down on the big desk too and took Hilda's hand in his.

For several moments there was a silence in the room that was broken only by the ticking of the clock and the incessant echo of hubbub that buzzed in through the windows, the other five all conspiring eagerly to hold and guard Mrs. Gregory's rest undisturbed until she broke it herself. Even the Chinese clerk who had come in just after Ah Wong, and who sat, with his face to the wall, writing in the farthest corner, began to drive a noiseless pen, without looking round.

But the clock struck three, and after a startled glance thrown up at it, Mr. Gregory said softly, "Florence."

"Yes?" his wife answered drearily, without moving; she did not even open her eyes.

The husband sighed remorsefully. "Dear, I'm afraid you'll have to go."

"Why?" she asked indifferently, as if the answer could not interest her, and still without moving her head or opening her eyes.

"Well, you see, I've made an appointment here at three—and it may, it just may, prove important, with—with a man."

"Who?" Her voice was still devoid of interest.

"I expect Mr. Wu here."

Before her husband had spoken the last word Mrs. Gregory was bolt upright in her chair, wide-eyed, alert—as if galvanized, revitalized, tense and acute.

"Mr. Wu?" she whispered eagerly.

"Yes," he told her.

And the amah fingered softly something hidden in her gown.

"About Basil!"

"About a lot of things," Gregory said grimly. "And Basil in particular."

"Oh! and he can help us! You think so, don't you, Robert?"

"He can help us all right, Mrs. Gregory," William Holman said sternly, "if he will."

"Oh! he must. He shall!" she said hoarsely.

"At any rate, he's coming. And that's more than I thought," Holman said, as a new degree and quality of hubbub belched up from the yard. And as he spoke Murray came in with two cards—a long, thin slip of crimson paper, the mandarin's name and title inscribed on it in black Chinese characters, and an ordinary English visiting card, simply engraved "Mr. Wu."

"He's getting out of his rickshaw, sir," Murray told his employer.

"And every man jack of the coolies is ko'towing to him as if he was a god," Holman grunted from the window.

Gregory rose to his feet with a careful show of calm. "Well," he remarked cheerfully, "we'll soon see now what sort of stuff this well-advertised Chinaman is made of. Show him in, Murray. Holman, take my wife to the den near the counting-house. She'll want to stay, of course, to hear the result. Now, please, off you all go."

The others turned to the door to which he had pointed—not the door that led to the hall, but at the other end of the long room—but Florence Gregory went up to her husband. "Robert——" she began, but she could not say more, and her eyes were swimming.

Her husband cupped her face in his hands. "There, Mother, there," he said tenderly, and just a little brokenly, "I know, dear, I know. I understand. There—there. It's all right. I'll be careful—very, very careful. Ah Wong!" But he need not have called Ah Wong—she was there already, waiting to serve; and though Hilda turned to her mother as if to help her, and Tom Carruthers and Holman did too, it was Ah Wong who led her out, Ah Wong to whose hand she held and leaned on a little as she went.

CHAPTER XXVII
THE BEGINNING OF THE DUEL

AT the door Holman, as devoted a servant in his masculine and British way as Ah Wong was in her way, turned back almost peremptorily, and coming close to Robert Gregory said sharply, "Governor!" There was entreaty in the word, and there was command.

Gregory recognized both, and accepted both loyally from so tried and loyal a servant. It was one of his strengths that he recognized and appreciated valuable subordinates. "Well?" he said.

"Handle this man carefully," the old clerk said, speaking more emphatically than he had ever spoken to any one before—and he was an emphatic man always.

Gregory nodded.

As Tom held open the door behind his chief's desk, Murray opened the other door and announced, "Mr. Wu, sir."

"Ah! show him in," Mr. Gregory said, rather too indifferently, and so scoring the first mistake in the duel of which it was the first thrust. Holman knotted vexed brows, and the wife threw an imploring look. But Gregory saw neither, but busied himself ostentatiously with his papers, writing with head down, posing as being deeply immersed in business—and just a little overdoing it.

The mandarin stood in the doorway.

It was dim there, and at first glance he might have been thought an Englishman. A second look showed his Chinese nationality but accentuated by his European clothes—a light summer suit, a little better cut, if that were possible, than Robert Gregory's, and more quietly worn. No silk handkerchief showed from a pocket, no gay cummerbund swathed his waist, and Wu wore no jewelry, for the short, black fob of watered silk that hung from his vest was plain as plain. He stood a moment in the doorway perfectly at ease, dignified but urbane. As tortured by the tragedy in which he had played high-sacrificial priest as Robert Gregory, who did not even guess at its crux, could possibly be, Wu showed of that torture no trace. In appearance, in demeanor and in breeding the advantage seemed with the Chinese man, not with the English. And why not? For the advantage in all was Wu's.

The slenderness of the Oxford days and the Alpine climbing was gone; but no man could have looked less "full of oil," less fat. "Mr. Wu" was tall and powerfully built, pleasant visaged and altogether gentlemanly, and unmistakably, in spite of his "smart" tailoring, an athlete.

The two English women in the other doorway turned to look at him, and he bowed to them quietly, catching the elder's eyes and for an instant holding them. Something in his quiet, respectful gaze fascinated while it disturbed her. She turned again to go, but on the door-ledge turned and looked at him again, almost as if some power of mesmerism had brushed against her. Wu almost smiled—not quite—and bowed again, lower than before, but not too low. And she went out a little hurriedly, the others with her. But Ah Wong, who naturally went last, looked at the great man deliberately—a strange thing for a Chinese woman of her caste to do. And as he looked, she read his face and saw the tragedy hidden there. But Ah Wong and the Mandarin Wu had met before.

The Chinese clerk had slid off his stool and crept cringing towards Wu—cringing, almost grovelling. Wu snarled at him noiselessly, and the fellow almost crawled from the room; and Murray went after him and closed the door. Holman had already closed the other. The duellists were alone.

They had no seconds.

Neither spoke. The clock tocked on.

Outside a new note, a note of exultation, had come into the incessant coolie chorus; and Wu's jinrickshaw man—for Wu had not come in state, but very simply—squatted between the shafts and smoked.

Gregory continued to write. Wu watched him with a faint, contemptuous smile, and then he made a slight gesture towards the Englishman. Gregory did not see, but he felt it, and he obeyed it, and fidgeted uncomfortably, and then spoke, saying, still writing and without looking up, "Sit down, Wu."

A deeper smile flitted across the Chinese face. "I beg your pardon, Mr. Gregory?"

At the man's voice Gregory almost started—it was at once so masterful, so pleasantly pitched and so highly bred. It was a clear voice—as the Chinese voice almost invariably is—but it was deep and rich, which in the Chinese is very rare. "I beg your pardon, Mr. Gregory?" Wu had said.

And Gregory recognized and regretted his blunder. But he stood by it—there was nothing else to do, he thought—and said again, "Sit down, Wu."

"I would suggest," the Chinese remarked smoothly, "that Mr. Gregory should not call me 'Wu,' but 'Mr. Wu'——"

Robert Gregory looked up sharply, and, when he had looked, rose less sharply and even a little less confidently. He had never seen Wu before. And he was not a little taken aback at the man's dress, his splendid size and undeniably superior manner. And with that first look something very like a touch of fear came to Robert Gregory, and a subtle, vague sense of the almost hypnotic power of Wu's personality.

"—Otherwise," the Chinese continued—just the faintest hint of amusement in the quiet, courteous voice—"I shall be compelled to call Mr. Gregory plain 'Gregory' to reciprocate the honor he has done me, and I do not think we are sufficiently intimate to allow of such a familiarity—on my part."

"Oh!" the other said, as nonchalantly as he could, and looking not at his visitor but at the letters he was holding, "I'm a busy man." He felt the prick. Wu had drawn first blood. The duel was far from fair—one foe played a rapier with a master-wrist; one bungled with a bludgeon awkwardly.

"Quite so," Wu agreed; "but such a fraction of a second only—Wu is so short a name that you could say 'Mr. Wu' while I was saying 'Gregory.'" A threat was never made more delicately—or with a nicer smile—but it was made, and recorded in both minds, and with it a sinister something of prophecy.

Robert Gregory winced. "Oh! sit down," he said uneasily.

The reply was easy and pleasant, "Thank you!" And, laying his hat on the desk, Wu sat.

Gregory remained standing—fussing at the papers and his pigeon-holes. And his tone was mandatory. "Now, Mr. Wu"—Wu inclined his head slightly—"I'm not given to fine shades, equivocations, diplomatic finesse or any other Eastern method of wasting time."

"Quite so." Wu's tone was as polite as his words. But the amusement—imperceptible to Gregory—was a little less, the contempt a little more.

"And so," the Englishman continued, "If I'm blunt, it's because—I mean business."

"Business!" the mandarin exclaimed, "Ah! I wondered what had procured me the honor of this invitation—somewhat peremptorily conveyed, I fear I must remark. But doubtless that was done to save time too. However, if it is upon a matter of business——"

"If you'll allow me to tell you first," Gregory broke in irritably (and he was irritated almost beyond endurance), "then you'll know better, won't you?"

"One moment," Wu interposed, slightly smilingly, "pardon me, but I do not like to remain seated whilst you are——"

"Never mind me," the other said gruffly.

"Oh!" Wu returned simply, "I don't. But still——"

"I think a man may please himself in his own office"—Gregory's voice was querulous with irritation.

"Quite so," the bland voice replied, "when he is alone."

"Then"—pugnaciously—"if you don't object, I think I'll remain as I am."

"Not at all," Wu said gravely, and rising; "in that case, we'll both stand."

For a moment the two men measured each other and themselves against each other—Wu very politely, but with a thin, cold smile just lurking at one corner of his mouth. Gregory fumbled for a cigarette, lit it clumsily, drew a whiff, then threw it down and stamped on it, Wu waiting patiently, and watching with an almost flattering evidence of interest.

"The fact is, Mr. Gregory," Wu continued, "I have my own little prejudices; and if you remain standing whilst I am seated, it will seem to me—possibly very unreasonably—that you are standing, not out of courtesy to me, but to exhibit to me a minatory and even overbearing presence."

For a moment Gregory fought with himself. He was hotly angry, and more chagrined than angry. And he knew now that he was completely at sea. But he made a brave effort to control himself. He had promised Holman and his wife—tacitly—in response to Holman's earnest word and the pleading in her eyes as she had turned to go. And he wanted to find or trace his son.

"Pray be seated, Mr. Wu," he said, after an instant, and indicated with a bow a chair. But Wu caught the irony, of course, in the elaborate bow and the mock-courtesy of the request. But he bowed quite gravely in return, and again said, "Thank you," as he sat down.

Gregory sat also; he did not dare to have his own way in this small thing, and the little defeat irked him and contributed to his thickening uneasiness. However, if he *had* to sit, whether he chose or not, he could sit as he liked, in his own chair, in his own office, he'd be damned if he couldn't—and he did. He put his elbows decidedly on the desk, rested his chin firmly on his knuckles, and faced Wu with a fixed look and fighting eyes, his face thrust forward aggressively.

Wu regarded the Englishman placidly.

"Now, Mr. Wu, what the hell are you up to?" Gregory spoke quietly but decisively, and he leaned still farther across the table.

Wu took his time before he returned blandly, "Would you mind repeating your question?"

"I think you heard it plainly enough."

"Quite plainly, thank you—quite. Most audible. But I thought you would perhaps welcome the opportunity of expressing yourself a little more politely."

"I'm not out for a ceremonious talk," Gregory blurted. "You'll notice there's none of your customary tea on the table—no whiskey and soda either—no cigars." He was too good a business man not to know that, young as the interview was, he was losing ground already, but he was not skilful enough, and far too overwrought, to conceal the anger he felt at the unwelcome knowledge.

"Thank you," Wu replied lazily, and with nice good humor, "I do not smoke"—that was not quite true. He smoked a water-pipe at home. He had smoked so with Nang Ping a thousand times. "I never drink whiskey, and I am degraded enough to prefer tea made in our Chinese way. However, I have perceived, as you say, that this is not—a ceremonious occasion."

"Meanwhile," Gregory snapped, "I'd like an answer to my question."

"Which was——" the Chinese asked gently, but there was a narrow glint of contemptuous laughter in his eyes.

"My question," Gregory almost thundered, "was—'what the hell are you up to, Mr. Wu?'"

"Pray be a little more explicit," Wu said coldly.

"I have every intention of being so," was the sharp reply. "Now, please listen to me very carefully."

"I am all attention." A very stupid listener might have thought the smoothness of the mandarin's voice meekness. Gregory did not make that mistake.

"Let me preface what I have to say," he said warningly, "by remarking that I have the reputation of being a very good friend—but a dangerous enemy."

"Who could doubt it?" Wu murmured, bowing admiringly.

"He is a rash man who dares to oppose me, Mr. Wu. Do you know my method of dealing with such a man?"

"I tremble to contemplate his fate. But I am never rash." Wu's voice *was* meek now—for no counterfeit could be so fine.

"I crush him, sir—crush him relentlessly."

"It is always interesting"—giving Gregory a half look—"to hear about the methods of great men."

"I mention these things to you by way of warning." The Englishman spoke gropingly; his irritation was growing.

"Warning?" Wu raised his delicate eyebrows delicately. "Really"—he sighed—"I'm almost afraid to follow you."

"I think my meaning is sufficiently clear."

"To yourself, no doubt; but to my limited understanding—if I might beg you to speak a little more plainly."

"I will. I will ask you a plain question. Are you my friend, Mr. Wu, or are you my enemy?"

Wu smiled openly, and there was a slight drawl in his voice answering, "Could I aspire to be the one, or presume to be the other? Can the rush-light claim friendship with the sun, or the mountain-stream declare war against the ocean?"

"Oh, yes, yes! you're very plausible!" Gregory threw himself back in his chair wearily, and he was weary.

"'Plausible' is not a very pleasant word, Mr. Gregory," Wu said quietly, but in a tone of curt resentment.

"You ask me to speak plainly."

"But not to speak rudely. I do not employ rudeness, nor do I accept it. And now may I ask how this hypothetical hostility of mine has been manifested?"

"In a number of ways," Gregory returned, a little sneeringly.

"Will you name *one*?" Wu was entirely bland again.

"You must be aware," the other told him, "that my firm has recently sustained a somewhat extraordinary series of setbacks."

"I regret to hear that you have been somewhat unfortunate"—Wu said it sympathetically.

"I am determined that these annoyances shall cease"—Robert Gregory said it doggedly.

"But even Mr. Gregory," the Chinese man said sadly, "can hardly hope to order the workings of Fate."

"But are they workings of Fate"—Gregory leaned across the table aggressively again, his bullet head thrust out—"or of Mr. Wu?"

For a moment Wu regarded him in silence. Then, "Surely you are joking?"

"I know pretty well as much about you as you know yourself"—Gregory's voice was as insolent as his words.

"Why should you not?" Wu replied cheerfully. "My life is an open book. All who run may read."

"But there's one thing I don't know!"

"Surely not?"

"Your object. Now you see I speak frankly—I lay my cards on the table. What is your motive? What do you want? Come, Mr. Wu, I'm willing to meet you on a friendly footing."

"You are very kind," Wu said subtly.

Gregory made an impatient gesture, and the framed picture fell between them. The Chinese picked it up—"Mrs. Gregory?" he said courteously.

"Our daughter." The English father bit his lip. He was convinced that to press the quarrel further with this opponent would be to press to his own defeat. But he restrained himself with heroism. To see Hilda's photograph in Wu's Chinese hand, Wu's Chinese eyes on Hilda's face, maddened him. Twenty Europeans had lifted the picture from his desk, held it so, and commented on it admiringly—and her father had been highly pleased. Wu merely bowed and replaced it quietly, face towards Gregory—and Gregory itched to throttle him.

If Robert Gregory had known of his son's spoiling of the Chinese girl—a girl of gentler birth and softer rearing than Hilda's—he would not have considered Basil's crime unforgivably heinous. "Damned foolish!" would have been his stricture. But that this Chinese man—a father too, as he knew, and, for all he knew, as clean-lived and as nice-minded as himself—had held Hilda's portrait in his hand, and look at it quietly, seemed to Gregory hideous, and his gorge rose at it.

Wu Li Chang read the other clearly, and, quite indifferent alike to the man and to his narrow folly, he stiffened coldly, for he knew what Robert Gregory did not, and he was thinking of Nang Ping as he had looked down upon her last, heaped and stricken in final expiation on his floor.

But, both through an instinct of breeding and through utter indifference, he made no comment on the picture, either in flattery or in admiration, as he replaced it. But he bent his head congratulatory toward the other and said: "Ah! yes. Miss Gregory reminds me—slightly—of some one I have known. Probably an English lady—I met years ago when I lived in England. I regretted not being at home when Mrs. Gregory and your daughter so honored my poor garden—and my daughter."

He did not admire Hilda's picture, and it was far too much trouble to pretend an appreciation he did not feel. And he thought her dress, or lack of it, disgusting, precisely as he had thought the décolletage of "honorable" (and entirely "honest") English ladies abominable when he had been a boy at Portland Place. And his Chinese taste (good or bad) would never have put a picture of Nang Ping in his offices, where casual callers and mere business acquaintances might scrutinize and comment on it. He had killed his girl— this man sitting easily there; calm and imperturbable—not a week since, and neither waking nor sleeping had he regretted it—not even for an instant. But a scented bead that he had found beneath her robe, when they had lifted up what had been his only child, lay now secure in an inner pocket. He could feel it where it lay.

"On a friendly footing, Mr. Gregory?" Wu took up the broken thread. "You Westerners are truly magnanimous. 'Friendship' is usually actuated either by hope of gain or by—fear."

"Don't you trifle with me, *Mister* Wu," Gregory said hotly, rising and beginning to pace up and down the long room—an ugly and determined look hardening on his face—"I'll have no more of this beating about the bush. To begin with,"—controlling himself a little better: there was so much at stake— "to begin with, Mr. Wu, the mysterious disappearance of my son is only one of the long series of unexplained disasters that have recently fallen on me, and concerning which I want an explanation."

"Then why not seek it from those who can enlighten you?"

"There's no one more capable of doing that than yourself," the Englishman said, swinging round on the Chinese fiercely. "What's behind it all, Mr. Wu? What's the game you are playing at? Why have you devoted your sinister attentions to me and mine? What have we done to start you on this career of kidnapping—of ship-scuttling—of incendiarism, among the coolies out there—and all the rest of it?"

Wu looked at his watch, put it back in his pocket, picked up his hat, and rose deliberately. "Mr. Gregory," he said coldly, "my time is of a certain value. Time is money, you Westerners say. Well, I never waste time—although I am never in a hurry. You will excuse me if I wish you a very good afternoon."

"No so fast, Mr. Wu," the shipper said ferociously, thrusting himself between Wu and the door. "My time's precious too, but I'm going to devote all that's requisite to getting an answer to my question. I've got the conviction lodged in this obstinate British head of mine that you know quite well what I want to know—and what I am going to know. And that's what I've got you here for—to tell me what I want to know. And, by the Lord, you will before you leave this room. I know that you can lay hands on my son—dead or alive. I know that you can—by God! I know that you can——"

"Can you lay hands on him?"

"I? No! No!" the English father almost sobbed it, recoiling.

"Well, when you can——"

"But I can lay hands on you if you don't satisfy me——"

"I do not think that Mr. Gregory will commit that—indiscretion," Wu said significantly.

There was a bitter pause. When Gregory broke it his voice wavered; he was greatly moved. "You're ruining my business," he cried, "you're hanging over me like a sword of Damocles."

"That sword may have had two edges, Mr. Gregory," Wu said quietly. "The man who wounds his enemy with one is apt to cut himself with the other. The sword," he added, strolling to the window, "is not my weapon."

Robert Gregory backed stealthily up to the door and fumbled with his right hand in his pocket. And Wu, turning to go, saw that his face was twitching.

Wu Li Chang had no thought of sparing this other father—Basil Gregory's father—but he was sorry for him now; and it may be recorded—as a modest contribution to the study of racial comparisons.

Wu moved to the door which Gregory stood barring. "And now, if you will kindly allow me to pass——"

And Robert Gregory thrust his revolver in Wu Li Chang's face.

The Chinese looked into the shining barrel. He smiled. "Ah! A Webley, I observe. Very good make. I have made excellent practice with them myself."

CHAPTER XXVIII
SOMETHING TO GO ON

GREGORY, nearly exasperated by the other's coolness, made a threatening gesture. And then came the sudden blazing out of ferocious rage that smolders always under the quietest Oriental seeming, and that, enkindled instantly by the tiniest spark, transforms a peaceful, obliging native into a spitting, hissing human volcano.

"You fool! You white-eyed dodderer, you green-hatted goat-man!" Wu Li Chang barked, "do you think I care for your shiny barrel? You English idiot! The slightest signal from me"—he pointed to the window—"and those coolies would swarm in here like so many devils."

"Yes, but you'd have gone to blazes first," Gregory said grimly, the revolver still well aimed, "to join those damned ancestors of yours."

Something as terrible as the death-rattle in a mad dog's throat tangled and gurgled in Wu's and a fiendish look leapt into his eyes—they narrowed until they were mere slits. But he recontrolled himself almost instantly—angry still, but coldly so, and imperturbable again. "I would have gone to blazes first?" There were snarl and sneer in the low-pitched voice. "Then we should have been able to resume this interesting conversation elsewhere! Come, come! Put your toy back into your pocket. If you insist upon playing the play out on these lines (but I think you will not), believe me, this is not the stage for it. And you know where I live. You also, I understand, broke and honored my unworthy bread the other day. And I am an easy man to find."

Robert Gregory deliberately pointed his revolver at Wu Li Chang's heart, and said as pointedly, "Pray be seated, Mr. Wu."

Wu bent his head politely to the pointed pistol, as if to thank it for the invitation. "With pleasure," he said, moving leisurely back to his chair. Gregory, eyeing Wu stormily, passed too to his own chair. For just a fraction of a second his back was turned to Wu; but that thin shred of time sufficed the Chinese to whip a revolver from his pocket, concealing it in his hand and in the loose sleeve of his tussore coat. Gregory banged down his chair, and, covered by the ill-humored noise, Wu clicked his revolver open.

They sat and faced each other in ugly silence, dislike and defiance very differently expressed, but expressed, on each face. Even wider apart by caste and by breeding than by race, Wu's tranquillity was terrible, his quiet at once a menace and a taunt, while Gregory's growing nervousness would have been a little comical if its primary cause had not been so pitiful.

"I perceive, Mr. Gregory," Wu Li Chang said pleasantly, "that you still keep your toy in your hand; kindly cease holding it. I do not fear it, but the implication of its presence is somewhat aggressive and offensive. Let us pretend, at least," he added lazily, "that we are gentlemen."

That taunt got through. Gregory winced, and after a moment of sulky hesitation put the revolver on his knee under the desk.

"Now then, Mr. Wu——" he began.

"One moment," Wu interrupted him. "Excuse my seeming so exacting, but I believe that revolver is loaded."

"It is—in every chamber," the other snapped.

"Well," the mandarin spoke so indifferently that he almost drawled, but his voice was honeyed, "if we are to arrive at an amicable understanding, I think I should prefer, as a matter of politeness—we Chinese lay such foolish stress on politeness—not to feel that I was discussing matters at the cannon's mouth, so to speak. Retain the weapon, by all means, but be so good as to remove the cartridges."

Gregory fidgeted, hesitating nervously.

"Merely as a matter of good faith," Wu urged conciliatorily. "That weapon might go off, you know—by pure accident." He stretched his hand, palm up, across the desk.

Gregory looked at the open palm oddly, embarrassed, and then looked round anxiously at the window. Then, shrugging his shoulders and trying to speak indifferently, "Why not?" he said, and lifting the pistol, jerked it, and the cartridges fell out onto the desk.

"Thank you," Wu said genially. "That makes the interesting conversation much more possible." He began playing with them lightly, throwing and catching them as nimble-fingered boys do jackstones; and Gregory watched the deft, sinewy yellow hand, fascinated. "One—two—three—four—five—beautifully made little things, are they not?" Wu's voice was dove-like. "Now we can start fair. Pray continue, Mr. Gregory, from the point where you left off." One yellow hand dropped nonchalantly on to Wu's knee below the table, two cartridges in the subtle fingers. "But please omit to make any further disrespectful allusion to my ancestors." He was leaning forward on the desk, both hands beneath it now, and the revolver had slipped from his sleeve. "I do not misunderstand your having made the offensive remark—it was a mere mark of difference of caste and education. But do not repeat it," he added smilingly, "or in any way allude to my ancestors"—the bullets were in his pistol, and Gregory was putting his emptied weapon irritably into a drawer. "You were asking me, I think, what I knew about the disappearance of your son and of certain commercial catastrophes which, I regret to hear, have lately overtaken you. Well, I will be perfectly frank with you—perfectly frank, Mr. Gregory, perfectly frank. I will conceal nothing." The yellow hands slipped up quietly on to the desk. "And the first thing I have to say is"—the barrel of the pistol thrust forward—"look at this!"

Robert Gregory sprang up with a smothered oath, and his hand went convulsively towards the bell on the desk, "Ah, no!" Wu said, "don't move, or it might go off by pure accident." Gregory shifted out of Wu's aim and made a foolish furtive attempt to ring. Wu covered him instantly, smiling still. "Don't move, I say! Sit down! Sit down, Gregory!"

And Robert Gregory very slowly sat down—obedient partly in fear, partly in defeat, and a little in a somewhat hypnotized subjection to a bigger, more skillful man. Then suddenly he pulled the drawer open to look at his own revolver.

"No," Wu told him, "not sleight of hand. This is not your revolver, but it's identical——"

"That's my son's revolver. I know. I gave it to him myself. Now, damn you, I have got something to go on!"

CHAPTER XXIX
"WILL YOU VISIT SING KUNG YAH?"

"QUITE right," Wu Li Chang said cordially. "This is—or was—your son's property. My servants found it in my garden, after your son had left there. I intended to give myself pleasure of returning it to you in person"—that was perfectly true—"although I hardly anticipated doing so in so—humorous a manner. Now kindly ring your bell"—his voice stiffened suddenly, still low and easy; it had a new percussive note, and the words came quicker. "When it is answered, merely say to whomever enters, 'Pray desire Mrs. Gregory to step this way.' Do nothing more, say nothing more. Because"—the voice grew beautifully soft again—"if you should draw attention to this, or anything of that kind, my hand might tremble so much with fear that it might go off, and that would be too ridiculous, with one of your own cartridges! Please ring."

At the mention of his wife—by Wu—Robert Gregory drew himself up stiffly. "What do you want with Mrs. Gregory?"

"I might merely wish to show her how foolish her husband has been in trying to bully and intimidate me instead of dealing with me reasonably. But also I have a message I have promised my daughter to deliver for her to your wife. Chancing to see Mrs. Gregory here reminds me of it, and it will be more convenient to me to deliver it here than to call at your hotel"—Gregory's eyes blazed—"and possibly as agreeable to the lady. Also I have a message—but less important—from Madame Sing, my relative." (Gregory grunted curtly.) "Ring!"

"Ring—yourself," the Englishman at bay said sullenly.

"That is a liberty I would not dream of taking in another man's office. You'll ring"—the revolver's barrel repointed insinuatingly. "You will ring now, Mr. Gregory."

Robert Gregory pressed the bell push on his desk and leaned back heavily in his chair, with an unhappy sigh, defeated.

As Murray came in, Wu so moved his body that the clerk could not see the little pistol which still covered Gregory. "Murray," his employer said wearily, "ask Mrs. Gregory to step this way a moment." Then he began breathlessly, "*Ce sacré Chinois me——*"

But Wu interrupted with a contented laugh and, "Oh! this damned Chinaman understands French perfectly. And I've often heard Englishmen pronounce it very much as you do. You are a linguist too, Mr. Murray? *E'um dom util—o dom das linguas—e de alto valar em cidades cosmopolitas!*"

Poor Murray stood bewildered, quite uncertain what to do. And Wu turned pleasantly to Mr. Gregory with, "Please repeat your instructions, as Mr. Murray does not seem to understand quite."

And Gregory said at once—broken, defeated—in a whipped tone his clerk had never heard from those thin lips before, "Please ask Mrs. Gregory to come here."

And indeed the hard little man was broken and defeated, and he knew it. The Chinese duellist had made but little lunge, but with a gentleness more cruel than any storm, and a suave persistence that under such circumstances no mere European nerve could outfight, he had borne his opponent to the knees; slowly, deftly had worn him out. His method and his touch had been—almost consistently—velvet, but through the velvet of the fur that hid them, relentless claws had found and torn and jagged the English adversary.

Robert Gregory was down and out.

"Now," Wu said in a changed tone, speaking briskly and quick, as the door closed on Murray, "I will open the matter to Mrs. Gregory—if you please."

"What's your object in wanting to humiliate me before my wife?" Gregory asked <u>drearily</u>.

Wu smiled. "Merely a 'Chinaman's' idea of—humor, let us say." He slid the Webley lazily into his sleeve.

Florence Gregory came in eagerly. Knowing less than her husband did of the mandarin's important place in international finance, yet she had a far clearer estimate of Wu Li Chang's personal potency than Gregory had. Ah Wong had coached her—if only with a hint or two—and she had her own woman's instinct, fine and alert.

Wu had risen instantly, and taken a courteous step towards her. He paused as she did. For a moment she stood looking from one man to the other questioningly, and then she fixed her anxious eyes on Wu, and they stood measuring each other quietly.

For once the English eyes were the quicker. Perhaps sex and motherhood combined outweighed any and every superiority of race. Perhaps he gave her a much more careless gaze than she gave him. Perhaps her exquisite anxiety gave her sharper sight. At all events, as they looked, she almost recognized him, but he had no such experience concerning her. For a puzzled instant her mind trembled towards "When? Where?" and in a few moments, or in less mental turbulence, her half-awakened memory might have caught up a broken thread, a forgotten acquaintance; but Wu spoke, and in the tension of her anxiety the chance passed.

"Mrs. Gregory," Wu Li Chang began, deferentially bowing and going a little nearer, "I am sorry to be compelled to ask your presence, but, before I explain, will you take this weapon from me? You see"——he laughed a little, lightly—"I present it to you with the barrel toward my own breast—but"—and this he added with quiet emphasis—"do not give it to your husband." As he indicated Gregory he gave him a straight look. "I trust to your honor." And he bowed again as he held the pistol out towards her.

She took it wonderingly, and held it so. She was not one of the women who have an exaggerated fear of weapons, but neither was she one of those who rather affect them. She had never hunted, and she had never practiced pistol shooting (Hilda had done both). Ordinarily Florence Gregory would have declined to hold a revolver. But she took this and held it steadily—puzzled but not afraid. She was in an abject terror for her boy that left no room for petty, personal, bodily qualms.

"What—what is all this?" she said ruefully. "Robert, what have you been doing?"

He sighed heavily before he answered her. "Mr. Wu has rather over-reached me in—a little transaction."

"Oh! pardon, pardon," Wu protested pleasantly. "You over-reached yourself. May we be seated?" he asked Florence Gregory; and as she sat down he drew himself a chair conveniently towards her, and convenient for an unimpeded view of Gregory. "I called here to-day," he continued suavely, "at your husband's invitation, on a matter of grave importance."

The woman leaned forward towards him quickly, her hands knotted at her knee. "Yes—yes—my son," she began eagerly.

"What the matter was," Wu went on smoothly, "he did not say. Of course, I knew of your son's disappearance—everybody in Hong Kong knows that—so I fancied that your husband wished, perhaps, to ask me that any influence I might possess among my countrymen should be exerted to assist you in your search——"

"Yes—yes," she said, "if you could!"

"Could!" Gregory muttered, "he knows all about it."

"To assist you in your search," Wu repeated blandly. "His reception of me, however, was strangely unlike that of a man—asking a favor."

"Favor!" Gregory flamed out—he couldn't help it—"I was going to ask no favor, I can tell you."

His wife sent him a peremptory glance, but Wu paid him no attention, but continued:

"And in the end, Mrs. Gregory, he presented a revolver at me, and practically held me prisoner."

"Yes," Gregory snarled, "and by a cunning ruse, like a man of your crafty nature——"

Wu Li Chang smiled deprecatingly. "Listen to him, Mrs. Gregory! It is cunning of me to endeavor to save my own life. It is not cunning of him to beguile me here under the pretext of——"

"Pretext be damned!" Gregory blustered, beside himself now, rising and going to the window. His face was twitching. He stood looking out at the seething humans on the dock-side, but it is doubtful if he saw them.

"You see," Wu said gently, "the strange means by which your husband seeks to enlist my help and sympathy."

Florence Gregory hung her head.

Wu moved his chair an inch towards hers. Gregory did not turn round at the sound. The Chinese spoke lower, and the sympathy in his voice seemed very real, "And all your natural maternal anxiety——" He paused eloquently, and the mother looked up at him, eagerly, gratefully. And in return he gave her a long direct look—there were respect and friendship in it. And after a moment she rose abruptly and went to the window.

"Robert!"

He did not answer. She touched his shoulder. He paid no attention. "Leave me to talk to Mr. Wu! Please!" But her tone was imperative.

A smile, a glint of triumph, flickered across the Chinese's face. "You, Mrs. Gregory?" he said, just stepping towards her—he had risen when she rose— "that would be different."

"He needs a man's methods of dealing with him!" Gregory growled, without turning.

"But they don't seem to have been very effective in your hands, do they? Robert," she urged more appealingly, "I want to find my boy! Let me try—my way."

"I'll send Ah Wong to you," was the grudging reply, and Robert Gregory shuffled awkwardly from the room. He did not even look at Wu again—and Wu barely looked at him.

"And who is Ah Wong, Mrs. Gregory?" Wu asked amiably, as the door closed.

"My servant," she told him.

"Your amah? But I do not need an interpreter," he laughed.

"She rarely leaves me."

"Who could?" he said with a little bow.

Ah Wong came noiselessly into the room.

"And now, Mr. Wu," the woman asked earnestly, her voice low and tense, "will you help us?"

"You, if I can—but—I am not sure if——" He broke off and gave Mrs. Gregory a little inquiring gesture that said, "Are you going to let her stand there?" For Ah Wong had come steadily across the room until she stood quite at his elbow.

"Wait, Ah Wong," her mistress told her, with a gesture of the head towards the door. And Ah Wong moved back as quietly as she had come, and waited just inside the door, immovable, expressionless. But not for an instant, never once, did her eyes leave Wu Li Chang. A critic at a "first night" could not have watched and listened more closely or seemed less interested.

Ah Wong and the mandarin were ill matched, but better matched than he and Robert Gregory had been.

Mrs. Gregory wasted no time on preliminaries. She forgot that he was a stranger. That he was man, she woman, she forgot that she was English and he Chinese. She had but one thought, one memory—Basil. "Oh! Mr. Wu," she pleaded—urged—at once, "if you can help us, if you could even give us your advice as to the best way of appealing to the natives or of offering a reward——"

"Ah!" Wu interjected gently, "for your sake, Mrs. Gregory—as his mother— I would do much." He picked up his hat and moved towards the door. But Ah Wong did not trouble to move from it—she knew that he was not going yet. But Florence Gregory did not know—and she followed him a step. Wu bowed to her with the utmost courtesy, and said—as if considering the situation—"Well, we must meet again."

"Oh! I hope so, Mr. Wu. But now—when every moment is so precious—— "

"I am thinking, Mrs. Gregory, and I will not waste one of them, you may trust me."

"I do," she said impulsively.

Wu bent his head gratefully—perhaps, too, to veil a smile—"But I will venture to take just two of those precious moments, to ask a great favor of you."

"Oh, anything!"

"You were visited yesterday by a lady of my house, Madame Sing, a kinswoman who has, since my wife's death, taken a mother's part—so far as it ever can be taken—to my daughter. Sing Kung Yah suffers a great humiliation and an intolerable loneliness——"

"I was sorry I was out——"

"And she was grieved to find you not at home. May I solicit your kindness for Madame Sing, Mrs. Gregory?"

"Oh—indeed—anything. But what can I do?"

"Much," Wu said. "She is ostracized by the ladies of our race. I am a powerful man among my own people, madame, but I cannot influence or soften the prejudices of Chinese femininity in the slightest. Because she is a widow, she should, according to one of the absurdest of the many absurd canons of our race, live in seclusion, sackcloth and discomfort. She is a nice creature, Mrs. Gregory, and she longs for friends. Will you visit Sing Kung Yah?"

"Oh—of course—gladly."

"It will open many doors to her, for Mr. Gregory's wife is a social power in Hong Kong. Chinese doors we are both powerless to open—in any real sense. Chinese cordiality I am not rich enough to buy for her or strong enough to seize. But life will be less dull for her if she can sometimes exchange visits with English ladies."

"I shall be so glad."

"Soon—perhaps?"

"Indeed, yes. Of course, until this terrible anxiety is removed——"

"It would be cruel of me to ask you to come to Kowloon to drink tea with Sing Kung Yah. And yet I do ask it—but for your own sake too. Yes, if you will be so kind—it will delight Sing—you shall be my guest."

"We have been already, Mr. Wu," she said a little sadly. "You remember it was in your house, or rather in your gardens, that I last saw my son. It was there he left us—and disappeared as completely as though the earth had swallowed him up."

"And it is from that point that we will begin our investigations—you and I—his mother and a Chinese who is honored to serve her. We will take the thread up from that moment—when you last saw him—from that place—my own house."

"But you know that he was seen afterwards here—in Hong Kong?"

"I know that it was said so," Wu replied judicially. "It may, or it may not, be true, and we will begin at the beginning—and end by discovering the truth. That at least I can promise you."

"Oh! You do?" she almost sobbed.

"I am sure of it."

"Then when may we come? If we must."

"Must," the man deprecated. "My dear Mrs. Gregory, I employ no such word where you are concerned. I merely point out to you, and I hope as delicately as possible, that—aside from the very real kindness your visit would be to a Chinese woman somewhat pathetically placed—that the—the circumstances of my visit here this afternoon hardly make this a—a propitious place— indeed, I am sure you will understand I am only too anxious to find myself outside this room—and to forget—as far as such things can be forgotten— —"

"Yes—yes!" Mrs. Gregory interjected contritely, "I do indeed understand. I am so ashamed———"

Wu waved that aside, and then he broke out with sudden feeling—it was finely done; even to Ah Wong it almost rang true—"Why, I wonder, do some Europeans—Mr. Robert Gregory and others—think God in heaven came to be guilty of making the Chinese race? You come here and reap the harvest of our centuries of sowing, and affront us while you fatten on our industry; teach the foolish among us to suck and smoke the poppy, and condemn us for it while it enriches you; brand the vice 'Chinese' while you revenue India from it—you treat us a thousand times worse than the leech-like fops of Venice treated the Jews they exploited and plundered—at least the Venetian cads were in their own country—you are in ours. I tell you, madame, a Chinese *hath* eyes, hands, organs, dimensions, senses, affections—*yes, affections*, passions—fed with the same food, hurt with the same weapons, subject to the same diseases, healed by the same means, warmed and cooled by the same winter and summer, as you English Christians are! If you prick us, we bleed. If you tickle us, we laugh. If you poison us, we die. If you wrong us, shall we not revenge? For sufferance is *not* the badge of *our* great tribe. Oh! forgive me, dear lady," and his voice that had been a shaking whirlwind was regretful, soft and humble. "Forgive me—not you—I do not mean you. Mrs. Gregory," he said with deep earnestness, "I *will* help *you*—to my utmost, to find your boy. And I *am* powerful. But, Mrs. Gregory, I will not help your husband. Nor shall he have the satisfaction of knowing that I have been instrumental in restoring Mr. Basil Gregory to you."

"Oh! I do not blame you," Basil Gregory's mother said. And her eyes were full of tears.

"Thank you," Wu said softly. "I will help you to find your son. I swear it. Trust me—and I shall not fail."

"I do."

Wu bent his head.

"And try to believe how much I regret to seem petty; but, really, Mrs. Gregory, frankly, if your husband and I were to meet again, even under the restraining influence of your presence, his strange animosity, his extraordinary prejudice against me, and his curious ideas of the language which a European may use to a Chinese gentleman—if I may so describe myself—would, I fear, tempt me to wash my hands of the whole affair. In short, I can not again enter any place that is Mr. Gregory's, and he has made it impossible for me to invite him to my house or to receive him there; but if you will so far honor me, and my kinswoman Sing Kung Yah, and my daughter—bring your amah with you" (he indicated Ah Wong with a gesture), "she has a loyal face, and I am sure you can trust her not to report your visit—and indeed," he added in a low tone, "she need not know how far I aid you. But all that I leave to you, naturally. All I ask is your promise that Mr. Gregory shall be ignorant always that your son has been restored to you by a 'damned Chinaman'; promise me that, and——"

She bowed her head.

"I promise you that it shall not be my fault if your son is not restored to you within a few hours."

"Then you know——"

"I know nothing," Wu Li Chang said earnestly, "Mrs. Gregory, that you yourself shall not know—at Kowloon."

"When may I come?" she begged.

"To-morrow, at four? I will be entirely at your service——"

"To-morrow?" Her voice broke on the word.

"To-night, then?" He glanced at the clock consideringly. "Yes, the time is short—but I think I can contrive it. I will employ myself so diligently in the meantime that I think I can promise you that your son shall be brought into your presence before you leave mine. I cannot put in words how much I shall rejoice to see that meeting—and how proud to have achieved it." His voice trembled at the last words. And she could scarcely command hers to say, "At what hour?"

"Six, or six-thirty? That will give time for the visit to which I shall so look forward—and my daughter and her aunt—and time to permit you to return while it is light, in time to dress for dinner."

"Return—with Basil?"

Wu Li Chang smiled kindly. "I believe—with—Basil." He spoke the name as tenderly as she had, or as Nang Ping might have done.

"Oh! Mr. Wu!" the woman cried, and held out to him both her hands. He took them and bent over them gravely.

"Oh! tell me," she begged, her hands still in his, "Mr. Wu, do you think he is safe and well?"

"I have no doubt of it," Wu said earnestly. "And that it is merely a question of making terms with those who are detaining him. And now," he said in a bright, brisk tone, turning alertly to the door, and this time Ah Wong drew aside, "there is so much to do, and I have put myself upon my honor not to fail in my—promise—if you do not fail——"

"I fail!" the mother said. "And you promise that I shall see my boy to-night?"

"I promise!"

"Oh!" she went to him impulsively again and held out her hand. But he seemed not to see it.

"Till six," he said bowing, and was gone.

The woman sat down in the nearest chair and began to cry softly. Ah Wong huddled over to her quickly and bundled down at her feet. "No, no," the amah said, catching her lady's hand, clutching her dress. "No, no, madame. Not go! Not go!"

CHAPTER XXX
SMILING WELCOME

AGAIN, as Wu Li Chang passed through the office yards, the coolies almost groveled at his feet, and this time he threw a curt but not unpleasant word to one or two of them.

He had been with the Gregorys some time, the afternoon seemed at its hottest, but he was as fresh and crisp as when the close duel began; and yet in a more resilient, a more stimulated way, he had felt the strain as they had not, for he had known the story of Basil and Nang Ping.

But "crisp" and "fresh" were the last words that could be applied to the shipper or his wife, or, for that matter, to any of their companions. Robert Gregory was having a stiff "peg," and needed it; and Mrs. Gregory, less unnerved, was tired and anxious enough. And Holman and his fellow faithful few were on desperate tenterhooks both for their chief (he was roughly lovable and not a mean master) and for the threatened business to which they were sincerely and doggedly devoted.

Perhaps Tom Carruthers and Ah Wong were the two Gregoryites least unhinged by the day's fusillade of miscarriage and by its recurrent stalemate. Ah Wong was anxious, but she had been racked by no surprise. Of the Steamship Company's business she knew little—and cared less. But, even so, she probably had, next to Wu Li Chang, a correcter estimate of the whole complicated situation than any one else. Bradley and Holman came next in prescience, but neither of them suspected, much less knew of, the particular slant the diabolism of Wu's vengeance had taken, or of the appointment he had made with Basil's mother.

Tom Carruthers was "no end" sorry, and sincerely so. But he could not quite help getting a certain enjoyment out of it all. He was built that way—and he was only twenty-four—and he had come to China to have an occasional nibble at the spice of things, almost as much as he had come to master the details of a business to which his father had assigned him not too sanguinely. The bankruptcy that positively seemed to threaten the great firm could not even embarrass him. His father was a very rich man (as mere British wealth went), and he himself an only child. Mr. Gregory's wealth had not in the least added to Hilda's charm in Tom Carruthers' eyes.

But the depression at the office was growing tormenting, and so was the heat, and Robert Gregory's nervous irritability was a bit trying, so when Hilda announced her determination to "go home" Tom resigned the affairs of the business cheerfully enough and picked up his hat.

Hilda saw that she could do nothing for her father by "hanging round." And "hanging round" was an occupation she particularly disliked. And when she learned that her mother had slipped off with Ah Wong without a word, she said, "How shabby!" and prepared to follow suit.

Robert Gregory scarcely noticed his wife's defalcation—and certainly did not resent it. The business turmoil did not lesson with the lessening day; it increased. His tired, unsteadied hands were overflowing full, and towards dinner-time (another whiskey and soda had taken the place of tea) he deputed Murray to 'phone Mrs. Gregory that he would not be home till very late that night, if at all. Hilda had answered the 'phone, and had said, "All right," Murray reported. And Gregory grunted an acknowledgment, paying little attention, engrossed in other things.

Florence Gregory was a just and a good-humored mistress, not an indulgent one. And she was in no way of the class of women who court or accept the advice of their servants. Even in the days of her modest Oxford housekeeping, when her own youthfulness and the deficiencies of the vicarage purse would have made most girls so placed peculiarly vulnerable to the insidious encroachment of hireling "I wills," and "I won'ts," she had been truly mistress of that manse, adamant towards would-be familiarity. And that natural smooth caste hardness had not softened under the flux of travel or the sunshine of affluence. From their first quarter of an hour together she had commanded distinctly, and Ah Wong, without comment, had obeyed. During the last week Mrs. Gregory had leaned not a little on her amah, sensing in the Chinese woman, who too was a mother, a something of sympathy that even Hilda could not give her, but she had in no way abrogated any of her personal autocracy to Ah Wong or let the space of discipline between them lessen. When Ah Wong had exclaimed, "No, no, madame! Not go!" the first liberty Ah Wong had ever taken, the mistress had scarcely heard and had not heeded; but when, on their return to the Peak, the amah had again urged "Not go!" Mrs. Gregory had checked her sternly, and Ah Wong had known that it was worse than useless to repeat the entreaty. To appeal to any one else, against her mistress—to Missee Hilda, to the master, or even to John Bradley—never occurred to her. And she submitted silently, only venturing a piteous, "Me clome? Madame take Ah Wong?"

"Of course," Mrs. Gregory said, not unkindly. "He expressly said I should bring you."

That there could be no question between them as to who "He" was told clearly of how Wu Li Chang had gripped the thought of both these women, and (at least of one) had gripped also the imagination.

At five o'clock—the hotness of the terrific day was scarcely waning yet, and Hilda and Tom in the darkened sitting-room were eating ices with their tea—

Mrs. Gregory and Ah Wong went quietly out and took the next car down the Peak. On the level (such level as terraced Victoria City can show) the amah hailed two rickshaws, and they bowled inconspicuously to the water's edge.

They did not use the ferry. A little boat was waiting for them. Ah Wong had secured it by messenger; and she took care that the jinrickshaw men should hear her tell the boatmen where they were to pole—which they already knew perfectly.

And then she sat down at her mistress's feet and waited. She had done all she could.

The boat slipped slowly through the gurgling water, the coolies sing-singing droningly as they poled her. Neither of the women spoke until the little vessel grated against the shore. Ah Wong was strangely calm, her very nerves hushed but alert in her lady's service, and the Englishwoman felt calmer than she had been for days, soothed that she was doing something definite at last, and not a little confident in the promise of Wu Li Chang.

She had made a special and somewhat magnificent toilet for this visit, pathetically anxious to seem to pay every honor to the Chinese lady for whose social peace of mind the mandarin had seemed so anxious. Mrs. Gregory was wearing more jewelry than she had ever worn before in the daytime, so thinking to do honor to a hostess who was of the inordinately jewelry-loving Chinese race. Even the wonderful bracelet—kept until now for functions of real importance—was hidden beneath the laces of her sleeve.

The boat grated in the gritty earth, and Mrs. Gregory looked up, glad to have arrived, confident of her reception and of the wisdom of her visit.

Wu Li Chang need not have been at such pains to tempt his prey and to bait his trap. Convention did not exist for Florence Gregory now, or fear. Basil and Basil's plight left her no thought, no consciousness of lesser things. And she had as little thought of the safety or danger of her act as she had of its propriety or impropriety. But if she had known her coming at Wu's bidding to Kowloon to be as imperilled as it was, and as Ah Wong sensed it, still she would have come, as unflinchingly, for Basil. Wu Li Chang had squandered inducement needlessly. And he need not have played poor Sing Kung Yah for trumps.

That widowed gentlewoman was greatly bewildered and scarcely less perturbed. Never before had she returned home ungreeted by Nang Ping. And of Nang Ping she could hear nothing. To all her questions the servants were deaf. The honorable master would tell his honorable kinslady all to interest her in his own honorable time. To them he had commanded silence.

She could not see Low Soong; it was forbidden—for a time. Wu Li Chang she scarcely saw; and, when she did, him she dared not question. He sent her to call on an English lady in the Barbarians' Hotel on the Peak, and she went, half dead with embarrassment, and carrying a splendid offering of flowers. The lady was out—the mandarin had almost counted on that—and Sing Kung Yah scudded back home, as fast as she could induce the servants to carry her, and burned a score of "thank-you" joss-sticks.

That she was to receive that same lady to-day, and at the very gates, was a care, but one that sat on her more lightly. She was at home here, surrounded by her customary servants, and she might know more or less what to do, how to conduct herself in the unprecedented presence of a foreign guest. And she was thinking of Nang Ping far more than of her own approaching social ordeal, as she sat in her own apartment eating perfumed ginger and quails dressed with sour clotted cream, and waiting for the summons to the gate.

Both were very good: the ginger embedded in jelly-of-rose leaves, and the hot, hot quail smothered in thick ice-cold sauce. She was very nervous, but somewhat phlegmatically resigned, plying her delicate chop-sticks industriously, now in the deep blue and white Nankin-ware jar of fragrant confiture, now in the silver dish where the sizzling, savory quail was too hot to be cooled by the icy cream, the sour cream too cold to be lukewarmed by the quail.

Just at six her summons came. She sighed a little, gulped down a tiny bowlful of bright green tea, and toddled off almost confidently to play hostess to the lady of the mandarin's latest whim, a little at a loss for herself, but happily and proudly confident that Wu Li Chang could do no wrong, much less blunder, and toddling fantastically because her feet were very small—Sing Kung Yah had no claim to Manchu blood, had had no traveled eccentric for a father and lord, and so, unlike Nang Ping, her feet had been well bound. Because she was a widow she used no cosmetics. But her clothes could not have been gayer: she was gorgeous.

She was standing smiling at the gate, servants on either side, when the Englishwoman reached it. And when Mrs. Gregory held out her hand she took it warmly, giggled and held it to her cheek, said a gurgling something that sounded Italian but wasn't, and drew her guest along the path to Wu Li Chang's threshold.

The two women went hand in hand, and Ah Wong walked close behind, carrying a tortoise-shell card-case in her hand. If anxiety and torture had made Basil's mother oblivious of conventions as they affected herself, they made her acutely careful to avoid every possible giving of offense and appearance of slight. And she would not forget to leave three cards, of her own and Hilda's, one for each of the ladies of Wu's household.

Her reception encouraged her. This little creature was very friendly, and it was nice of Mr. Wu to have stationed her at the gate, for he was master of the smallest details here, she made no doubt of that. She wondered at what point Miss Wu would appear, and the funny, pigeon-plump cousin.

They went along the tortuous paths, through the lovely, elaborate gardens (not Nang Ping's garden), hand in hand up to the very door, and Sing Kung Yah chatted incessantly in her pretty, musical mandarin Chinese, and the guest said an amiable word now and then. Neither understood a word the other said, or ever could, and Sing Kung Yah thought that screamingly funny—and screamed with high-pitched, tinkly laughter.

 The sun was brilliant still. Flowers leaned with friendly welcome from every ledge and corner. How perfectly absurd Ah Wong had been!

And Ah Wong kept closer and closer, growing more terrified every moment.

At the door Sing Kung Yah slid her hand gently away, and, toddling back a step, gestured laughing that Mrs. Gregory was to go in first.

When the door had closed again, the guest was surprised to find that the hostess had stayed outside. On what "Martha" errand had the little housewife thought it necessary to go herself, in this household overflowing with servants? But she was not altogether sorry. It was the mandarin she wished to see—to hear what his success had been. Perhaps it was his kindness that had arranged it so. But she must not forget to ask the Wu ladies to lunch, and, above all, she must remember to leave cards. The Chinese set such store on such things.

She caught her breath. The servant who was conducting her paused at a door. Probably she would see the mandarin now.

CHAPTER XXXI
FACE TO FACE

IT was four when Wu Li Chang reached Kowloon and his own home. Barely two hours in which to arrange the details, the scenic background, of the last act of the tragedy—the exquisitely horrible details of his revenge. But it was time enough, for he had planned it all down to the smallest point as he sat with Nang Ping dead at his feet. A few moments would suffice for the orders he had still to give Ah Sing, and upon the implicit obedience of his servants he could depend absolutely.

He bathed, dressed in the garments of his country, took rice, spoke briefly to Ah Sing, then sent for Sing Kung Yah and coached that surprised and flustered lady in the part she was to play in the events of the afternoon. She was not a particularly skillful or astute coadjutor—indeed, for a Chinese woman, she was dull, inept and dense; but for seventeen years it had been her invariable habit to give him minute obedience, and the habit would stand her in good stead to-day. And, too, she had, of course, a Chinese memory—the most wonderful memory bestowed on any race. He had little fear of Sing Kung Yah, and, for that matter, the rôle he had assigned to her was but that of a well-dressed supernumerary with a few unimportant lines to speak. She was not essential to the movement of the piece, and her rôle might well enough have been "cut" from the cast, but with the evil seething at his heart all the native artist in him was aflame. He intended to carve his victims delicately—a dish for the gods. On the terrible altar of his hatred, yes, and of his just resentment, he would lay an English woman who had never wronged him and an English son who————. But he intended it all to be done as exquisitely as some finest ivory carving cut by a master Chinese hand.

When he had dismissed Sing Kung Yah he went into his study and waited.

It was the room in which perhaps he had lived most. It was here he studied; and in the many long hours of leisure which he always relentlessly kept for himself, Wu Li Chang was a devoted student. It was here he wrote; and Wu was an author of some distinction in the current literature of China—the land in which a genuine love of letters counts as nothing else does, a fine skill in literature is respected as no other human quality is. There were poems to his credit in the Imperial library at the pink-walled palace in Pekin, a book of philosophy, a comedy, and a history of the women of his house. And he contributed almost regularly to the *Pekin Gazette* and at long intervals to *Le Journal Asiatique*—in French, of course.

The hour-glass—he had turned it when Sing Kung Yah had left him—was running down; almost was run.

Wu rose, and stood looking out into his garden, saying good-night to it something as Nang Ping had said "good-by" to hers four mornings ago— saying good-night, for it would be dark when Mrs. Gregory left him.

He had no doubt that she would come.

He turned from the window, and walked gravely into the next room, where he intended—in less than an hour now—to receive his guest.

It was a curious room: Chinese, but with some differences from other Chinese rooms. For this man dared to tamper with custom when it suited his convenience, and to modify an architecture that had been unaltered almost since Kublai Khan ordered every grave in China to be plowed up remorselessly, and so made room for homes and crops for the living, till then out-crowded by the honorable dead.

This was a very beautiful room, and so richly furnished that its opulence must have been oppressive had it been less beautiful, its taste less distinguished.

Essentially and strikingly like Nang Ping's room, unlike hers it was not so exclusively Chinese, and it was more nearly crowded. The Chinese—like all Orientals—are fantastic collectors, even of European flotsam and jetsam, though more discriminatingly so than the Turk, the Indian, or the Japanese. In the remotest yamên in Honan or Kwei Chau you may find a Dresden vase, a music-box from Geneva, a silver dish from Regent Street, and—most probably of all—half a dozen clocks, made anywhere from Newhaven, Connecticut to Novgorod, and all ticking away together, but quite independently, and all giving a different lie to the old dial in the sunny Chinese garden. (There were eighty-five clocks—and all "going"—in one of the Pekin throne-rooms.) But you are not apt to find, except in the poorer quarters of the treaty ports, the gimcrack chandeliers and tawdry vases, Europe-made, which will astonish and shame you in a palace in Patialla or Kashmere.

Wu had collected in princely fashion during his years in Europe. There was a Venetian harp, a German grand piano, and an English organ in an adjacent music-room. And in this, the smaller of his own reception rooms, there were several European treasures. Unlike most Chinese rooms, this was carpeted, not with one of the beautiful native carpets, but with a great mat of silk and mellow splendor—Constantinople was the poorer since Wu had purchased it.

It was an octagonal room—perhaps the only one in China—and when all the sliding panels were closed its only ventilation came from a small window or opening high up against the ceiling. The panels were made to slide back or up, and out of sight; each was in the center of one of the apartment's eight walls, and cut into about half of the wall's width. The widest panel was open wide, and through it Wu could see his garden, with all its pretty architecture of pagoda, bridge, pavilion and "tinkly temple bells," all its lush and flush of flowers, all its affected labyrinth of yellow path and costly forests of dwarf trees, and, beyond the garden, the bay, terraced Hong Kong, the imperial Chinese sky.

The room was furnished in ebony, as costly and as carved as ebony could be made. There were no chairs, but several stools. A stool stood on each side of the moderately-sized square table, behind which stood the most noticeable article in the room—the huge bronze gong, swinging in a frame of chiselled ebony lace and silver and onyx, which no hand but the mandarin's ever struck.

There were several cabinets, Chinese masterpieces, holding china and bric-à-brac, chiefly Chinese and all priceless.

Chinese antiquities of every description were on the walls and on narrow tables against the walls—bronze from Soochow, porcelain from Kintêching, cornelians from Luchow cut into gods and reptiles, jades from the quarries of Central Asia, bowls, weapons, vases, statues, armor, a piece of Satsuma that Yeddo could not match.

There were two scrolls inscribed with lofty sentiments Tze-Shi herself had brushed one, and Kwang-Hsu had given it to Wu with his yellow-jacket. Aside from its imperial association it was very beautiful—even a European could see that, and Bradley had spent much covetous time gazing on it—for in all China, where the cult of "handwriting" is an obsession, no one has ever written more beautifully than her majesty. The other said in the original Arabic, "Es-salam aleika." (John Bradley had another verse from the same Sura over his bed.)

And, as in Nang Ping's room, there was just one picture—this one a bird perched on a spray of azalea painted by Ting Yüch'uan.

Wu prostrated himself before the altar which proclaimed the owner's importance. He had come here to do worse than butchery, but to do it as a priest—to sacrifice to his gods and to his ancestors, to scourge in their service a woman who had never injured him or them, as much as to scourge a man who had; but he had vocation in his heart rather than personal vengeance—and such is Chinese justice.

Fantastic—is it not?—the Chinese code that ennobles and flagellates the dead ancestors and the living kindred in punishment of the raw present sin! And yet, even for it, there is a poor, feeble something to be said. We dig down into the earth and uproot the diseased tree, burn it *all*, search out and burn, too, its suckers and its saplings lest all our orchard suffer worm-breeding blight.

From an alabaster box, gold-lined, he took a handful of yellow powder, dribbled it into the tiny saucer of sacred oil burning before the tablet, and as the pungent blue flames hissed up, prostrated himself again, and knelt for a long time—in prayer.

When he rose Ah Sing had entered, and stood waiting to say, "Your honorable instructions have been obeyed."

"Good," Wu said grimly, throwing more powder, from a different box, on to the votive oil. A thin smoke curled up, thickening as it rose into perfumed clouds that broke in waves of jade hues until all the room was a glow of green.

"Bring him now!" the mandarin said, seating himself beside the table and waiting with an expressionless face.

Ah Sing said something to a servant waiting outside the door through which he had come, and presently feet came along the passage. They were bringing Basil Gregory to Wu Li Chang.

They had not met or exchanged a message since Wu had bent and gathered up Nang Ping where she had swooned at Basil's feet. Since then no slightest message from the outer world had reached the prisoner in the pagoda. Wu's servants had brought him food, and, on the second night, even a rug; but not once had they spoken to him or appeared to hear what he said to them.

The hours in the pagoda had marked him. And—why not? Those other hours there had marked Nang Ping down to doom. The man does not go scot-free. Never! That is immemorial fallacy. Nature would be full-moon mad if that were so—and nature is very wise and sane, as wise as she is old. The partners foot the bill both—always. Nang Ping had paid her share. Now he was paying his.

He looked ill and haggard, and his wrists were bound together. Two Chinese servants stood guarding him, close on either side. Almost at the threshold Ah Sing halted the three.

Basil Gregory had no doubt that he was about to die and little hope that he would not be tortured first. And the horrors of Chinese tortures lose little hideousness in the telling at English clubs in China. Basil was abjectly tormented.

The mandarin sat and studied his prisoner curiously. His lip curled, and his soul. What had his daughter, bred for centuries from China's best and finest, descended from Wu Sankwei and from the two supreme Sages, and who might well have made an Imperial marriage, seen in this? He had known such slight men by the dozens and twenties at Oxford, scant-minded, uncultured, clad like popinjays; and for this—this English nothing, this manling thing too slight for Wu Li Chang's hate, almost unworth his crushing—she had made the father that had adored and cherished her grandsire to a mongrel of shame. The pain at Wu Li Chang's heart was greater and gnawed sharper than that at Basil Gregory's. The Chinese was the bigger man, and paid the bigger penalty.

And Nang Ping had died for this: degraded herself beneath Chinese forgiveness, beyond pity, for this: disgraced him, her father, and the great ancestry of a thousand years for this! *This!*—and she might have been the bride of a *man*!—loved as he had loved her mother, cherished as he had cherished Wu Lu—and the mother of sons, honorable, love-begotten Chinese sons!

Almost Wu Li Chang's Chinese imperturbability cracked under his strain. His sorrow and his rage panted in his throat, battled, almost squealed aloud. But he was master yet a little, and he said smoothly, "Well, are your thumbs more comfortable?"

"If I were only free, I'd throttle you." Basil said it, of course, to cover his own terror—but, too, he meant it. He was insanely angry with Wu. The offender rarely forgives!

"The heated language of youth!" the mandarin said with contemptuous patronage. "But I will be indulgent. You will admit, I think, that, so far, you have been dealt with leniently—considering the resourcefulness usually attributed to us in the matter of ingenious torture."

"I presume you have not yet exhausted your ingenuity," Gregory said with sullen, trembling lips.

"By no means," was the bland reply.

"And that is why I am brought here; I supposed so."

"Partly," the Chinese replied coldly; "also to prepare you for a shock."

"Death"—Basil tried to say it stoically. And, too, since it was to come, it would almost be welcome in place of such suspense.

"Nothing so pleasant," Wu replied.

CHAPTER XXXII
"Cur!"

"NOTHING so pleasant"—and the perfect placidity of his voice was more cruel than any outburst could have been.

"Well," the other said desperately, "but there'll be a reckoning for all this—my father——"

"Not necessarily, my young seducer," the Chinese said softly. "Your father I do not regard as a man at all formidable. I had a most interesting interview with him—to-day. And I formed a low opinion of his abilities. There is a positive hue and cry after you, of course—almost a paper-chase. The walls of Hong Kong city are plastered with your portrait, and even here, on the mainland, it is to be seen. It is a very nice portrait, too—the nice likeness of a nice English—gentleman—the portrait of a very handsome young—seducer." Wu Li Chang was not quite his own master now. The storm was rising, threatening his own insolent calm. He rose and moved a little up and down the carpet—quietly but stealthily, as hungry-for-flesh and thirstily-dry-for-blood cats move through the jungle in the night.

His last word cut Basil Gregory. Wu was behaving like the yellow dog he was; but he—Basil—was not entirely blameless: he had said as much to himself, alone in the pagoda—that cursed pagoda. Oh, well!

"Your daughter loved me," he began. And at a something manlier in his tone than Wu Li Chang had expected to hear, Wu paused still and met the English eyes squarely. "We are both young." And after a pause, so throbbing that even the three automaton servants must have felt it beat, he added slowly, "Except that the two races don't mingle, I would——"

"Marry her?" Wu interrupted haughtily.

"Yes," Gregory replied, as if proclaiming a determination and a promise. "Yes—if she still wishes it."

"A very interesting suggestion," Wu sneered. "In your country, when a woman has been dishonored, marriage is called 'making an honest woman of her.' It is a quaint notion. To me it seems a nasty one—plastering some putrid sore with gold-leaf! *Here* we have other methods. To us a woman's honor, once stained, no more can be clean again than the petals of a rose, torn and scattered by the storm, can be gathered back into their opening bud to perfume the dawn and glisten with its dew. If marriage, and with such as you, would redeem the honor of a ruined girl, what would redeem the honor of a father and a house so desecrated as mine? Nothing! And nothing is left me but to avenge. And I avenge it now." He turned and confronted the trembling wretch with a look before which a braver and a less guilt-stained man might well have quailed, and each word curled and hissed from his mouth like a snake.

Basil moistened his lips, tried to speak, but failed.

"However," Wu continued, "I was going to say that although your disappearance has become a matter of public advertisement, yet the last place where you are looked for happens to be your present, if temporary, abode. I say 'temporary' because in this life everything is temporary—even life itself. You might be buried here—though I don't say you will be—without any one being the wiser outside my own household. At one word from me you would be taken and crucified beside the pagoda, and left there until the carrion birds came and plucked your vitals out, and your eyes, and no one would suspect, or, if they suspected, dare make a move. Your people at your Government House! They could do nothing. My Government would dare do nothing, *even if they wished to*, for in an hour I could pull half China tumbling down about their ears. By the way, your father is a ruined man to-day. His ships are sinking, his credit gone. In China we punish parents for their children's sin— and our gods have punished Robert Gregory for yours and for his own: his own sin in having begotten such a *thing* as you, and his daily sin of impertinence to my countrymen. Well, my virtuous young English gentleman, our interview is drawing to its close. What is it that you wish to say—if your quivering nerves will let you speak?"

"If"—Basil Gregory spoke humbly enough now—"if you would grant me one favor."

Wu Li Chang laughed aloud. "Optimist!" he sneered. "Well?"

"That—that before anything"—his voice shook, and the words were not very clear—"anything happens to me, you will let me write a letter to my mother."

"To your mother?" Wu said softly. But his triumph leapt in his veins.

"To my mother! I—I *beg* you that one thing. It would not mention this place or your name, of course"—Wu laughed—"but," the tortured man went on, "but if you would see that it reached her——" There was a sob in his voice.

"And—so you would like to write to your mother?"

"Oh!" Basil Gregory cried, "double the torture you have planned, but let me write to my mother."

"This is very interesting," the mandarin said, sitting down again. "Very interesting—very. As for the torture I am preparing for you, I shall not increase it, because it cannot be increased. Largest cannot be enlarged. To the utmost one cannot add. So," he laughed softly, "you wish very much to write to your mother—a virtuous lady who bore a son in wedlock!"

Basil Gregory dropped his head. He could no longer meet the eyes of the father of Nang Ping.

"I suppose you would scarcely credit," the Chinese voice went on softly, "that my consideration for you had gone even beyond that? Would you like—not to write to your mother—but to *see* her?"

"See her!"

"Because you shall."

"See her!" Basil cried, trembling as he had not trembled before. "Oh! Mr. Wu!"

"Yes," Wu said slowly (and it says something of him and of his race that it did not occur to the other to doubt him—nor would have occurred to any one), "you shall. And you shall see her soon. You may even go home with her this very evening and sail for Europe next week. It is quite possible." He spoke with quiet emphasis.

"Mr. Wu!" the blanched face was twitching hideously, "oh! I would do anything!" The frightened eyes leapt and burned. Gregory's revulsion was terrible—the great revulsion of reprieve, or nightmare torture past and gone, the revulsion of a starving man at sudden meat and plenty, of one dying of thirst who finds a brimming mountain-pool cool to his reach, of the mother who from hours of agony slips towards sleep with the warm velvet of her baby snuggled to her breast. He took one eager step forward, and so far the men beside him let him go, and Ah Sing made no sign. "If you would give me your daughter——" he said earnestly, but at a look from Wu he paused.

"Give you my daughter?" Wu Li Chang said terribly. He rose and crossed to Gregory and stood before him—very near. "I have no daughter," he said gravely, and his meaning was unmistakable, "to give you or any man!"

The pinioned man recoiled with a sob. "Oh! my God!" he cried under his breath. And he knew himself for the murderer of a girl who had given him— all—and a child. And his own soul rose against him, and cursed him, and called him "Cur!"

CHAPTER XXXIII
A CHINESE TEACHING

THERE was terrible silence between them. Great puffs of sweet smell came in at the window where the headheavy wistaria hung and the lemon verbena crowded at its gnarled roots, and bursts of sweet sound from birds singing in the sun.

They looked at each other, weighing each the other—the man who had given Nang Ping life and the man who had given her shame.

They each had given her death: one in guilt, one in love.

Basil Gregory looked into Wu's eyes and could not look away—fascinated, horror-held.

Wu looked his fill, then turned away and went slowly to the shrine.

Again he put the pungent votive powders to the flame, and all the room quivered with deeply opalescent lights, and the odors of the garden were as naught.

The mandarin bent his head to the tablet, and walked away from the shrine, speaking in a changed tone—quite lightly.

"But I was speaking of your mother. I am expecting her here."

"Expecting her! Here?"

"Here," the Chinese repeated, standing close to Basil, eyeing him narrowly.

"Then they know——" Basil began, but could not finish.

"No"—Wu smiled faintly—"they do not know. She is coming here, your mother, as my guest—to learn, amongst other things, the truth about you!"

"If you could spare me that!" Basil said hoarsely. "We have been more like brother and sister," he pleaded.

Wu took it up as a cue, and on it began, with a little leer, the hideous part he had planned to play. "Yes, she is very young——"

"Tell my father, if you will——"

"Your father?" Wu said sharply.

"Yes, tell *him*, but——"

"I have nothing to do with your father!" Wu Li Chang said sternly, each word an emphasis.

"But you said——"

"I said that your mother was coming here. She is coming—alone. She is a devoted mother. I am going to test her devotion."

Again there was a pause—while the horror sank in. Basil Gregory did not grasp it at first, and could not grasp it very quickly. But it crept into his soul little by little, and while its agony seized and strangled him, Wu stood and watched him intently, Wu with the panther light of intensest hatred in his half-closed eyes.

"You—you fiend!" The Englishwoman's son screamed it, writhing.

Ah Sing slid a little nearer him. The two guarding moved on his either side a little closer. But neither on their faces nor on Ah Sing's was there the slightest expression or any sign of interest.

"Why?" Wu laughed as he spoke. "Other countries, other ways! In China a daughter often sacrifices herself for a father, a son for his mother—to the utmost. You—English—reverse it, and the mother sacrifices herself for her son."

"You fiend of hell!" And with a yell of torment the Englishman sprang almost too quick for the vigilants beside him. He wrenched one pinioned hand free and swung it up mightily. But Ah Sing—still with an expressionless face—leaned across the table, leaned between the blow and Wu Li Chang.

And almost as Gregory sprang the other servants seized and held him—they, too, with indifferent, blank faces. They would have shown far more interest sweeping wistaria leaves from the graveled paths, far, far more watching a quail fight.

"An eye for an eye!" the mandarin cried fiercely. "A tooth for a tooth. *That is what you teach us, you Christian gentlemen!* And," he hissed, from enfoamed, protruding lips, "Woman for woman! *We'll teach you that!*"

Basil Gregory hid his face in his hand and buried it on his shoulder.

For a space Wu Li Chang stood looking grimly at the foreigner. He did not mean to see him again. Then he spoke emphatically to Ah Sing—in Chinese—and at each sentence of the master's Ah Sing bowed his head with an earnestness that was a promise that each word of Wu Li Chang's should be obeyed strictly and minutely.

"Ah Sing," the mandarin said, rising slowly and taking the beater from where it hung beside the gong. He said something slowly, and then struck once on the great brazen disk, gave a further direction, and struck the gong twice. And Basil Gregory uncovered his eyes, lifted his head limply and stood watching and listening, agonized, fascinated. When Wu had finished his orders Ah Sing bowed still lower than he had done before, and then went slowly from the room, but not by the door through which they had brought Basil into it.

Wu turned to the Englishman. "You do not understand our barbaric tongue. I have been telling my servants that when they next hear me strike upon that gong they may release you to come here. You will find your mother here. It will be a tremendous meeting. Back to the pagoda! To-morrow it will be destroyed. Back to the pagoda, and wait there, thinking of my daughter, and listen for the gong to sound—for when it strikes you will know that you are free. These doors and all the gates of my garden will be reopened then, and you will be free to go—wherever you will—with her."

"With her?" Basil Gregory gasped, bewildered and dazed.

"Yes," Wu Li Chang told him with a curt smile, "for with my striking of this gong your debt will be fully discharged. Your mother will have paid it."

Gregory made one supreme, straining effort to get at Wu. "You monster!" he sobbed, "you monster of hell!"

"Quite so," the Chinese said calmly. "Western logic is an unfathomable mystery. You dishonored my daughter," he began fiercely, and then broke off abruptly. He'd waste no more words on this English thing. He'd punish—strike to the quick, flay to the raw nerve—but not wrangle with his condemned. "The sound of that gong will ring in your ears as long as you live. Go where you will, you will hear it. Go where you will, you will see, waking and sleeping, a pagoda by a lotus lake, while you live; and when you die, you will feel the vengeance of a Wu. Never again will you look upon your mother's face without seeing too the dead face of Wu Nang Ping—and mine."

"Oh!" Basil moaned imploringly, "you can't—you can't do this awful thing."

"Take him away," the mandarin said in his own tongue.

Basil Gregory understood the tone, though not the words. Dumb with terror, he scarcely resisted as the two servants dragged him through the door.

Wu Li Chang stood motionless. He heard the bolts shut. He heard the footsteps die away. But still he did not move.

He was thinking of Nang Ping—not as he had seen her last, not as he had known her for years now, but of Nang Ping, a laughing, imperious baby. And then he thought of that other, dearer baby—the baby he had married in Pekin—and a great, silent sob shook him roughly as he stood.

CHAPTER XXXIV
ALONE IN CHINA

"THE lady has arrived," Ah Sing said with an obeisance, and speaking, of course, as he always did to his master, in Chinese; "she is coming through the honorable garden."

"Show her in." Ah Sing went out again, leaving open the wide sliding doors through which he had come. And Wu, too, went from the room, lifting his hands high in symbol to the altar as he passed it. He left the room through its fourth door and closed it close behind him. He had gone into his sleeping-room.

In a few moments Ah Sing returned, bowing at the threshold for Mrs. Gregory to enter. She came in eagerly, Ah Wong close at her heel. Absorbed as the mother was in her own exquisite anxiety and in the paramount errand that had brought her here, still she was struck with the distinction and the character of the room; and at any time less engrossed it would have delighted and absorbed her. She had seen many rich interiors in Europe, and not a little of colonial extravagance in home decoration, but she had not seen such luxury as this. And the quiet taste of the place, for some reason, surprised her, but not more than its spotless cleanliness did.

Ah Sing watched the English lady with inscrutable eyes as she moved a little curiously about the room; and to Ah Wong, watching him, it was significant that for this once his scrutiny was open, almost frank. And as he passed from the room, the two Chinese servants interchanged a long, grave look. Ah Sing closed the door behind him.

"How stifling it is here!" Mrs. Gregory said, unfastening her cloak and drawing off her gloves. "I wonder where my hostess has gone off to. How very droll of her! Ah Wong"—putting her hand a moment on the other's arm—"I'm glad I have you with me!" The amah took the cloak and the gloves; put the gloves in the cloak, the cloak over her arm. And after a moment Mrs. Gregory moved wearily across the room.

Ah Wong looked hurriedly about the room—searchingly. She gave a little quick breath when she saw the one high window. Without a sound she went to Mrs. Gregory and touched her arm. Florence turned questioningly, and Ah Wong pointed eloquently up to the high orifice; then, watching first one door and then another, she moved a carved bench a little nearer the window—without a sound—while the mistress stood and watched her half curious, half amused. Again the amah pointed—this time from bench to window, and from the window to the bench. She thrust her hand into her dress, clutching at something hidden there, and bent her face close to her mistress's ear. But her own ear caught an almost imperceptible sound, and when Wu came from his bedroom Ah Wong was standing some distance from her lady, stolid but bored, her empty hands folded in front of her, idly.

The mandarin stood just inside the door, gravely watching. He did not speak. His face was very calm, priestly even.

Florence Gregory felt his presence, and turned with eager, welcoming eyes. But when she saw him she recoiled a little, with a slight breath of surprise. This morning in Hong Kong Wu had only half seemed to her un-English. Here, in his own house, and clad as she had never seen any one—stiff, gorgeous robes, tiny fan of ivory and silk, a mandarin's necklace of cornelian beads—he was intensely Chinese, barbarian, unknown, and she felt very far from home.

Wu made the motion of salutation with his fan—it is so the Chinese "bow"—before he said reverentially, "This is indeed an honor—none the less felt because it was expected."

Mrs. Gregory laughed a little nervously, but somewhat reassured by his voice, as he had intended her to be. "You startled me, Mr. Wu," she said. "I hardly expected——"

"This dress?" he said pleasantly. "It is put on in your honor. To have received you in my Chinese home in other than Chinese garb would have been a rudeness—and so, impossible. Hong Kong is your Queen's now, even its city's legal name—though custom-ridden tongues still stubbornly say 'Hong Kong'—and there, where I am but a business man among business men, I dress as Europeans do. I find it more convenient. And a long residence in Europe makes it easy. But this is China. You are indeed in China now, madame—as truly in China as if you were within the vermilion walls of the great imperial palace or in evil Hwangchukki. The Kowloon territory ceded to England in 1860 ends a yard beyond my gates. My kinswoman seems remiss to you, I fear," he continued. "But pray dismiss the thought. She has gone to give an order for your entertainment and to assume her best robes in your honor—robes she may not wear to the gate."

"Oh! but she was very splendid, and I thought how beautifully dressed." The mandarin fluttered his fan in grateful acknowledgment. "And your daughter? I hope Miss Wu is well?"

Wu Li Chang bowed—his head as well as his fan this time.

"And now, Mr. Wu"—she could wait no longer, and as she spoke she moved a few steps towards him—"what news?"

"Good," Wu said assuringly. "So that it does not need to travel fast," he added suavely, moving to the table, motioning her deferentially to a seat beyond it.

"Ah! thank God!" She was tremulous with the intensity of her relief, for she had feared the worst. It's a sorry trick that mother-hearts have. "And thank you, Mr. Wu," she added earnestly, with a pretty, friendly gesture that was very womanly and very English. But she was too restless, and too anxious still for details, to take at once the seat Wu again indicated. And she moved about the room a little, hoping Wu would volunteer more, and a little at a loss what to say next if he did not of his own accord immediately slake in full the burning torment of her anxiety. "Ah Wong, take my scarf," she said, unwinding it. It was light and lacy, but even it seemed to stifle her. Ah Wong came for the gauze, and backed away again, standing immovable, uninterested, by the door.

Mrs. Gregory waited, a little pantingly, but Wu said nothing. She looked round the room, not at its treasures, but looking for her own next words, piteously afraid of blundering, unable to be patient.

Wu Li Chang did not misunderstand, but he pretended to, and said in a pleased voice, "You find my modest treasures interesting?"

"Very," she forced herself to lie. She had heard a great deal of Oriental deliberateness, and she was heroically determined to commit no social solecism, give this man no smallest affront. "Oh! very." If he wished his possessions admired by her, admired by her they should be, and to his vanity's content, cost her heart the delay what it might. "I had no idea——" she nerved herself to begin, but stopped abruptly, embarrassed and at a loss.

"That a Chinese house could be so civilized a place?" Wu quizzed good-naturedly.

Really, she must do better than this. She *would not* give offense. "Not only civilized," she said, contriving a slight laugh—it was an awkward one—"but refined to the last degree."

There was very fine sarcasm and some contempt in the little bow he gave her—not a Chinese bow—but his voice was sincere and almost pleading. "My dear Mrs. Gregory," he began, "there is not so very much difference between the East and West, after all. Perhaps we in the East have a finer sense of art; certainly we care more for nature. But we *all* have the same desires—ambitions—the same passions, hate, revenge—and love!" There was honey in the slow, well-bred voice now—honey and something else. It jarred on the Englishwoman, and she turned with a slightly uncomfortable look. Instantly his tone changed to one entirely courteous still, but ordinary and commonplace. "Will you not be seated?" he said simply. "Or shall I describe some of my ornaments? You look about you as if you were good enough to be interested in my Chinese bric-à-brac."

"Yes—do—do," she stammered desperately; "that—that wonderful thing there? That gorgeous-looking duck!"

"Ah!" Wu said, "that is a very precious treasure. Our Chinese potters, as probably you know, are very fond of reproducing members of the animal kingdom."

"I have never seen a finer piece of that kind of pottery in my life," Mrs. Gregory said with almost breathless enthusiasm, gazing at the curio with eyes that scarcely saw it and fumbling her rings.

Wu Li Chang smiled. "And it is a very sacred object," he said.

"Oh?" she asked.

"It is a mandarin duck," Wu told her significantly. "And the mandarin duck with us, you know, is the emblem of conjugal fidelity!" He ended with a strange, low, sinister laugh. It was slight and very low, but it affected Florence Gregory weirdly. To cover up her own disconcerted inquietude she moved— at random—to one of the magnificent carved cedar columns beside the altar (Wu watching her with a grinning face) and pointed to the weapon hanging there. "And that sword up there?"

"That?" Wu laughed, and at the sound Ah Wong's blood curdled in her breast; "yes, that's an interesting thing. It has rather a curious history."

Her procrastinated anxiety for her son, her thwarted hunger to see him, were unnerving her, and she was growing anxious on her own account, though that she scarcely realized and in no way could have explained.

"Oh?" she forced herself to say. But she said it lamely, and she could say no more.

Apparently Wu noticed nothing amiss. "Perhaps rather a gruesome one," he said with a note of apology.

"Oh!" his guest said with a shudder; "well, then, don't tell me! At the moment I don't quite feel———"

"Then," Wu interrupted her quickly, solicitously, even, "I will spare you its story," but added more crisply, "for the present, at any rate."

He moved easily about the room and proceeded in the most leisurely way to point out his treasures. "This," he said, lifting a bowl from its place in one of the cabinets and bringing it to her, "will interest you very much. This is one of the famous dragon bowls—one of the first three ever made."

"Indeed," she said, "how very interesting!" But she could not hide her torture or her indifference.

Wu smiled cruelly into the priceless dragon bowl, and carried it back to its shelf even more slowly than he had brought it. "Up here"—he pointed to over one door—"I have what your English collectors call a three-border plate. I have a set of six. Up there"—he pointed to the top of another cabinet—"is another with five borders. It is almost unique. Li Hung Chang has one, Her Imperial Majesty the Dowager Empress has one, but they are very, very rare. And this"—indicating another bowl conspicuously placed on a carved ebony stand of its own on a malachite pedestal—malachite carved into coarse but exquisite lace—"is a Shangsi bowl. There are several in the house. Each one is worth something like two thousand pounds." He took it in his hands and turned it about very, very slowly, now this way, now that, gloating over it as if he'd never be done. The woman could have screamed; and, in spite of her, a heavy sigh escaped. But Wu seemed not to hear it. He returned the Shangsi to its stand at last and crossed the room to a larger stand, and, laying down his fan, which he had held till now, took up a sea-green vase, beautifully molded, enormously glazed. "You must look at this, dear Mrs. Gregory," he told her cordially, "you must look at this well. This is a particularly fine piece—this sea green glaze, Mrs. Gregory—one of the earliest productions of the ceramic art."

Her face was twitching now with nervousness. He seemed to notice her perturbation for the first time, and said contritely, "But I fear I weary you with my treasures," and carried the glaze back, very, very slowly, and put it down.

"No—no," she said hastily, "no, Mr. Wu, not that—not that at all. But I have come here with only one object——"

"With two, dear lady," he interrupted her gently; "you forget Madame Sing."

"Indeed, oh, no—I—I did not mean that, forgive me—but my boy—his safety—to see him—my mind is full of that——" The mandarin smiled indulgently and took up his fan again. "I should like to come again, if I may, some other time—when we are older friends"—she was pleading now—"I should like to come again and spend hours examining all your wonderful treasures—if you will let me. I hope you will. But now—now—I have only one thought in my mind. I can have but the one." Her voice trembled pitifully.

Wu Li Chang smiled indulgently. "I have been waiting, Mrs. Gregory," he said explanatorily, "for you to dismiss your servant."

Ah Wong fixed her eyes on her mistress, entreaty and misery in their narrow depths.

Mrs. Gregory looked at Wu in startled astonishment. "Dismiss her—Ah Wong? Do you mean send her away?"

"Only out of the room," the mandarin said carelessly. "She can wait in the courtyard."

"But—but I couldn't possibly do that," the visitor stammered. She was frightened now, and knew that she was.

"Nevertheless," Wu returned, in a tone he had not used before, "I fear I must insist."

Their eyes met. The Chinese eyes of the man, inscrutable, the English eyes of the woman, appealing, terrorized. And Ah Wong half thrust a hand in her bosom, then dropped it back quickly to her side.

"But, Mr. Wu," Mrs. Gregory faltered, "it is such an extraordinary request to make—under the circumstances."

"Not in the least," Wu said smoothly—and he seemed somewhat amused. "Do you in England usually bring your servants into the drawing-rooms of your friends?"

"No-o. No," she admitted lamely, "but—that seems different, somehow. I think, under the circumstances—and Madame Sing——"

Sing Kung Yah's remissness as a hostess received no further comment from her kinsman. But he said emphatically, "I could not possibly offend the spirits of my ancestors by sitting down in the room with your servant."

"Your ancestors, Mr. Wu! What on earth have they to do with a matter of modern propriety?"

"I said I should offend them," the mandarin replied with ominous quietude.

"Well then," the Englishwoman retorted, just a shade contemptuously, "they must be very thin-skinned."

"Mrs. Gregory!" Wu Li Chang said so sternly that she turned and looked at him alarmed, "this afternoon your husband grievously offended me by certain disrespectful allusions to my ancestors. He knew better—or he should have done. You do not, for you are unacquainted with China. So you must pardon me if I point out to you that in China we pay the memory of our ancestors the deepest respect."

"Oh!" she said unhappily, "I'm sorry—I'm so sorry. I wouldn't offend you for the world."

"Then will you kindly send your servant away?" Wu put his words in the sequence of a question, but there was neither interrogation nor request in his voice: it was cold, imperative and final.

The Englishwoman hesitated miserably. She was thoroughly alarmed now. "But," she begged (for it was supplication—open, not implied), "Mr. Wu, I—I hope that I shall myself be going soon."

Wu took no notice of what she said, and, for the time no further notice of Florence Gregory. He clapped his hands sharply, and at their sound Ah Sing stood in the doorway.

"Analiaotang," the mandarin said quietly. The frightened Englishwoman understood no Chinese. But Wu's tone—quiet as it was—said unmistakably, "Take her away."

Ah Sing moved quietly on Ah Wong, and she, looking pathetically at her mistress, backed as slowly as she dared through the open door, from the room. But at the threshold she paused, glanced for an instant up at the high window, looked her mistress squarely in the eyes, bowed her head and was gone.

And Mrs. Gregory had returned her amah's signal, look for look.

It was two women against one man; and one of those women was Chinese.

- 166 -

CHAPTER XXXV
THE STORY OF THE SWORD

"YOU—you shouldn't have done that," Mrs. Gregory faltered as the door closed again behind Ah Sing. "She is very devoted to me," she added feebly.

"No doubt," the mandarin answered tersely. "But I fancy my authority is even more powerful than her devotion."

The woman's uneasiness was growing rapidly. "I don't think I ought to have come," she said, looking about her nervously. "But now," with an effort to speak ordinarily and to assume an unconcern she no longer felt, "Mr. Wu, what is the news?"

"Oh! pray, Mrs. Gregory," the Chinese begged, all the blandness in his voice again, "do not let so trifling an incident disturb you in the least."

A sudden throb of Chinese music came from the garden, and at the first note a change crept into his face. It was such music—but softly thrummed, almost timid—as he and Wu Lu had heard together on their first hours alone in Szechuan. Chinese music is strange to European ears; they rarely learn to hear it for what it is. It is not discord. It is not crude. At its best it is the pulse of passion turned into sound. No other music is so passionate, no other music so provocative. And this was Chinese music at its best. Wu laid down his fan softly, and stood listening, his head thrust a little towards the sound. Mrs. Gregory listened too for a moment, startled; then, in a spasm of nervous tension, she covered her ears with her hands.

Wu took a step towards her. "Do you not find the music agreeable?" he asked her in a creamy voice.

"No," she almost sobbed, "it is horrible! Horrible! I—I can't bear it—as I feel now." And she sank down miserably on a stool and leaned a little against the table.

Wu smiled—a cruel, relentless smile. But he moved to the low, wide window, pushed back the opaque slide, and called out abruptly, "Changhoopoh." The music stopped instantly.

"Oh, thank you!" the woman cried.

"I am sorry it distressed you," he said in an odd voice; "perhaps these notes——"

"They jarred on me dreadfully," she sighed.

"It is a pity," the mandarin told her, "for the music was in your honor."

"I'm sorry," she faltered, twisting and untwisting her little handkerchief—Wu was fanning himself again, slowly, contentedly—"not to appreciate it more. You must please forgive me," she pled, "but I am so dreadfully overwrought." She turned to him with a wan smile that tried to be confident, but failed, and with a brave attempt to appear at ease that was sadder than her tears would have been, "Now, Mr. Wu, please tell me. Where is my son? What do you know about him? Oh! if you only understood a mother's anxiety!"

Wu Li Chang looked into her eyes with a narrow smile that was half a taunt, half a caress. "Ah!" he said, laughing a little, "the old, old mother-vanity. Why is it, I wonder, that motherhood lays claim to all the love, all the tenderness, and to all the misery of parentage? And it is so, world-wide. Our own women are so. But"—his voice grew stern—"fathers feel too! Fathers love their young. Fathers dote, brood, fear, suffer." He ended with a slight, bitter laugh that was a sneer and frightened the woman oddly, and then he added smoothly, imperturbably, "I was about to say, Mrs. Gregory, that that music, performed in your honor, is one of our classical love-songs."

"Really," she responded lamely. "Well, I hope your love-making is not so——" She broke off, painfully at a loss, and turned her head away.

Wu, still standing, leaned towards her, resting his hands on the table between them. "Not so—violent?" he suggested with a leer, "Displeasing? Passionate? What was the word you were about to use, Mrs. Gregory?" He almost whispered her name.

"Oh! Mr. Wu!" Florence exclaimed, rising hysterically—the torture was telling on her cruelly now; the handkerchief was torn and knotted—"please have mercy on a mother's agony!"

Wu Li Chang bent down, across the table still, and laid a hand very gently on hers. At his touch her self-control, already worn to a thread, snapped, and she screamed violently. Wu moved his fingers softly across her wrist, and smiled down at her amiably. "I'll scream the house down!" she gasped pantingly. Wu looked at her calmly, shook his head deprecatingly, and folded his hands upon his arms beneath his sleeves. Nothing answered her cry of terror—unless the absolute stillness of the garden did, or its rich, penetrating perfume. "I'm sorry," she murmured distractedly, recognizing her mistake, and that to show fear would both affront him and invite annoyance. "I didn't mean that," she said, choking back a second scream; "I only mean that—oh! I'm tortured by all this suspense." In spite of her new resolve, a low sob broke from her, and she huddled down upon the stool again, crying like a tired and frightened child.

The man stood a moment watching her grimly. Her head was bowed and she could not see his face. There was bitter determination on it, remorselessness, but no desire. He moved slowly across the room and closed and fastened the thick screen-slide of the window that looked upon the garden. And now again, except for the high narrow window, through which no one could look out or in, the room was shut and barred from all the rest of the world.

They two were entirely alone.

The mandarin moved slowly back until he stood beside the woman. "Pray compose yourself, dear lady," he said very quietly. "That weakness was unworthy of you, and hardly complimentary to your host." He took her hand quietly in his, and she made no remonstrance, made no attempt to draw her hand away again. He put his other hand on her arm, and pushed her gently down upon her seat, and released his hold.

"I'm so sorry," the woman said brokenly, brushing her hand across her eyes. "I—I am not myself. Please forgive me." Wu flicked that aside with a courteous gesture. "And now," her voice was little more than a whispered gasp, "Mr. Wu, please tell me———"

"I am about to do so. Patience!" Wu said silkenly. "In China things move slowly. China is the tortoise of the world, not the hare. I was going to tell you"—he spoke with a deliberation that was a torture in itself.

"Yes?" she interrupted his vindictive procrastination feverishly.

"About that sword." The mandarin pointed to where it hung.

Mrs. Gregory half smothered a moan.

"The sword with rather a gruesome history———"

"Oh! don't, please, Mr. Wu," she broke in, "please—I—I couldn't bear it now."

"But, my dear Mrs. Gregory," he persisted blandly, "good news will keep. Time is not pressing. Besides, tea has not yet been brought in."

"Tea!" she panted distractedly; "oh! Mr. Wu, you must please excuse me."

"I beg *you* to excuse *me*," the Chinese corrected, a little arrogantly. "For countless generations my ancestors have drunk tea at this hour, and our tradition must be kept up. You have been long enough in China to know, perhaps, that tea-drinking with us as a matter of ceremony is an indispensable custom———"

"Yes, I do know that," she said quickly, "but—I———"

"And so," Wu continued pleasantly, "whilst we are waiting for tea I will tell you the story of the sword." And he moved as if to lift it down.

With half-closed eyes, wearied with terror, Florence Gregory half crouched against the table, prepared to listen. Her rings were cutting into her hands. Her handkerchief lay at her feet, a ball of rag. Suddenly Wu turned from the weapon, left it hanging in its place and swung back to her; standing behind her, his hands on the table, almost touching her, bending over her, he said, "By the way, Mrs. Gregory, you must love your son very much."

"Oh!" she told him, rising and turning to him with supplication in voice and gesture, "I do."

"Otherwise you would not be here?" the Chinese asked her calmly.

"Otherwise I should not be here," she said a little proudly, stung for the moment back to a sort of self-assertiveness.

"Alone," he added with a horrid emphasis. "But a mother's love is capable of any sacrifice, is it not?"

"It is capable of *much* sacrifice," the woman returned, some dignity lingering in her voice.

"If your son were in any peril, you would——"

"Oh!" the mother said sadly, "I would give—my very life."

"Your life!" the mandarin exclaimed almost contemptuously. "In China life is cheap. Is there nothing you value even more?"

"Why?" she asked feebly, at bay now, and putting up such poor fight as she could for time, in the desperate hope that some outside help might come— from Ah Wong or from somewhere. "Why, what can one value more than life?"

"Let us rather say," the Chinese insinuated, bending until his breath fanned her cheek, "what can a woman value more than her own life—or the life of her son?" He paused, not for a reply—he expected none—but to watch the effect upon her of his poisoned words; to watch and gloat. She, poor creature, no longer made any pretense. Her strength was gone: worn away by the persistent drip, drip of his long, slow cruelty. She looked about the room wildly, saw the face leering close to hers, and shrank away shuddering. "When I have your attention, Mrs. Gregory," Wu said determinedly, but falling back a pace or two.

The entrapped woman summoned up all her courage. "You shall have it, Mr. Wu," she said steadily, rising, "from the moment you tell me what I came to hear."

"If you will be seated again," the mandarin said suavely, "I will proceed to do so. But you must allow me to choose my own route."

Florence Gregory looked at her tormentor squarely, then beseechingly. She hesitated. And then she sank back listlessly on to the seat.

"And so," the man continued, "I will commence with—the sword."

Mrs. Gregory closed her aching eyes and caught her cold hands together—and waited.

The mandarin moved, and spoke more and more deliberately. Slowness could not be slower than his was now. He took down the sword—he remembered how he had touched it last—his face was ice, his voice as cold. "As I told you," he began, standing in front of her, the sword resting on its point, held between them, "it belonged to an ancestor of mine who lived many generations ago, Wu Li Chang, whose name I bear. Perhaps you would like to look at it more closely." There was a note of command in his voice, and the woman, obeying, lifted her head a little and fixed her agonized eyes on the weapon he held, edge towards her. "I will show it to you, and then restore it to its place. You see, the blade is no longer keen——" But the point was. She saw neither. "I keep it merely for its history." He laid it on the table, laid it between the Englishwoman and himself, as he might have laid a covenant or some vital document of evidence, a terrible accusation, a great deed of gift.

The torture of the merciless leisurely recital was telling on the woman visibly. She had held a pistol stoically enough this morning. But when, at a weary movement of her own, the lace in her sleeve caught in the old sword's hilt, she shuddered and shrank back. She made no pretense of listening. She was "done," for then at least; and of her diplomatic courteousness not a shred was left. But yet she heard each word.

Wu sat down again, and the slow, cold voice went on evenly. "My ancestor had only one child, a very beautiful daughter. He worshiped her with more devotion than is common in China—for you know we do not often (unless of pure Manchu blood) esteem daughters so highly as sons. But he was an admirable man—a good neighbor, unselfish, upright, charitable (and—is it not strange?—for all this was before the missionaries came to China), a faithful husband—he was a very devoted father. She was, in your Western phrase, the apple of his eye. Well, one day when the time came for her marriage to a mandarin to whom she was betrothed, her father discovered that she—that her marriage was no longer possible." Basil Gregory's mother was listening now, not listlessly. The ears of a mother's soul are terribly acute. "He dragged from her her lover's name, and then, without a word of reproach or of warning, he slew the being that he loved—with that sword."

The English mother moaned. She understood.

"And after that, her lover too was slain; and not only he, but also his sister, his mother, his entire family. My old sword has drunk deep, Mrs. Gregory," and he drew a finger lovingly along its blade.

"Don't—don't tell me any more," Florence Gregory whispered.

Wu lifted the weapon and laid it across his knee—reverently. "I warned you that it was rather a gruesome story," he said gravely.

"Yes—well," she stumbled, playing still for time, trying to think, "thank Heaven we are more civilized to-day than—than anything so horrible as that!"

Wu smiled. "Much more civilized, no doubt. Methods change; and since I have had the advantage of a European education, if I found myself in such a case, I would not adopt so bloodthirsty a revenge. Indeed I think, if anything, my ancestors erred on the side of leniency." Wu Li Chang paused. Less light was coming through the one high window now. Florence Gregory was well-nigh strangled by the beating of her tortured, frightened heart. And almost Wu could hear its beat.

"He was robbed of honor," he said sternly; "he took merely life in exchange, whilst he might have taken—from the sister or the mother—that which they would have held dearer than life. Are you listening to me, Mrs. Gregory?" for she had buried her face in her hands on the table where the sword had laid.

She lifted her head heavily—her face was ashen and lifeless—and looked at him with stricken, agonized eyes.

"I have wearied you," Wu said contritely. "Your husband would reproach me—or your honorable son. My story was too long, and unpleasant in an English lady's ears. Yet I have said no word that does not bring me nearer to my point. I, too, had a daughter——"

"Had!" the woman's lips just breathed it.

"And family history has repeated itself—so far."

For some moments there was silence in the room—a silence far more poignant than any words—a silence chill and kindless as the voicelessness of death. Then Florence Gregory started up at the sounds of bolts withdrawn and of panels sliding in their grooves.

Wu rose too, carried the sword, and put it beside the gong. "It is growing dark," he said.

CHAPTER XXXVI
In the Pagoda and on the Bench

SO long as he may live Basil Gregory will never understand how he lived through those hours in the pagoda—his last hours in the pagoda by the lotus lake. So long as he lives he must remember them, and shudder newly at each remembering—waiting again in torture and alone to hear the deep-throated damnation of Wu Li Chang's gong telling him that—that he was branded forever, soul-scarred. Wu Li Chang had hit upon something that not even a man could forget.

How he got there he never knew. He remembered being taken to the mandarin, the terrible interview, the news of Nang Ping's death, the demoniac threat of his mother's ordeal and agony, but nothing of his return to the pagoda. For a time—he had no way of knowing how long or how brief—a merciful space of blank had been vouchsafed him. And the utmost fury need not have grudged him it. For, if the mother in the house suffered more than a death, the son in the pagoda, when consciousness crept back, suffered her sufferings multiplied. She was his mother, and he loved her. Always she had been very good to him. And he had been so proud of her. Could he ever feel quite that pride again? Her very sacrifice must smirch her in the eyes of the son for whom it was made, and whose crime it punished. Even his love for her must be a little tarnished, a little weaker, after the clang out of that brazen gong. Wu Li Chang had found a great revenge. His own honor had never burdened Basil Gregory; but his mother's honor—ah! Or, for that matter, even Hilda's, or his cousin May Gregory's—for, like so many such men, Basil Gregory leaned his soul (such as he had) and his pride upon the women of his blood. To be virtuous vicariously is a positive talent with some men.

His mother! He writhed. His mother! He tore against the pagoda's walls with his hands, all pinioned as they were—for his freed hand was bound again—until his knuckles bled. If such punishment as Wu had devised could be shown vividly, anticipatorily, to men about to stray, the gravest of the social problems must be so somewhat solved, the most stinging of the burning questions somewhat answered. If sons, light, selfish, weak, could expect such chastisement as Basil Gregory was enduring now, a famous commandment would be honored in observance an hundredfold, dishonored by breach miraculously less. A daughter's shame—a sister's—that scourges most men; a wife's—oh! well, there are wives and wives, there are men and men, but a mother's—ah! That touches all manhood on its quick. Brand the scarlet initial of adultery on his mother's brow in punishment of him, and what son would commit the fault? Fewer!

From the sun—for there were spaces pierced in the elaborate stonework of the pagoda's thick sides, and he could see through some of them—he thought that he must have escaped nearly an hour of the misery of consciousness.

Heaven knows the scene enacted in the smaller audience hall was exquisitely terrible enough; but the man alone in the pagoda pictured it ten times more terrible, more hideous, more stenched than it was. Made an artist in fiendishness by his love for his child, Wu was most fiendish, most exquisite, in his enmaddening deliberateness. He drew out the woman's agony until the sinews of her soul seemed to crack and bleat. The hideous hour seemed an age to her. To Basil, waiting alone in the pagoda, the hour seemed ages piled on ages.

Alone? But no, he was not alone. This was Nang Ping's pagoda. She had given him "free" of it, and shared it with him. She shared it with him still. A ghost—a girlish Chinese ghost—stood beside him and looked at him adoringly, accusingly, with death and motherhood in her eyes. "Oh! Nang Ping! Nang Ping! Forgive, forgive!" he cried, and hid his face on his pinioned arm. Then he looked up with a cry—wide-eyed, for he had seen his mother in the room he'd left, the room where the gong was, and Wu—he saw his mother, and the Chinese moving towards her, and he turned and cursed the girl-ghost at his side—the poor dishonored ghost with a tiny nestling in her arms.

Angry at punishment self-entailed, to shift, or seek to shift, the blame, or some part of it, upon shoulders other than our own, is a common phase of human frailty. "The woman tempted me." And so the fault is really hers. Punish the temptress and let me go. "The woman tempted me": it is the oldest and the meanest of the complaints. But sadly often it is true enough.

A man never had less cause to urge it, in self-extenuation, or even in explanation, than Basil Gregory had. Nang Ping had never tempted him. Even in the consummation of their loves, the heyday of her infatuation, she had never wooed him. In their first acquaintance, contrived in part by him, brought about in part by a fan of Low Soong's, lost and found, Nang Ping had been as shy and unassertive as a violet. She had never tempted except with her own sweet reserve and the fragrant piquancy of her picturesque novelty. And that she had not sought him, or, for some time, allowed him advance, had been her chief charm for him. And on the day that he had told her that he was returning to Europe, and at once, leaving her to face their dilemma alone, she had uttered no reproach, made no outcry—just a quiet expostulation abandoned as soon as made. "You will not come back," she had said quietly, and had gone from him calmly, with dignity.

Never lover had less just cause to reproach mistress than he had to reproach or blame Nang Ping. But for his mother's sake, and, too, perhaps, for his craven own, he did, and cursed the girl who had died for him, as he raged futilely here in the pagoda, where he had taken, and she had given, her all.

It is a big thing to be a manly man.

It is a tragedy to be a woman—except when it's the very best of great good luck.

Very little of the good luck of life, very little of the joyousness of womanhood, had ever been Ah Wong's. All her life she had worked hard for scant pay and no thanks. All her life she had yearned passionately for companionship, and been lonely. From a brutal father she had escaped to a brutal husband. Her children were dead, and had not promised much while they lived. God knows, Mrs. Gregory had given her little enough—almost nothing. And yet Mrs. Gregory had given her her best time—the nearest approach to a "good time" she'd ever known. And she was pathetically grateful to have had even so much of creature comfort, such crumbs of kindness, so shabby and lukewarm a sipping of the wine of life. The Englishwoman did not even know that she had been kind to the amah. Indeed, Ah Wong had merely warmed her cramped and frozen being in the careless overflow of a nature that, by happy accident, was full of sunshine and brimmed with radiance.

Ah Wong was grateful, and Ah Wong was honest. She meant to repay. She hated debt; almost all Chinese do. She had loyalty. She had grit. She had Chinese wit. And she had the light wrist of her sex at subterfuge: it is world-wide.

Ejected from the house, she sat down contentedly in the courtyard and began to knit—an industry foreign to Chinese eyes. It brought curious women of the household about her. She had intended that it should. They brought her liangkao and melon seeds—for hospitality was the rule of the house—and she ate all the liangkao and cracked all the melon seeds while the other women chattered to her and to each other.

She said that she was very tired—her lady was a hard taskmistress. She didn't like the English. She was very tired, but she'd like to see something of so beautiful a place, now that she was here, and she tottered about a little wearily from treasure to treasure, but never far from the house, from tiny forest trees a few inches high, in pots the size of thimbles, to an evergreen that was a century old and that had its widest branches cut into birds in full flight. She cried out in ecstasy at a great dragon sprawling on the grass, a dragon of geraniums and foliage plants. And presently she yawned and said that she was very tired, and sat down heavily on a carved stone bench. After a little she fell asleep, and the women giggled at her good-naturedly and left her. The bench was not far from the window that high up looked into the mandarin's sitting-room.

CHAPTER XXXVII
THE FAN

"IT is growing dark," Wu said, as he put the sword down beside the gong.

Three other servants followed Ah Sing through the sliding door that he had opened from the other side. Two were tea-bearers and the other a servant of the lamps.

The tray of tea was laid on the table. The lamp-man moved about the room, and a dozen dim lights broke out, like disks of radiant alabaster, so dim, so beautiful, and so unexpectedly placed that their shrouded brilliance made the wonderful room seem even eerier than before.

The woman watched it all, inert and motionless. She felt, without thinking about it—she was almost worn past thinking now—how more than useless it would be to appeal to these wooden-faced Chinese, the creatures and automatons of Wu Li Chang. And an instinct of dignity that was very English held her from making to foreign servants a prayer that would, she knew, be denied. She would make no exhibition of a plight they would not pity or of an emotion that would not move them—unless it moved them to mirth.

But when, their service done, the servants went out, soft-footed as they had come, and after the door closed, bolts clanged, she realized that she and Wu were again alone—the room locked—and she sprang up and dashed to the door.

Wu watched her, smiling. "Come," he said—almost as he might have spoken to a restless child—"tea is served."

And she turned, in obedience to his voice, and looked at him. "I couldn't, Mr. Wu," she said with plaintive petulance, "I couldn't possibly." The distress in her voice was more than the annoyance.

Wu ignored her words good-naturedly, and began pouring out the tea. "I have sugar and cream, you see, quite in the Western way."

"No—no, I couldn't," she reiterated impatiently, but coming back to the table and watching the cups as he filled them. "Please tell me of my son and let me go."

For answer, the mandarin held out to her a cup of tea. "Pray take this cup of tea, Mrs. Gregory," he said with grave politeness. "Oh! I understand," he added with a slight, chill smile, when she paid no attention to the cup he proffered her. He put it down. "You would prefer to see me drink first." With an inclination of his head to her, he lifted his own cup and drained it at a draught. "So! perhaps that will reassure you." He put his cup down and refilled it. "Pray take the tea," he urged hospitably: "it will not only be refreshing—and your lips look dry and parched—but it will also be a politeness to do so."

She stood looking at him dully, and then sank slowly down on to a stool.

"Sugar—and—cream," the mandarin said brightly. There was more of Mayfair and of Oxford in tone and in manner than there was of Cathay. And the anachronism was gruesome rather than droll, as he stood in his mandarin's robes fanning himself with his left hand (the sons of Han are more nearly ambidextrous than they of any other race) and with his right hand plying the silver sugar-tongs with slow dexterity. "So!" he held out the perfected cup. "It is the choicest growth of the Empire, Mrs. Gregory, sun-dried with the flowers of jasmine."

She took the cup, and he took up his. Just as she was forcing herself to drink—his own cup almost to his lip—he said with the same suave manner, "Have you no curiosity, Mrs. Gregory, to learn the name"—a poisonous change came in his voice—"of my daughter's seducer?"

The Englishwoman put down her cup quickly, with a hand so unnerved and trembling that it scarcely served to guide its small burden. She tried to drop her eyes, but she couldn't—he held them with his relentlessly. "I don't understand you," she faltered. "Your—your manner is so strange."

Wu said nothing, but he smiled into her gaze coldly, and she rose with a shudder. Wu smiled at her still, and with a sudden wild cry she darted to the sliding doors and beat on them hysterically. But she realized at once that they were locked and were strong. And she turned around, at bay but hopeless, leaning her back against the door, and faced Wu miserably, her smarting hands hanging limp at her sides.

Wu Li Chang unfolded his fan and began to churn the air towards his face with it.

No European ever has understood what his fan means to a Chinese. Probably no European ever will be able to understand that. With their fans the Chinese hide emotion, express emotion, and, when it reaches the danger point, give it vent. Often a Chinese man's frail, tiny fan is his safety valve. China's greatest warriors have carried their fans into battle. Criminals fan themselves on the execution ground. Frightened Chinese girls, in the torment of first child-birth, fan themselves. Wu was fanning himself in triumph. And he spoke to her quickly, his voice ringing with triumph. "There are several ways into this room, Mrs. Gregory, but only one way out." The fan shut with an ominous click—a rattle of ivory, a hiss and a rustle of silk. "It lies by that door"—he pointed it with his fan—"which leads to *my own inner chamber.*"

The woman smothered a scream, but she could not smother a groan.

Wu laughed. He took a step towards her. "Have you no desire to hear my news of your son?" he asked softly. "Good news? I promised that you should—I am here to keep my promise." The terrible significance of his words could not have been clearer, but he emphasized it hideously by gliding still a little nearer to the stricken, appalled woman.

"Oh! don't torture me," she implored, moving away.

"He is well—comparatively. His hands have received a trifling injury—quite trifling. But he is quite well"—nearing the woman again—"and he is here."

"Here?" she sobbed, "here?"

"Almost within sound of your voice"—still nearer.

"O my God! where?" she cried, looking about her frantically. The third door caught her attention, and she ran to it weakly and beat against it, crying, "Basil! Basil!"

"Do not be so impetuous, dear lady," Wu said with insolent gentleness; "I did not say he was there. And it is not good that he should hear your voice, for the sound would only distress him."

She looked at Wu questioningly, and he gave her the cruel explanation. "You see, he is not at liberty to come until the right signal is given. It lies with you whether that signal shall be given or not!" He was very close to her now.

Wu Li Chang intended to use no physical force with this woman. He would not grant her degradation even that poor loop-hole of excuse.

That she would yield, he had no doubt. And her own tortured soul knew that it wavered now, and it was sick.

Wu laid his hand on her arm. And she scarcely shrank back, but drew herself up, proud in her sorrow, and said slowly in his smiling face, "You—you devil!"

"Harsh words will not help him, Mrs. Gregory," the mandarin said. "Only one thing can." Face almost brushed face—they were so close.

She hid hers in her hands and sobbed in fear.

"I will leave you whilst you decide," Wu said, and turned to the door that was, he had told her, her only way "out."

In a sudden frenzy and palsied with nausea, she dashed at the other doors, sobbing, "Let me go!"—panting—"let me go, I tell you!"

Wu watched her a little before he said calmly, still smiling gravely, "This door is the only door which remains unlocked. If you should decide to enter it before I return, I should not be unresponsive to the honor you will do me. If not, I shall return soon myself—to assist you, if I may, to decide."

"My husband knows that I have come here!" Mrs. Gregory cried defiantly. "I told him!" (Wu smiled.) "He will be here at any moment, and then———! Oh! I am not afraid of you!"

"Oh! I am glad of that!" Wu Li Chang said eagerly, "I desire only to inspire trust—and confidence—and the tenderest sympathy! But I know that your husband—that amiable, estimable Mr. Gregory—an odd, subtle creature, but so lovable—does not know you are here. You have not the remotest hope of seeing him—or you would not have told me! You would have temporized—delayed—said nothing."

"He *does* know!" she stormed. "He may be here at any moment! And if he is not admitted he will batter your gates and doors down!"

The mandarin laughed softly and shook his head at her indulgently.

"You scoundrel!" she told him, infuriated.

"Oh! I forgive your trying to deceive me, Mrs. Gregory," Wu said calmly; "it is only natural. Oh! that window," he added, in answer to an involuntary look toward it. "Yes, it leads out on to the courtyard where your devoted servant is waiting; but the architect has placed it so very high, and has made it so very small. Now"—he made her a little bow—"I will leave you, but not for long." And he passed through the unlocked door and closed it behind him very gently.

CHAPTER XXXVIII
THE GONG

DISTRACTED, not knowing what she did, or why, like some wild thing trapped and helpless, Florence Gregory looked about the room, searching it with eyes almost too fright-blinded for sight. Again she tried the doors—all but one. She made a desperate, useless effort to push the window apart. "Basil!" she cried, "Basil!" Then she checked herself. "No! I mustn't do that! O God!" she moaned, turning to driven humanity's last great resort, "help me!"

She groped her way unsteadily across the room, and climbed with trembling legs upon the bench and reached her hands up toward the little window.

"No," she sobbed in a whisper, "I can't," for she could not reach to half the opening's height. She looked about her stealthily, rose on her very tiptoes, and called towards the window, "Ah Wong! Ah Wong! can you hear me? Go quickly, for the love of Heaven! Fetch them! Help me, Ah Wong! Help me! I am alone, Ah Wong—but he will be back—very soon. Quick, amah, quick! Ah Wong, are you there?"

And then she waited.

Oh! that waiting.

There was no sound except the panting of her heart. From Wu's inner room nothing came but silence. The house and the garden were midnight-still.

Ah!

Through the window came a sound so soft it scarcely grazed the silence.

Something fell, almost noiselessly, at her feet. She swooped upon it with a smothered sob of thankfulness. It was her own scarf. Her hands shook so she could scarcely unroll it for the message or the help it hid. She knew it hid one or the other, or Ah Wong would not have thrown it. Or was it only a signal that the other woman heard her? With her eyes riveted in agony on Wu's door, her heart beating almost to her suffocation, her cold fingers worked distractedly at the matted gauze. Yes—there was something there. Oh! Ah Wong! Ah Wong! It was something hard and small.

She looked at the tiny phial wonderingly. But only for a moment. Then she knew. And her white face grew whiter. The last drop of coward blood dripped back from her quivering lips. Poison, of course! Must she? Dared she? Could she? And Basil? The boy that she had borne—her son and chum. Should she desert him so? Save her honor and leave him to death and to long fiendish torture ten thousand times worse than death? Was *any* price too great, too hideous to pay for his rescue from such burning hell? To so save herself at such cost to him, was not that an even greater dishonor than the other? The woman began to whimper, like some terrified child. And could she die? Could she face such death? Here—all alone—in China? God hear her prayer!—she could not think to word it. God have mercy! Life was sweet—the sun warm on the grass. And there were cowslips in the meadows at home, and the lilacs were wine-sweet, and the roses wine-red against the sun-drenched old stone wall in the vicarage garden—in England.

She tottered, sobbing silently, across the room, clutching the phial in her ice-cold hand.

England! At the thought of England she stiffened—proudly. She was English—and a woman. English and a woman: the two proudest things under Heaven. Basil must suffer. The body that had borne him must not, even for him, be dishonored. The unalterable chastity of centuries of gentle womanhood reasserted itself and claimed her—pure of soul, pure of body— claimed her and made her proud and strong as it had the English women of an earlier day who threw themselves rejoicing upon the horns of the Roman cattle rather than yield themselves—English women—to the lust of the Roman legionaries. As Abraham had prepared to sacrifice Isaac—Abraham! Abraham was only a man, only a father. She was a woman—she was a mother—and English!

With a smile as cold as any smile of Wu's, and more superb than smile ever ermined on the lip of man—she looked about for means: determined now— yet hoping still against hope for escape. She would die. Oh yes! she would die—here—now. But she hoped the stuff was not too bitter. She drew out the cork and smelt the liquid. It had no smell. Or had fright paralyzed her gift of smell? And all her senses? Her fingers could scarcely feel the glass they clutched. And need she drink it yet? Help might come. Surely Ah Wong had gone! But dared she wait? Wu would be back. Hark! Was he coming? Did his door move? He must not see her drink it. He would prevent her. But need she die quite yet?

She saw the cup of tea she had put down, and gave a little gasp of hope: at such poor straws do we clutch!

Yes—yes—she'd pour the poison into her tea—and drink it, if she must!

The cup was full. She drank a little chokingly. That was enough. Room now! She looked in terror at Wu's door, then emptied the tiny phial into her cup.

Wu's cup did not occur to her—she was too distraught.

Shaking pitifully, she wound the scarf again about the little bottle and dropped both into a satsuma vase.

She tottered gropingly back to her seat beside the table, the poisoned cup close to her hand. "My God!" she whispered, not to herself, "if it must come to that, give me strength."

Until the door opened and Wu came in, she sat cowering, her eyes riveted on her cup, her fingers knotting and unknotting in her lap, and under the lace of her sleeve the costly jewel she had worn to pay honor to Sing Kung Yah winked and danced.

She did not look up at the mandarin's step, and for a space he stood and studied her, hatred and contempt for Basil Gregory's mother ugly on his face, pity for his vicarious victim—and she a woman—in his Chinese eyes. And in his heart there was self-pity too: his sacrificial office was in no way to the liking of Wu Li Chang. He was sacrificing to his ancestors and to his gods. But the flesh reeking from his priestly knife, hissing in the fire, smoking on the altar of his tremendous rage, was repugnant to his appetite, a stench in the nostrils of this Chinese.

He wore now loosened garments of crimson crêpe—color and stuff an Empress might don for her bridal. He carried no fan. It was laid away. But on the hem of his gorgeous negligée a border of peacocks' feathers was embroidered, each plume the fine work of an artist.

"Well, chère madame!" he said softly, and then she looked up and saw him and his relentless purpose, and shrank back with a little moan.

Wu smiled and drew nearer. "Do I now find favor in your eyes?" he murmured wickedly—insinuation and masterly in his honeyed tone. "No? Oh! unhappy Wu Li Chang! My heart bleeds, stabbed by your coldness, you lovely and oh! so desired English creature, you fair, fair rose of English womanhood. Ah! well—I have no vanity, luckily for me, and so that is not hurt also, since it does not exist. One important matter," he said, almost at his side, drawing slowly nearer still, "I did not mention. It is only fair that you should understand fully my terms—only fair to say that your son knows that your sacrifice will set him free———"

Florence Gregory rose to her feet. She searched his face. "You—you *will* set him free?"

Wu Li Chang bowed his head in promise. And she did not for one instant doubt his word. It was her unconscious tribute paid to his individuality—and, too, it was tribute of Christian Europe to heathen China. Undeserved? That's as you read history and the sorry story of the treaty ports. Verdicts differ.

"That, of course, is understood—and pledged," the mandarin said quietly, "when—you—have paid—his debt."

She shuddered sickly. Wu smiled, and then his choler broke a little through its smooth veneer. "It is just payment I exact—no jot of usury: virtue for virtue. I might have seized your daughter—for myself, or to toss to one of my servants—but that could not have been payment in full. You, you in your country, you of your race, prize virginity above all else; we hold maternity to be the highest expression of human being, and the most sacred. So, because he took what should have been most sacred in the eyes of an English gentleman—and he a guest, both in my daughter's country and in her home—I take what is, in my eyes, a higher, purer thing—and I your host. And, too"—his voice hissed and quivered with hate—"the degradation of his sister would not have afflicted him enough—he does not love his sister with any great love. His love of you, his mother, is the one quality of manhood in his abominable being. He would have suffered at her shame and outlived the pain; yours he will remember while he lives—and writhe. It will spoil his life, make every hour of his life more bitter than any death, every inch of earth a burning hell." He paused and waited, and then—he slid behind the table, put his arms about the palsied woman, and whispered, pointing to the other room, his face brushing hers, "And now, dear lady, will you not come to me?"

For an instant they two stood so—she paralyzed, unable to move.

Music high and sublimely sweet pierced through the shuttered window: a nightingale was singing in Nang Ping's garden, near the pagoda by the lotus lake. Wu Li Chang had heard many nightingales, and from his babyhood. Florence Gregory had heard but one before—once, long ago, in England.

She wrenched away from Wu with a cry—of despair; and he let her go.

She sank on to her stool and took up her cup—she tried to do it meaninglessly—and slowly raised it to her lips.

"Oh!" Wu told her tenderly, "my lips also are dry and parched with the heat of my desire——"

But he had no desire of her. And even in her torment she knew it, and that in the coldness of his intention lay the inflexibility of her peril.

"I too would drink." He lifted up his own cup. "Ah!" he exclaimed, putting it quickly down again, "I see that you have sipped from your cup—your lips have blessed its rim." Standing behind her, he slipped his hands slowly about her neck, took her cup in them, and lifted it over her head, and faced her. "Let me also drink from the cup that has touched your lovely lips."

With a cruel look of mock love—to torment her even this little more, and in no way because he suspected the contents of either cup—with a slow look into her terror-dilating eyes, he slowly drained the cup. And Florence

Gregory watched him, motionless, horror-stricken—scarcely realizing that he had given her her release—by a way it had not occurred to her even to attempt.

"So," Wu said, putting down the cup, "I have paid you the highest compliment. For I do not like your sugar or your cream. Indeed, I cannot imagine how any one can spoil the delicious beverage——" His voice broke on the word. Something gurgled in his throat. "It was even nastier than I thought," he whispered hoarsely.

Suddenly he reeled. He staggered and caught at the table's edge. Had he gone drunk, he wondered, with the intoxication of his smothered, inexorable rage? The room was spinning like a top plaything. His head ached. He thought a vein must burst. The room was turning more maddeningly now—like a dervish at the climax of his dance. And he was spinning too—not with the room but in a counter-circle. He tottered to a stool and sank on to it, his face horribly contorted with pain.

Mrs. Gregory moaned, half in fear for herself, half in horror at the ugly agony from which she could not take her eyes. She moaned, and then Wu knew.

He gripped the table with hands as contorted as his face, and leaned towards her muttering in his own Chinese words of terrible imprecation of her and hers. Curses and hatred beyond words even the most terrible blazed from his dying eyes.

He was dying like a dog—outwitted by an Englishwoman. And then he laughed, a laugh more terrible than the death-rattle already crackling in his throat like spun glass burning or dry salt aflame: the damnéd burning may laugh so. Dying like a pariah dog! He laughed with glee—hell's own mirth; for now the signal would never be given, the Englishman would never go free. He would starve and rot in Nang Ping's pagoda. Did she realize that? Oh! for the strength to make her know it! But only Chinese words would come to his thickening tongue or to his reeling brain. Of all that he had learned or known of English, or of the England where he had lived so long, nothing was left him—nothing but his hate.

Was it for this—this death degraded and worse than alone, no son to worship at his tomb—that Wu Ching Yu had banished him to exile and to excruciating homesickness?

Where was the old sword? He would slay this foreign devil where she stood. Who was she? Why was she here—here in the room with the tablets of his ancestors? Who was she? Ah! he remembered now: she was the mother-pig—the foul thing that had borne the seducer of Nang Ping!

With a hideous yell, with a supreme effort, he tottered to his feet and lunged at her with his writhing hands outstretched like claws, his feet fumbling beneath him.

She shrank back in terror, and raised her arm as if to ward off a blow.

And the jewel on her arm slipped down and flashed and blazed and jangled on her wrist.

And Wu Li Chang knew it. His eyes were glazing now and setting in death, but he knew her too. He remembered now—Oxford, the purgatory of Portland Place, the country vicarage, an organ he'd given a church, an English girl he had liked and befriended in a gentle, reverent way. And this—*this*—was the reaping of the kindness and the tolerance he had sown—in England!

Rage heroic and terrible convulsed and nerved him. With an effort that almost tore the sinews of his passing soul asunder he turned and looked—yes—there it was—he wanted it—he reached it—and with a scream of fury he caught it up—the sword—and lunged again at the woman cringing and panting there—he gained upon her—she screamed and ran from him feebly—he followed—he lifted the great weapon and clove the air—he struck out wildly with it again, and again cut only the air.

Twice they circled the room—she sobbing in terror, he blubbering with rage and with the agony of death.

Ah! he had almost reached her. One more effort!—he knew it was his last.

He raised the sword with both his hands, raised it above his head, and struck.

It only missed her, and in missing her it struck the gong—once, then twice.

At the tragedy of that miscarriage, life throbbed again through all his tortured pores. Meaning to kill, he had saved. And he had released the Englishman. That knowledge broke his heart—a mighty Chinese heart—the great heart of the mandarin Wu Li Chang.

For a moment he stood very still, motionless but not quelled, silent, superb in his defeat. And then he fell, and moved no more.

When Florence Gregory looked about her—when she was able to—the doors were open, and the wide window opened noiselessly from without. No one had entered the room. They were quite alone, she and what had been Wu Li Chang. And there was not a sound except the love-sick ecstasy of a nightingale singing his devoted desire through the jasmine-scented garden.

Very slowly, horror-stricken, watching him till the last, she crept from the room, leaving it, by chance, through the door at which she had entered it.

She had aged in that room.

CHAPTER XXXIX
AFTERWARDS

AS she passed from the house into the garden, moving crazily on—not knowing why, how or where—the frenzied mother met her son coming blindly toward the door, his arms still trussed at his sides.

Neither could speak.

But a Chinese woman, coming to them stealthily through the gloaming, spoke as she reached them. "Clome, me tlake," she said.

And almost literally she did take them, one on either side of her, each touched by her hand, impelled by her will.

"No talk," she whispered sternly.

But she need not have said it. Neither of them had word or voice.

They met no one. They heard nothing—except once the far-off trilling of a nightingale, telling the day good-by.

For such was the quality of Wu Li Chang. He had commanded the servants to their quarters, on the other side of the estate, when they should have undone the doors and gates.

But Ah Wong did not slacken her anxious pace, or let them slacken theirs, until the shore was almost reached.

Then, just before they were within sight of the waiting boat and of the boatmen's eyes, she stopped and untied Basil's arms. It was not easy work, although she had a knife. And Mrs. Gregory could give no help.

They stumbled into the boat as best they could, but not without aiding hands, the mother and son. Ah Wong scrambled in nimbly. And at a word from her the watermen lifted their poles—and they had left Kowloon.

They leaned against each other, the English mother and her boy, as the small craft crossed the bay, but not a word was spoken by either of them or to either of them. They huddled together dumb with relief and with exhaustion, and almost numb with the horror they had known.

Unobtrusive, stolid, commonplace in manner as in her humble amah garb, Ah Wong directed and enforced everything.

Ten million stars came out and specked with diamond dust the grave, blue sky. The moon came up and rippled with silver and with gold the rippling water. And before the night-flowers of Kowloon had ceased to lave their faces with the fragrance which was "good-night," the fragrance of the night-flowers of Hong Kong Island rushed out to them and buffeted them with sweetness.

The world was very placid. The night was radiant. The night was very still. And the smiling indifference of the night was cruel. At least, the English woman felt it so. Basil felt nothing. Ah Wong was scheming.

She disembarked them. She paid the boatmen. She tidied her mistress, and tidied Basil as best she could. She got them up the Peak, and she smuggled them into the hotel at last, almost unobserved.

"Too tired talk to-night," she told Hilda imperatively. And she said it as imperatively to Robert Gregory himself when he hurried in from the office in answer to Hilda's telephoned good news.

It was Ah Wong who sent the news of Basil Gregory's safe return spreading like wildest fire through gossipy Hong Kong—not only the news of the return but the detailed story of his absence. It was a very pretty story, and beautifully simple: nothing more out of the common than a slightly sprained ankle and an undelivered chit. The chit had been entrusted to one vellee bad coolie man—needless to say, a victim of the opium habit of which one hears so much in books on China and sees so absurdly little in China itself. Some believed the story—as started by Ah Wong—some did not. But it might have been true (a merit such fabrications often lack) and it served, although one cynic at the English Club said of it that it reminded him of the curate's celebrated egg, "quite good in parts."

And John Bradley wondered.

But the next day the Gregorys and their affairs were well-nigh forgotten in the greater flare of news that flamed from the mainland. Mr. Wu was dead, and so was his daughter, an only child. She had died suddenly, and the shock had killed him—his heart, you know—fatty degeneration, probably—all those rich Chinamen over-eat.

Again, some believed the story as it was told, and more did not. But Wu had died on the mainland, not on English soil, and it was no one's business in Hong Kong.

John Bradley's face grew very stern when he heard that Wu Li Chang had "become a guest on high," and he went at once to Kowloon. And, almost to his surprise, Ah Sing admitted him. The mandarin would have commanded it so, Ah Sing thought.

Bradley learnt nothing on the mainland. He saw his dead friend, and prayed an English prayer beside him, kneeling down between him and a grinning, long, red-tongued Chinese god. That was all.

When he reached his own bungalow, he went into his tiny study, locked its door, and knelt again—at the *prie-Dieu* that stood against the wall between the little silver crucifix and an engraving of a tender, sorrowful face beneath a crown of thorns.

Between the elder Gregory's relief at his son's return and his exultation at Wu's death, the younger Gregory came off nearly scot-free of paternal reprimand, and quite free of any real parental wrath.

"Where the very dickens have you been?" was the father's greeting when they met at breakfast. "A pretty state we've been in!—upsetting the entire family—and me—and the business! You shall answer to me for this, young man. Why the devil don't you pass that toast?"

"I've—I've only been a short trip, pater, off the island," Basil replied, not greatly perturbed.

"I'll short trip you!" the father said with beetling brows; and the tone in which he laconically said, "More," as he thrust his coffee cup to Hilda was very fierce indeed, but he winked at her with just the corner of his left eye; Basil was on his other side. And presently Robert Gregory chuckled openly as he helped himself to marmalade. And when he was leaving the table he slapped his boy on the back, but not too roughly.

"Dead broke?" he demanded.

Basil was about to say, "No, indeed!" but he caught Ah Wong's sudden eye, and said instead, "Well, yes, I'm afraid I am rather."

Robert Gregory chuckled again. "I've a damned good notion to send you home in the steerage—jolly good idea; and while I'm thinking it over, you'd better mind your P's and your little Q's. Show up at the office about three, and I dare say I'll be ass enough to find you a fiver."

Hilda followed her father to the door. She always "saw him off."

Ah Wong at the sideboard continued to select tit-bits for the tray she was going to carry to her mistress's room. She intended, by fair means or by foul, to coax Florence Gregory to eat.

Basil pushed back his plate. He had been pretending to eat, but the food was revolting.

He was longing to see his mother, and he was dreading it. They had not spoken together yet.

He was terribly anxious to know if there were any truth in the report of Wu's death. Probably Ah Wong knew. He looked at her curiously as she carried her tray away; but somehow he could not question her.

On the whole, he wished his mother would send for him and get it over. This suspense was only a little less terrible than his suspense in the pagoda had been.

But all Robert Gregory's anxieties were laid. He reached the office in high good humor. Government House confirmed the rumor of Wu's death. And Gregory felt assured that, his formidable (for the Chink had been formidable) rival wiped out, the only heavy disasters that had ever threatened his own almost monotonously successful business career would disperse under his astute, firm management as summer clouds beneath the sun, and that disaster would not menace him again.

And by the time he reached the club for lunch, he was quite too highly pleased with himself and with his world, and more particularly with his share in it, to keep up any longer even a pretended anger at his son. He chuckled boastfully over "the usual sort of escapade," and said he'd "be glad to get the rascal home—back in sober old England"—"no harm done"—"devil of a good time, no doubt; hadn't got a yen, and only had his allowance eight days ago, a quarterly allowance, and the Lord Harry only knows how much he's bled his mother!" "But, after all"—and then he delivered himself of the amazing originality that "Boys will be boys!"

If there are many men who like to be virtuous vicariously, there are a few, even odder specimens of our wonderfully variegated humanity, who like to sin—in one direction—by proxy. Robert Gregory, in the big thing of life, was an exemplary husband. If Florence Gregory dwelt but in the suburbs of his good pleasure, he lived—in the one sense—on an island on to which no other woman ever put her foot. The Gregory Steamship Company was his adored mistress and his wedded wife. But Florence came next nearest to his warmth—and she had no human rival, never had had or would have one. She knew this. Even a much duller woman must have known it. And perhaps it had enabled her to hold up her head and go smiling through some hard years of disillusion and chagrin.

But Robert Gregory had a very soft spot in his stupid heart for his boy's gallantries. Secretly he was not a little proud of them—of course, they mustn't go too far or cost too much—and of this last escapade he almost boasted as he smoked his after-tiffin cigar—boasted with an unctuous hint of reminiscent glee that insinuated—and was meant to—that he'd been a bit gay "in the same old way" in his younger days.

Which most emphatically he had not.

CHAPTER XL
A GUEST ON HIGH

AND in the K'o-tang—the smaller audience hall—where he had died, Wu Li Chang lay as he had fallen. For none had dared to disturb him for a long time, unless he summoned them. And now, discovered by an early sweeper whose duty it was to open the casements to the summer dawn, he still lay undisturbed, and would lay so until the soothsayer had determined to where the body should be lifted and just how.

He lay upon his back, his face lifted to the paneled and painted ceiling.

Almost as Florence Gregory's footsteps died from his house, a great change swept his face. The contortions of poisoned death had left it set and agonized. That passed away. He was smiling when they found him, as even Nang Ping had never seen him smile. Only one had ever seen that look upon his face. And she had only seen it once—in quite the fullness of its beauty, the majesty of its declaration, all its exquisite tenderness. A living man smiles so but once. Some men never smile so—they have frittered its possibility away—some of them, and some are small men, and it is not for them. It is a hall-mark.

It is a hall-mark, and now and again death stamps it caressingly and regally upon some dead man's face; and always he is a man who has put up a fine good fight, and always it tells that there *is* marriage in Heaven.

Wu Lu had seen that smile—once—in Sze-chuan; and now, in that near garden-place where she had waited for him all these years, he took her in his arms and held her close; and she gave all herself to him again. And he looked down and smiled at her, his bride.

Wu Li Chang lay dead on the K'o-tang floor, and his face was very beautiful.

CHAPTER XLI
"Just With Us"

BETWEEN breakfast and tiffin Florence Gregory sent for Basil, and he went to her heavily. His feet were lead, his heart, his head; and his hands grew very cold.

The interview was inevitable. They each knew that.

It would be difficult to say which dreaded it the more, or which suffered more during it: probably the mother—both; for she was guiltless and made of the finer clay.

It was simple—almost commonplace, the meeting and the short talk between the weary woman and her son; as every interview of intense and indeterminable human tragedy is apt to be. There are no fripperies in true tragedy, but little romance, no poetry. The rocks of life are hard and naked. Not even a stunted lichen can grow on such soilless barrenness.

But this was a very different reckoning from that with his father, jocund and magnificently indifferent to details. Basil realized, of course, that settling up with his mother must be—very different.

She was dressed for going out, elaborately dressed; for she and Ah Wong had decided that she must be seen about Hong Kong to-day, carefully dressed and debonair.

She sat in a low chair beside her dressing-table, her long gloves and her purse of gold mesh at her hand. And because her reputation, and Basil's, were at stake, she and Ah Wong between them had contrived to banish the yesterday's ravages from her face—almost.

Basil looked shockingly ill. Any eyes less self-satisfied than a Robert Gregory's must have seen it.

"You should go and lie down," his mother greeted him.

"Yes, I must," he nodded, "when you've done with me."

Ah Wong went out and closed the door.

Florence Gregory waited then for him to begin. It was the first unkindness she had ever done him. But she was very, very tired. And in the sleepless watches of the night, she had seen clearly Wu Li Chang's point of view, and not altogether without some sharp, acrid conviction that it had some justice on its side—rough, terrible, primeval, barbaric, but still undeniable justice of a sort.

Mrs. Gregory waited for her son to speak, and he did not speak soon.

"Are you all right, Mother?" he said at last.

"I am very tired," she told him.

"Yes—yes, of course you are. But——"

"Oh—yes," she said gently, "I am all right."

"Sure?"

"Yes, Basil!"

"Quite, Mother?" he persisted.

"Yes, Basil!" she told him again, with emphasis this time. And then she smiled a little, very sadly, thinking how sardonic it was that he should be standing there cross-examining her.

"Thank God!" he whispered fervently—all that was best in him welling up in gratitude that his mother had escaped a more cruel wrong than he had inflicted on murdered Nang. For Nang had loved him!

And then he shuddered sickly at the sudden thought that always his mother would know that he had betrayed a girl to her death and worse, a girl who had trusted him—that always his mother would be thinking of it, condemning him—that all the clean sweetness of their old-time, life-long intimacy was tainted—gone! Always his mother must feel towards him regret—despisal. Could he ever wipe that out? Never. Banish it or even dim it for a moment? Be "her boy" again, if but for an hour?

He looked at her searchingly, and at his eyes she blanched. For she read in them his fear, and knew its echo in her own heart. It would be with them both—always; nothing could ever allay it: the estrangement that was born to-day! She saw it all! She read it all—his soul, and hers—and suffered as she had not suffered in the K'o-tang of Wu Li Chang. And her soul quailed and grew very sick before the vengeance of Wu, a greater vengeance and a more terrible even than he had planned.

We need never snatch at vengeance with our poor, feeble, fumbling hands. God always repays. And sometimes it seems as if He, like the Chinese, enforces vicarious atonement—daughters scourged for fathers, mothers for sons, and even friend for friend. But sooner or later the great ax of retribution always falls.

Basil Gregory saw the grief and the torture in his mother's face. "Oh! well, then," he said, strolling to the window, and standing there looking out across the bay—towards Kowloon—"that's all right. They say he's dead—Wu—you've heard it?"

"Yes."

"I wish I knew if it's true."

"It is true."

He turned back to her quickly. "How do you know, Mother? Are you dead sure?"

"I saw him die," she said.

At that her boy came and knelt down and took her hands in his.

And she told him—just the bare facts of yesterday.

Nang Ping, or his own fault, was not mentioned between them, then or ever. Florence Gregory uttered no reproach. She said none, and she tried to look none. It is so that such women most reproach the men that they have borne—and nursed.

She asked no details of his amour or of his capture and detention; and he offered none.

And it was better so. The burden of their common memory was heavy enough—a memory from which nothing could ever purge her soul or his.

"What will happen—about it all? He was a devil of a big man among the Chinks," Basil said anxiously when he spoke again.

"Yes, I know. What will happen? By the Chinese, you mean? Ah Wong thinks nothing——"

"Ah Wong!" Basil said contemptuously.

"She saved my life—and yours——"

"By a Chinese trick."

"It served," Mrs. Gregory said gravely. "Ah Wong knows her people. And she thinks nothing will be done—soon, if ever. And we will leave China at once. I think your father'll be glad to—he's been anxious enough to get back to float the new Company. But, if for any reason he wishes to wait even a little, why, I must get Hilda to coax him to go at once. You, at least, must go by the next boat."

Basil nodded. "Yes, I'd like to catch the next comfortable boat."

"We'll all catch it, if we can," his mother said emphatically.

"Is that all, Mother?" he asked her gently.

"All?" she was puzzled.

"All you want of me?"

"Oh! Yes, dear," she said brightly.

"Then I believe I'll go and lie down again. I'm jolly tired and jolly weak."

"Yes—do," Florence said.

But at the door he turned back and came to her and took her in his arms.

"God bless you, Mother!" he whispered with his lips against her hair.

"God bless my boy!" she answered brokenly.

Then he kissed her passionately, and turned away sobbing.

"Wait a moment," she said when he had smothered back his emotion and had put his hand again on the door. "I did forget one thing. Make no explanation—not to any one."

"What about the governor?"

"Least of all to him. Your father will ask you not another question; he has promised me."

"I say, Mother," Basil said, flushing painfully, "you are a bit of a brick—aren't you?"

"I am your mother, Basil," she returned, smiling into his eyes. "Remember, not one word to any human creature. Promise me. Let it rest where it is forever—just with us."

And there they left it—glad to be rid of it, as far as words went, but knowing that, waking or sleeping, neither could ever be rid of it in thought again. It was a poison cooked into their blood.

For years they did not speak of it again, except that Basil said when she came to him later with a cup of tea—he had slept through tiffin, and she would not have him called—"What about Ah Wong? She knows."

His mother answered him proudly: "I trust Ah Wong. Ah Wong knows, of course—part at least. But it will be always precisely as if she knew nothing."

Basil shrugged skeptically, sitting up among his pillows. And his mother put the tray down and left him a little hurriedly. There is little a woman finds harder to bear than a man's ingratitude. Florence Gregory was ashamed of her son.

She had tiffined early, and before tiffin and since she had been out and about: shopping, paying calls, laughing, chatting, the brightest woman in Hong Kong, the best dressed, and the most care-free. And now she went out again, sitting radiant and chic in her smart chair, carried wherever she would be most seen. She stayed a little at the racquets court and at the cricket club. But she did not leave her chair. She was too tired—almost at the end of her woman's long tether.

CHAPTER XLII
THE DUST OF CHINA FROM THEIR FEET

THE Gregorys sailed from Hong Kong the next week, and half the Colony saw them off. One means, of course, half the Europeans: the Chinese don't count—in China. But John Bradley did not see them off—nor had he come to wish them good-by. Hilda was offended, and Basil was grateful. (He could be grateful at times.) Except Florence, none of them had seen the priest since the night Basil had consulted him. Mrs. Gregory called upon him two days after her escape. She had sent a note asking him to come to her at the hotel. He had replied asking if she could, and kindly would, come to him instead; he knew she'd been out continuously the day before. And she had gone at once.

Of Kowloon she had told him nothing: when she had enjoined silence on Basil, she had meant silence; and she had no thought of breaking it towards any one.

She had wished to see him before they left Hong Kong, she said, and they were going home at once now.

Mrs. Gregory had a very sincere affection for John Bradley. If she had been in Hilda's shoes, she'd not have given him for a wilderness of Tom Carrutherses, she thought. And in leaving Hong Kong she was leaving behind her nothing that she regretted more than her talks with Bradley; except Ah Wong. That was her great regret, for she was leaving Ah Wong.

The amah had refused to quit her country. Mrs. Gregory had pleaded at last. Ah Wong would not budge. Hilda was indifferent, Mr. Gregory not sorry, and Basil Gregory was meanly glad.

And John Bradley was glad, too, when he heard it, but not meanly. He knew that the amah knew more than any other living person did of all that had happened—far more than he knew or even suspected—and he was sure that her presence with them in England would make for a blight upon the entire Gregory family—a blight which all her devotion and all her deft service could not counterbalance.

It was partly concerning Ah Wong that Mrs. Gregory had called. Would he befriend the woman—her amah, perhaps he'd noticed her?—if he could ever?

"Oh, yes!" he said, he "had noticed her, several times." He did not add how well he knew her, or how highly he valued her, or that he had received her in this very room, and in the middle of the night, not long ago. But he promised cordially to do any earthly thing he ever could for the Chinese woman. It was a queer legacy for a bachelor priest, he said, laughing, but all was fish that came to his net—pastoral or otherwise—and he accepted Ah Wong heartily. She should come into his service, if she would—potter about the bungalow, sit hunched up on the verandah and sew, or play a guitar or a native drum or something in the compound—and, if she declined his service, still he'd try to contrive to look after her some other way. He'd keep an eye on her, a friendly, helpful eye—if she'd let him—seriously he would.

And he echoed fervently the amah's entreaty that the Gregorys should leave China at once—*at once*—let the order of their going be what it would, the comforts or discomforts of the first outgoing boat just what they might. Nothing mattered, absolutely nothing, except for them to go—to go at once, and never to return.

"You'll say good-by to them all for me?" he begged, "I—I may be called away for a few days by any post. But please say my good-bys to them all: your husband—and Basil—and to your daughter. And, Mrs. Gregory, young Carruthers is staying here, you said. I'll look him up as soon as I know you've sailed, and I'll look after him a bit, be a sort of parson his-man-Friday, if the boy'll let me."

"Tom?—Tom's a nice boy—I think," Mrs. Gregory said a trifle hesitantly.

"I think so too," the priest said cordially.

She was going into the city when she left him, and he went almost to the level with her, walking beside her chair.

"Remember," he said at parting, "you'll go at once. And you'll none of you come back—ever."

"We will go at once," she told him earnestly. "And we will not come back." But to that last there was a small reservation at the far back of her mind. She thought it just possible that Hilda might come back—some day. Not that Hilda particularly liked China; she did not—she greatly preferred Kensington. But, if Holman thought well of Tom Carruthers, it was probable that he—now that Basil was definitely out of the Hong Kong running— might be permanently attached to that branch, and ultimately its head.

And with one slight deviation, Mrs. Gregory kept the promise she made John Bradley as he stood bare-headed beside her chair. For they did sail—almost at once. And only one of them ever came back—Hilda.

The long voyage home differed in nothing from all other such voyages. Not one voyage in ten thousand ever does differ from other voyages. It is impossible. They made the same stops, the same changes, ate the same food, had the same fellow passengers. Nothing short of pirates or a shoal of ship-devouring Jonah's whales could differentiate one P. & O. passage from another.

But Hilda Gregory found this one a little dull at first, and was driven in self-respect to appropriate the ship's surgeon and two homing subalterns.

For Basil and their mother were inseparable, and the father who heretofore had been her faithful, if not too picturesque, knight lived in the smoking-room, telling again and again the story of his cowing of the great Chinese "I Am," Wu Li Chang. Robert Gregory, never a wordless man, had never talked so much in all his life.

It was impossible to pass the smoking-room door without catching some such scrap of English masterpiece as: "I put him through it." "The damned nigger was only bluffing. Well, I damn well called his bluff!" "... and that's where a knowledge of the Chinaman comes in—an inside, intelligent knowledge. They like to be thought clever, I tell you. Don't you see that it flattered him that I should think—*seem* to think, of course—that he was a sort of Mister Know-All?—and he was sly enough to play up to it. Oh! he was sly, I grant you that. But no match for me; no real ability." "Yes; as I told you, he hummed and hawed a bit at first, until I simply turned him inside out, and then I could see he knew nothing. It was only tickling his vanity to let him imagine I thought he was a little local god. That's why I left him to Mrs. Gregory. I saw it was a mere waste of my time. And it pleased her, and, too, it took her mind off the boy a bit. She was fretting over him—the young dog!—until I thought she'd make herself downright ill." "Oh! we flatter these damned Chinamen too much in thinking them so clever." "Oh! if you know the way to manage Chinamen. You should have seen the way I talked to that compradore. I frightened the beggar—just as I'd frightened Wu the day before. He saw it was a bit dangerous to play any games with me, by the Lord Harry, and so he called off the strike. I scared him stiff. And I scared Wu half to death, I can tell you." "Oh, yes! he's dead, right enough. No, I don't know how he died. Perhaps he was ordered to commit suicide. Well, I had no objection, I can tell you. And I shan't go into much black for him." "He always was a bit of a handful. Kept his school-masters busy. But that did them good and him no harm. And they were well paid for it. Boys will be boys, you know. Why, when I was his age...."

In the smoking-room other men came and went all day and a good bit of the night, but Robert Gregory's voice went on forever. And Mrs. Gregory and Basil, walking up and down, grew careful to keep at the other end of the big ship. For the smoking-room was near the front, and opened on to both sides of the promenade deck.

Basil Gregory scarcely left his mother from Hong Kong to Liverpool.

As the great ship drew anchor, he drew her arm in his, and they stood together so and watched Hong Kong until their sight had gone from it quite.

This was their passing from China, but not from tragedy, and the woman knew it.

They did not speak of Wu Li Chang. They had spoken of him definitely together for the last time. They did not speak at all as the island faded slowly away from them. But they knew that to-day the mandarin's interminable funeral cortège started from Kowloon to Sze-chuan. For they were taking the dead man to his old home—taking him tenderly with shriek of fife and howl of drum, coffined almost as splendidly as the Macedonian in his casket of gold. And no son followed Wu Li Chang! But behind the mandarin's coffin they carried, more meekly, a simpler, smaller one. And Sing Kung Yah walked behind them both, almost bare-footed, clad in coarse unbleached hemp. This was her last secular function, if one may speak so of any human burial rite; for when at last Wu Li Chang and Wu Nang Ping were laid beside their dead ancestors in far-off Sze-chuan, Sing Kung Yah, if she lived so far—the road was long and rough—would seek life-long sanctuary in the Taoist nunnery of her abbess cousin.

As long as Anglo-Hong Kong's eyes had been upon her, Mrs. Gregory had borne herself bravely—gayly even. But she was breaking now, and with each revolution of the ship's great wheel she showed a little older, a little more limp. "You're looking downright washed out," Gregory told her; "high time we got you home." Already she was no longer Basil Gregory's young and pretty mother. No passenger among them all mistook her for his sister. She would never be so mistaken again. But he was very tender of her, and offered her a daily atonement of constant companionship and of those little tendings which mean so much more to a woman than any great sacrifice or big climax of devotion ever can. (If women are small in this, they are also exquisite by it.)

They clung together pathetically. And, at the same time, each shrank from the other a little, almost unconsciously, and quite in spite of themselves. Their souls shrank; their hearts clung.

Basil sensed that she grieved over his crime, and, as he thought, out of all proportion to its real seriousness, and that also she condemned and despised it. He was far from self-absolution. His conscience was not dead. But he resented her disapproval and the implied "charity" of her careful considerateness and studied cheerfulness.

Her soul-withdrawal from him was more justified, and of more moment and dignity than his from her. For once or twice she just glimpsed almost an antagonism, a seed of hatred—born of his writhing conscience—that was slowly cankering in his mind. That he should doubt the all-forgiveness of her love grieved her sorely, but she recognized that it certainly was involuntary, and probably was inevitable; but that, even so, he presumed to arraign her at the judgment seat of his peccant soul, blaming her that she could not forget, could not quite condone, incensed her bitterly.

The grave secret that they shared, and that no one else now of their world even suspected, linked them tightly—too tightly: the gyves hurt. And while it linked it separated. They were closer together than they had ever been before; closer than even a mother and son should be; closer than any two human creatures should be. They violated, with the hideousness of their mutual knowledge, each other's utmost right of privacy—the soul-privacy which God and nature command that with each human entity shall be forever inviolable.

He suffered at her suffering. He brooded over her. He was very tender of his mother. But between them, and in them mutually, a poison worked. Their love was exquisite and human still; their companionship, and even their sympathy, warm and sincere. But a slight cloud hung over them, a cloud no bigger than a dead man's hand. It grew a little darker every day.

CHAPTER XLIII
ENGLISH WEDDING BELLS

BASIL Gregory's wedding day was warm and clear. June and England were at their best.

It was a sweetly pretty wedding. Every one said so.

And the girlish bride was prettier than her wedding—prettier than any mere picture could be; as pretty and as sweet as the June roses she wore, and very like them: pink and white, delicate, fair-haired, violet-eyed Alice Lee, the motherless daughter of the incumbent of the old gray vicarage in which Basil Gregory's mother had been born.

Homesick for the old days and the old ways, Florence Gregory had gone to Oxfordshire soon after their return to England, hoping to bathe and to heal her stained and torn spirit in the quiet of old places, the ointment of pure memories. She had failed. But she had made fast friends with her dead father's successor, and had gone back to the cordial hospice of her old home again and again in the three years that had elapsed since she had come from China. A year ago Basil had accompanied her, none too willingly, for a week-end, had stayed a month; hence these wedding bells!

Florence Gregory was an old woman now, old and limp. Robert Gregory was no longer proud of his wife. Her white hair was very beautiful, but he resented it, and it rasped and angered him that she had prematurely aged. He had married her, as he had loved her, for her buoyant good looks, and he felt that he was defrauded by the change in her—a change so marked that even his careless and ledger-bound eyes could not fail to see it. And secretly his poor mundane spirit groaned aloud that *his* missus—the best-dressed woman in Hong Kong three years ago, and every bit as smart as her clothes—had degenerated into a frumpish nobody, looked older than he did, by the Lord Harry, and without an ounce of snap in her or a word to say to any one. Greatly to his credit, he had kept all this to himself loyally. He had never spoken of it, not even hinted at it, to any one, beyond plaintive and repeated entreaties to Hilda to help him find some way to buck Mother up. He had never been unkind to his wife. He still bought flowers for her—the bouquet she carried at their son's wedding had cost five guineas—and burdened her with gifts of jewelry almost inappropriate to his means. And Mr. Gregory was growing very rich indeed. The wounds that "Mr. Wu" had dealt his fortune had soon healed, and left no scar. He was still a faithful husband. Such pride and consolation as a woman may take from the continence that is chiefly the outcome of a husband's indifference to her sex and of his absorption in business and in self were Mrs. Gregory's. And in all their married life they had had but one quarrel—a unique quarrel, as husbands and wives go. It had occurred two years ago, and had been over a dressmaker's bill.

Such quarrels are common? They are scarcely uncommon—certainly not unique. But this was one with a difference. Mr. Gregory had always seen and paid his wife's dressmakers' bills. It had been one of his greatest pleasures. Madame Eloise had taken less pleasure in concocting those princely accounts, and in receipting them, than Robert Gregory had taken in writing the cheques that had discharged them. Two years ago a quarterly account had come in in two figures. That was too much. Gregory raged at his wife, and after an impatient word or two, she had bit her lip, smiled and promised reform. And she had kept her word; for she had seen his point of view and the justice of his complaint. But the latest fashions no longer suited her. Still less did she now suit them. Wu Li Chang and Basil Gregory had sapped her of the courage and the carriage to wear smart gowns. Her *beauté de diable* was quite gone—she had left it in a Chinese K'o-tang; and the finer beauty that had replaced it this husband had no eyes to see.

But Hilda saw, and between the mother and daughter had grown a tenderness and a friendship that had not been theirs before. "Your mouth is the most beautiful thing I ever saw, Mother," the girl said sometimes. And it was very beautiful, with an exquisite loveliness that only the lips that have been steeped in hyssop can ever show.

Hilda was the only bridesmaid to-day. She had none of the bride's soft prettiness, and only a fair amount of the splendid good looks that her own mother had lost. But she had gained in charm, in tact, in womanliness, and, too, even in girlishness.

Her engagement to Tom Carruthers was broken. The breaking had grieved her—at the time. The day Carruthers had sailed for England to claim Hilda and to take her back to China, a Chinese girl had thrown herself into Hong Kong harbor. Oddly, the story had reached England—oddly, because such stories are so common. But this one had in some way trickled across the world, and to Hilda. Hilda had probed it, and had given Tom back his ring. It had not been a very black case, as such things go. The Chinese girl was nobody's daughter. Carruthers had never deceived her, and had promised her nothing that he had not given. But she had grown to care for him. O curse of womanhood!

And Hilda had a sturdy, wholesome instinct of virtue, a matter-of-course as towards herself, relentless towards others, that she had inherited from her mother, but not from her mother alone; and she also had a quick, curt, businesslike method of dealing with the facts and incidents of life that she had inherited solely from Robert Gregory. She considered her engagement to Tom Carruthers a bad debt; and she wrote it off with a steady hand. Basil was angry with her, and had upbraided her. "Girls don't understand such things!" he told her petulantly. "But I thought you had more sense."

"I understand myself," she had retorted haughtily.

Needless to say, Carruthers also was angry, and shared his anger with generous, masculine impartiality between Hilda Gregory and I Matt So. Mrs. Gregory was glad. And it was she who mentioned the news (but not its circumstance) in her next letter to Hong Kong. Hilda's father was indifferent. There was time enough for so rich a man's daughter, and the finest girl in England, by the Lord Harry, any day; and as for Tom, she might do worse, of course, but, on the other hand, she might do a long sight better.

It was not Basil's old misdemeanor that had so broken his mother, nor was it her experience in the K'o-tang of Wu Li Chang. It was the estrangement that had grown between her and her son—an estrangement that had become almost a bitterness. At times it was a bitterness.

A great secret shared between two, and inviolably kept by both, must be either a great bond or a great alienation. The terrific secret shared by Florence Gregory and her boy proved both. They never spoke of it. But, for that, it burdened and haunted them the more.

So far as she blamed him for his old fault his mother had quite forgiven Basil.

But he could not forgive her.

It cut her to the quick. But she could not blame Basil for it. And she sorrowed for him, more than she did for herself, that she was powerless to give him conviction of the good truth that her forgiveness was "perfect and entire, wanting nothing," her love unchanged.

And sometimes when the soul-poison scummed thickest in him, because of it, Basil Gregory loved his mother a little less. The high place to which sons in their souls set mothers carries a great price.

But this was not the worst between them. At times—and these were his blackest—Basil Gregory wondered if, at the absolute last, his mother would have failed him, would have refused to spare, at her supremest cost, the life she had given him. Would she at the last hideous resort have grudged him her all? Sometimes he thought that she would. And when he thought so he blamed her. And for that blame, his mother, who read his very soul, a little despised him, and she could not forgive it.

Wu Li Chang had wreaked a vengeance more terrible than he had planned. For when in a mother's soul there is something that she cannot forgive the son she has borne and nursed and still loves, human tragedy has reached its depth.

CHAPTER XLIV
THE SOUND OF A CHINESE GONG

IT was a pretty wedding, and very simple. The Lees were simple English gentlefolk.

It was a quiet ceremony, quietly performed. There was but little music; no fife, no drum, no clang. The old organist played softly. (Neither he nor Mrs. Gregory gave a thought to who had given the instrument; and no one else there had ever known.) No incense burned. The English sunshine, perfumed by the roses that grew about the village graves, drifted softly through the old church windows and dappled on the chancel floor and on the altar rails and on the organ's pipes. And the holy place was sweet with quiet harmony.

Even Robert Gregory, spruce and straight, wearing the whitest pair of gloves, and almost tightest into which human hands were ever packed, was content. He was glad to see Basil settled. The girl had no "dot," but she was pretty enough to eat; and his manliness was of a straight, sturdy stuff, and held that a man should earn and provide for his wife, by the Lord Harry, every time. And for once he was satisfied again with Mrs. Gregory's appearance. She looked fine in her gray and gold, and the emeralds at her breast and pinning the scrap of bonnet on her white curls were some style.

Hilda listened to the old service with a rapt, tender face. John Bradley was coming home for six months of holiday next week. She had no doubt that he'd come to see her mother.

Mrs. Gregory was not displeased. It was no part of her regret to wish that Basil should live all his life wifeless and childless. And the rift between her boy and her saved her the jealousy that happier mothers must suffer when their first-born son weds. Sorry recompense—but recompense.

Basil Gregory did not make a very brave bridegroom. But only his mother noticed it. Most wedding-guests have little eye to spare for mere bridegrooms. And there is something about the function so trying to masculine sensitiveness that before now kings and heroes have carried themselves a little craven at their happiest triumph.

Basil Gregory saw two girls beside him at God's altar.

As he passed down the aisle with his wife's shy hand on his arm, he felt the touch of a smaller, tawnier hand. Its weight hurt him; it was heavy with fabulous nail-protectors and with priceless rings. He was madly in love with his wife, and, too, he was madly miserable, because he knew now that they two would never be quite alone—neither by day nor by night. His mother saw and knew. Just before they passed her he stumbled a little, startled by the sound of a Chinese gong.

And a few hours later, in the still sweetness of the dark, it smote him again.

Rest, Wu Li Chang! Be satisfied! The Englishman is punished. He has broken his mother's heart. Your curse is fulfilled. Basil Gregory heard your gong cry out a soul's damnation to-day above his wife's "I will." So long as he lives he will hear it, a bitter, relentless knell. When ginger is hottest in his mouth, when wine bubbles reddest in his cup, when the English girl he loves lifts with tired, triumphant hands their firstborn toward his arms, through the young mother's misty smile he will see Nang's face, above the baby's first cry he will hear the throbbing note of a Chinese gong.

Rest! Sleep in your Sze-chuan grave! Your hideous vengeance is complete, life-long, soul-deep. It is greater than even you could have planned. Almost it is adequate.

"The great mountain must crumble,

The strong beam must break,

The wise man must wither away like a plant,"

Confucius crooned as he died.

THE END

- 207 -

Milton Keynes UK
Ingram Content Group UK Ltd.
UKHW010709240424
441619UK00004B/385